Praise for the Gethsemane Brown Mystery Series

MURDER IN G MAJOR (#1)

"The captivating southwestern Irish countryside adds a delightful element to this paranormal series launch. Gethsemane is an appealing protagonist who is doing the best she can against overwhelming odds."

– *Library Journal* (starred review)

"Gordon strikes a harmonious chord in this enchanting spellbinder of a mystery."

– Susan M. Boyer,
USA Today Bestselling Author of *Lowcountry Book Club*

"Charming debut."

– *Kirkus Reviews*

"A fantastic story with a great ghost, with bad timing. There are parts that are extremely comical, and Gethsemane is a fantastic character that you root for as the pressure continually builds for her to succeed...in more ways than one."

– *Suspense Magazine*

"Just when you think you've seen everything, here comes Gethsemane Brown, baton in one hand, bourbon in the other....There's charm to spare in this highly original debut."

– Catriona McPherson,
Agatha Award-Winning Author of *The Reek of Red Herrings*

"Gethsemane Brown is a fast-thinking, fast-talking dynamic sleuth (with a great wardrobe) who is more than a match for the unraveling murders and cover-ups, aided by her various–handsome–allies and her irascible ghost."

– Chloe Green,
Author of the Dallas O'Connor Mysteries

DEATH IN D MINOR

The Gethsemane Brown Mystery Series
by Alexia Gordon

MURDER IN G MAJOR (#1)
DEATH IN D MINOR (#2)

A Gethsemane Brown Mystery

DEATH IN D MINOR

ALEXIA GORDON

HENERY PRESS

DEATH IN D MINOR
A Gethsemane Brown Mystery
Part of the Henery Press Mystery Collection

First Edition | July 2017

Henery Press, LLC
www.henerypress.com

Author photograph by Peter Larsen

Trade Paperback ISBN-13: 978-1-63511-231-3
Digital epub ISBN-13: 978-1-63511-232-0
Kindle ISBN-13: 978-1-63511-233-7
Hardcover ISBN-13: 978-1-63511-234-4

Printed in the United States of America

To Mom and Dad
To Nancy Willard, 1936-2017

ACKNOWLEDGMENTS

Thank you, Rachel and Erin, for turning my messy manuscripts into good books.

Thank you, Kendel, Art, Amber, and the rest of the Hen House, for believing a cozy mystery series with an African American sleuth and a snarky ghost is something people want to read.

Thank you, Paula and Gina at Talcott Notch.

Thank you, Wendy at Lifeworking.

Thank you, Professor Terry Myers of the College of William and Mary, for teaching me about the Bray School.

Thank you, "Ann Wager" and "Gowan Pamphlet," for sharing your stories with me at Colonial Williamsburg's St. George Tucker House.

Thank you, Charlotte Courtney of the Colonial Williamsburg Foundation, for going above and beyond to help me find answers when I asked you a random question about embroidery and Colonial-era black schoolgirls.

Thank you to all my friends for your unwavering support and your hilarious Facebook posts.

Thank you to all of the authors who ungrudgingly shared your time and advice to help a newbie figure out what this writing business is all about.

Thank you, Mom and Dad, for that first library card. This is all your fault and I love you for it.

One

He showed up two days after Christmas.

Gethsemane Brown awoke to the crunch of tires pulling into the gravel drive of Carraigfaire Cottage, home for the past few months. She'd moved into the whitewashed thatched-roof house perched near the base of Carrick Point lighthouse after a job loss and a theft stranded her in Dunmullach, a cliffside village in southwestern Ireland. She found a new job as music director at the local boys' school. Which was closed for the Christmas holidays. Which was why she was still in bed at—she reached for the clock on her bedside table—seven thirty in the morning. A night owl since childhood, she'd chosen a career—concert musician—that allowed her to stay up late and sleep in. However, in the three months she'd been in Ireland, solving murders and preparing a school orchestra for an important competition had robbed her of the chance to sleep late.

She threw back the covers and got up, shivering as her bare feet hit the cold floor. She reached the cottage's entrance hall by the time her unexpected visitor knocked. No one she knew from the village would trek up to Carrick Point to make a wake-up call. She grabbed the shillelagh her students had given her as a Christmas present.

"Who is it?" she asked through the heavy wooden door.

"Hank Wayne," came the reply in an American-accented voice

like hers. Not *just* like hers. Her Virginia drawl rang far more melodious than the flat tones of the man's Midwestern English. Although her loathing for the speaker may have biased her. He'd been after Carraigfaire Cottage since before their first meeting several weeks ago.

"It's early," she said to the hotel developer. "What do you want?"

"I want to come in. Billy didn't think you'd mind."

She hadn't spoken to Billy McCarthy, the cottage's owner and her landlord, since he brought Hank around to look at the cottage. He'd gone off on another business trip right after. Billy hadn't come right out and admitted it during the visit, but the men's talk made it clear he planned to sell Carraigfaire to Hank. Who'd convert this quaint postcard-perfect two-hundred-year-old cottage into one of his tacky tourist monstrosities and destroy the cultural and historical character of the area. Gethsemane knew his track record. She'd even stayed in a few of his horrid pink motels while on tour with the Cleveland Symphony. That had been four orchestras before she landed in Dunmullach. A lifetime ago.

"Billy didn't say anything to me." She put down the heavy walking stick and tugged at her pajamas. "I'm not really dressed for company."

"Miss Brown." A note of irritation crept into the practiced, businesslike tone. "My assistant and I have a flight to catch this afternoon and this is the only convenient time for us to do a walk-through. I can get McCarthy on the phone so you can discuss it with him, but it would streamline the process if you'd just let us in now. This will only take a few moments, then we'll be out of your way." He spoke like a man used to getting what he wanted.

Gethsemane eyed the shillelagh. Would it be worth spending life in an Irish prison to *really* get him out of her way?

More knocking. "Miss Brown?"

Why prolong it? She opened the door wide enough to see onto the porch. Hank stood closest to her, bundled in the familiar gray cashmere overcoat and scarf, silver pompadour with every hair in place unchanged from his last visit. A woman in a leather car coat huddled behind him. Her tight bun pulled veins into high relief on her temples. She wore a fake tan that failed to hide the underlying paleness of her skin. She muttered about the deficiencies of gravel driveways as she stood on one foot, the other leg flexed at the knee, and examined a stiletto-heeled boot.

Hank stepped forward. Gethsemane stepped back to avoid a collision and opened the door wide enough for Hank and his assistant to come in.

"Thank you, Miss Brown," Hank said.

"Doctor Brown," she corrected.

"Oh, that's right, you do have some sort of degree in, what is it, music?"

"A Ph.D. From Yale."

"You must forgive me, Doctor Brown. I believe I mentioned before I don't pay much attention to music. Too busy earning money."

Gethsemane clenched her jaw as the duo filed past. Sarcastic comebacks filled her head, but she suspected Hank would prolong his walk-through in retaliation for any comments. Best to keep silent for now and wait for a better opportunity to deal with Hank. An opportunity when she had the upper hand and could deal with him on her terms.

Hank led the way to the music room. His assistant trotted behind him. She paused by the coat rack and lifted the sleeve of a mackintosh between a gloved thumb and forefinger. She sneered, then let the sleeve fall as if she feared it might be infectious or vermin might crawl from it.

She wiped her fingertips on her coat. "How do you stand it?"

Gethsemane pegged her accent as New York, filtered through vocal coaching. "Stand what?"

"Living out here with the leprechauns? Mr. Wayne's is-it-miss-or-is-it-doctor routine is for show. He knows exactly who you are. He paid people to find out."

Gethsemane held her tongue as she vacillated between anger

at being spied on and being creeped out. At least Hank did his homework.

The assistant continued. "We know all about you. Degrees from Vassar and Yale. Certification in orchestral conducting. Multi-instrumentalist. Prize-winner in several important competitions, often the youngest female and only African American to win some of them. World traveler who's performed with first-class orchestras on nearly every continent. And you turned down a job offer back in Boston—an offer from Peter Nolan, no less—for the privilege of being stuck out here in some dreary cottage straight from a Brontë novel without a Starbucks or a Neimans or a nail bar in a hundred-mile radius. I'd throw myself off the nearest cliff. How do you manage?"

Gethsemane couldn't hold back. Her inner snark demon won out over discretion. "Being out here's not so bad. Fresh air, beautiful view. And it could be worse. I could be playing flunky to a megalomaniacal narcissist with the aesthetic sensibility of a toddler beauty pageant coordinator."

The woman gasped. Hank's voice bellowed down the hall. "Where the hell are you?" The woman sniffled and hurried after her boss. Gethsemane followed. The assistant whipped out a tablet and stylus and scribbled as Hank gestured at walls. "We'll knock that one out, push that one back a few feet," he said.

Gethsemane slammed the Steinway's keyboard, interrupting Hank's soliloquy with a cacophony of notes. She strode to Hank and stared up at him, hands on hips. "You have no right to barge in here and talk about knocking out walls and auctioning off furniture. This is Eamon McCarthy's cottage—"

Hank cut her off. "Was Eamon McCarthy's cottage. Eamon McCarthy's been dead a quarter century. Now it's Billy McCarthy's cottage, and once he sells it to me, it will be my cottage. In no case is it any concern of yours."

"Carraigfaire isn't some random building no one's going to miss. Eamon and Orla McCarthy made important contributions to music and literature. Their home was their creative space and has major cultural significance. As an artist, and a decent human being, what happens to this cottage concerns me and would even if I didn't live here. Your mutilating this place just so you can install a cocktail bar and park an extra car or two in the front is—is—sacrilege. Eamon's and Orla's fans won't sit quiet while you destroy their legacy." She counted herself among those fans. Eamon McCarthy, brilliant composer and pianist, inspired her musical career.

"Dr. Brown." Hank's tone dripped oil. Gethsemane wanted to run upstairs and shower. "I don't want to destroy Carraigfaire. I want to enhance it, make it accessible to the *new* legions of McCarthy fans—fans garnered thanks to you."

Leave it to Hank to throw her success in her face. Twenty-five years ago, Eamon McCarthy had been suspected of murdering his wife in a jealous rage then killing himself in a fit of remorse. A month ago, Gethsemane proved him innocent and uncovered the real killer. Her investigation made the news, and news generated publicity. She pictured oversized tourist buses lining the road and a parking lot crowded with cars where the garden used to be. And the thought it might be partly her fault...Hank rubbed salt in her wound. She'd pull the scab off one of his.

"Aren't you afraid remodeling the cottage will upset the ghost?"

Hank had been terrorized by traumatic childhood paranormal experiences. Violent entities drove his entire family from their Michigan home in a well-publicized incident dubbed "The Wayne Terror" by the press. Gethsemane only hinted Carraigfaire was haunted the last time Hank visited and he'd gone into near apoplexy and scurried from the cottage. His reaction this time differed.

He laughed. "No need to worry about a ghost, once again, thanks to you. Billy assured me his uncle's ghost rested in peace after you cleared him of those dreadful false charges. Well done."

Damn. Damn. And damn. Bluff called. Carraigfaire *had* been haunted when she'd moved in, by Eamon's ghost. The ghost convinced her to investigate the murders and became her friend in the process. But she hadn't seen him since she'd solved the mystery.

"Too bad the cottage isn't haunted," Hank's assistant said. "Paranormal tours are still trending."

Hank's eyes narrowed and he clenched his fists. The woman froze like an animal caught in the crosshairs of a high-powered rifle.

"I, I mean, I, um," she sputtered.

Hank's voice dropped and he spoke through a clenched jaw. "Out."

"But, Mr. Wayne, I—"

He lowered his voice further, to almost a whisper. "Now." The cold intensity of his tone seemed to drop the room temperature several degrees. Veins pulsed in his temples.

The assistant clamped a hand over her mouth and ran from the room. The front door slammed.

Hank scowled at Gethsemane, all pretense of nothing-personal-it's-just-business gone. "Are you religious, Dr. Brown?"

Gethsemane nodded. "I'm an Episcopalian."

"Then you're familiar with Twelfth Night."

Epiphany. What did the magi's arrival at Jesus's manger have to do with anything?

Hank didn't wait for her answer. "Billy invited me to his Twelfth Night party. I'm expecting him to give me a gift. One that beats the hell out of twelve drummers drumming. I suggest you start looking for other living arrangements before then."

Hank headed for the hall. Gethsemane followed him out. His assistant held his car's rear passenger-side door open, but Hank ignored her and got behind the wheel. He peeled out with a spray of gravel. His assistant hung her head as the car disappeared around the corner and walked after it.

"I can call a taxi," Gethsemane said.

The woman halted, tugged her coat, squared her shoulders, and continued down the hill without looking back.

Gethsemane paced the hall and tried to calm her nerves. "Floyd Gardner, two-eighty-four; Vic Harris, two-ninety-two;

Smokey Joe Williams, three-thirty-three; Buck Ewing, three-seventy-five." Reciting Negro League batting averages usually worked to calm her nerves. Not this time. Hank had a point. The sale and destruction of Carraigfaire didn't concern her. She loved the cottage as much as Eamon had, but she had no rights to it. She didn't even pay rent. Billy let her stay in exchange for upkeep. Billy had every right to sell what he owned, and Hank undoubtedly made him an obscenely generous offer. So why did the thought of walking away feel like betraying a friend? She went to the piano. Eamon's piano. The piano where his ghost had composed "St. Brennan's Ascendant," the concerto she'd used to lead the school's honors orchestra to victory in the All-County School Orchestra Competition. She played. The concerto's movements flowed from allegro to andante to allegretto, mirroring the school orchestra's journey from defeat and humiliation to sacrifice and determination and, finally, to triumph and restoration of pride. During the competition, Gethsemane had ridden the notes, along with the musicians and audience, from despair to hope for a bright future. Today, however, the music only highlighted her sense of loss and desperation and brought her to the brink of tears.

She slammed the keyboard. "Eamon McCarthy, where are you? I need you. Carraigfaire needs you."

She listened. Silence. She searched the cottage. No dimpled smile, no curly hair, no green eyes, not even a blue orb. She sniffed. No trace of leather-and-tobacco cologne mixed with the freshness of soap, the telltale sign Eamon was about to appear. Nothing. She had nothing.

She caught sight of herself in a mirror. Rumpled pajamas, red-rimmed eyes, hair sticking out in all directions. She scolded herself. "Stop it. Get a grip. You don't quit. You didn't quit when you had six weeks to lead a boys' orchestra from zero to first place, you didn't quit when the body count rose and everyone told you to go home before you got killed. You don't quit." The only way to save Carraigfaire from Hank's "improvement" plan was to convince Hank he didn't want the property. And a full-scale haunting was the only way to do that. She needed a ghost to save this house from that smarmy SOB. She'd find a ghost.

A cold winter wind snaked beneath Gethsemane's collar as she stood in front of a Vodafone store window still bedecked with Christmas decorations. She'd paused on her way to Arcana Arcanora, Dunmullach's occult bookshop and New Age store. If she was going to bring Eamon back from beyond the veil, she'd need to do more than mope around and shout at empty rooms. She pulled her Helly Hansen trench coat tighter and stooped for a closer look at the smartphones. She needed to replace hers, stolen in her luggage along with almost everything she owned the day she arrived in Dunmullach. Stranded with her violin and the dress on her back, she'd made do with Orla's old clothes until her first paycheck afforded her a shopping trip to Cork. Not that she could complain. The late Mrs. McCarthy had excellent taste. A twenty-five-year-old Chanel suit was still a Chanel suit.

"Apple or Android?" asked a voice behind her.

Gethsemane recognized the baritone and greeted *An Garda Síochána* Inspector Iollan O'Reilly. His trademark stingy-brimmed fedora, pulled low against the wind, obscured his salt-and-pepper hair. His eyes shone smoke gray this morning, not the thunderstorm-dark gray they'd often appeared while she investigated the McCarthy murders. A red scarf insulated his neck above his black wool car coat. He wore black leather chukka boots, Cole Haan, she guessed. The inspector had a thing for quality footwear, a tip he'd picked up, like his hat, from his policeman father.

"How go the cold cases, Inspector O'Reilly?" she asked the head—and sole member—of the Dunmullach garda's cold case unit.

"Still on ice, a fair number. I'm following up leads on one or two. And call me Niall."

"Your name's Iollan."

"My name's Iollan to my ma and my ex-girlfriend. And to my

baby sis when she wants to borrow money. Everyone else calls me by my middle name."

"Niall, then. I'm afraid you'll have to settle for calling me Gethsemane."

"No nickname?"

"What? Get? Simi?" She made a face. Her paternal grandmother had insisted all the grandchildren receive Biblical names. She'd been the only one of the five siblings christened with a name not easily shortened. Close family called her by a pet name, Sissy, bestowed on her as a child when her younger siblings struggled to pronounce Gethsemane. She'd rather hear fingers on a chalkboard than have anyone outside the family use it.

"What's your middle name?"

"Anna."

O'Reilly cocked his head and studied her. "Nah, Gethsemane it is."

"Halloo!" The call sounded across the village square. The postmistress waved an envelope from the porch of the century-old red brick post office. "You've a letter, Dr. Brown. Had it nearly a fortnight."

Mail delivery didn't extend up to Carraigfaire Cottage and Gethsemane hadn't thought to stop by the post office and check.

"It's from America," added the postmistress.

"No trouble, I hope," O'Reilly said.

Gethsemane listened. Tchaikovsky's "Pathétique," her internal early warning system, didn't sound off in her head. Probably an offer for a credit card or car insurance. Junk mail tracked her down no matter where she traveled. "One way to find out. Excuse me." She crossed the green.

Neat, almost calligraphic, script graced the front of the envelope and told her who sent it even before she read the return address. Her brother-in-law, Jackson Applethwaite. She opened the envelope and extracted several pages covered in the same precise handwriting. She read to the end of the letter's first page before she noticed the spicy scent of sandalwood and clove wafting near her cheek. Her forehead caught the brim of the inspector's hat as she turned to face him reading over her shoulder.

"Sorry." He kept reading. "Nosy habit. Occupational."

"Here." She handed him the letter. "Make it easy on yourself."

"Who's Jackson?"

"My brother-in-law."

"He's coming for a visit." He handed her the letter.

"Strictly speaking, he's coming for an auction. In someplace called," she referred to the letter, "Ballytuam. Where's Ballytuam?"

"Not far. About twenty kilometers from here. Brilliant town with a class art museum. Is brother Jack an art collector?"

"Museum curator. He's head of the Bayview Museum of Textile and Design. He specializes in early American embroidery, schoolgirl samplers in particular."

"Makes sense, then, his coming to Ballytuam. Olivia McCarthy-Boyle lives there. She's an important collector, some paintings and antiques but mostly textiles. Some of her pieces are like hen's teeth. She owns a chasuble rumored to've been worn by Thomas Aquinas. She's put a few pieces up for auction in recent months. Bet she's got a lot or two on offer at this auction your brother-in-law's coming to."

"McCarthy-Boyle? Any relation to the Dunmullach McCarthys?"

O'Reilly explained, "Cousins. Half the county's McCarthy. Olivia and her late sister were the black sheep of the family on account of their marrying Anglo-Irish landowners."

"Which is some sort of problem?"

"It is if the English stole your Roman Catholic ancestors' lands during the Plantations."

"How do you know so much about this woman?" Gethsemane raised an eyebrow. "Either she's cute or you arrested her."

"She's old enough to be my grandma—at least my ma—and she's out of my jurisdiction." O'Reilly's smile brought out the dimple in his right cheek. "I studied art history at college. Dated a beure in the textile conservation program and she sparked my interest in collecting. But my interest in Mrs. McCarthy-Boyle is professional. The old girl's become a philanthropist since her husband died. Hosts loads of charity fundraisers and benefit galas and whatnot. Sometimes we Dunmullach guards help the fellas in Ballytuam with security for the hooleys. Big bash coming up at week's end. Benefits Children's Hospital, I think. Rare artwork means big money, which means crime risk. Scuttlebutt has it an art theft ring's active in the area. We're on alert."

"You think thieves are going to strike the charity ball?"

"More likely one of the auction houses," he said. "Items turned up missing at three so far: one in Dublin, one in Shannon, and one in Limerick. Ballytuam is lousy with auction houses. But we're not taking any chances. We're watching the party, too."

"I'm trying to picture a gang in ski masks ambushing an auction."

"Nothing that dramatic. No one even noticed the thefts until the auctioneers started the bidding. They called for the lots, but the lots weren't there."

"Sounds like inside jobs," she said.

"Listen to you. You've been watching too many gangster films."

"How else would someone be able to steal an item from an auction without anyone noticing until show time? Shoplift? It's not like people can wander in off the street and paw the merchandise."

"No, but the public can attend auction previews and get a good look at what's being sold."

"I've been to some," Gethsemane said. "I could look, but I couldn't touch."

"We suspect the thieves case the venue at the preview then pose as buyers at the auction. They wait for an opportune moment during a bidding frenzy, then *poof*." O'Reilly made a vanishing gesture with his hands. "Auction houses have been warned to be dog wide and several gardaí will be undercover at the events." He paused. "You understand what I told you isn't public knowledge?"

"Don't worry, I'm not going to sell the story to the *Dunmullach*

Dispatch." O'Reilly opened his mouth, but she continued before he could say anything. "Or mention it to anyone at the Rabbit. Speaking of auctions, if Mrs. McCarthy-Boyle can afford to host fancy dress balls, why's she selling off the family silver?"

O'Reilly shrugged. "She's only recently started selling. It's expensive maintaining those estates Oliver Cromwell handed her husband's ancestors."

"So she auctions a Vermeer from time to time to pay the light bill." She turned pages of the letter. "Jackson doesn't say anything about attending any fundraisers. He only mentions the auction. Doesn't say what he plans to bid on. Not that he would." She adopted a melodramatic tone. "In case the letter fell into the wrong hands. Curators are both paranoid and competitive." Her eyes fell on a line on the last page. She spewed a string of Virginia-accented Irish swear words.

"Good mastery of the language. Brogue needs work."

Eamon used to tease her about her accent. Sadness crept into her chest.

It must've shown on her face because O'Reilly apologized. "I was only coddin'."

"It's not that, it's—never mind. Jackson arrives the day after tomorrow. I haven't cleaned, there's no food in the house—"

"He's family. He's coming to see you, not the house."

"He's *Southern* family." She swore again. "Advanced warning would've been nice."

"Letter's been waiting a fortnight."

"Ten days. Thanks for pointing out it's my fault."

"You need a mobile phone. Then people can text or email. You know, like people do in the twenty-first century."

"Jackson would've written anyway. He's an antiquarian. He's got one foot in the nineteenth century and the other in the eighteenth. Except when it comes to art fraud. He's pretty cutting edge when it comes to new methods to detect forgeries. He wrote several papers on antique textile fraud and acted as a consultant to the FBI's art crimes unit once or twice."

"A fellow crime fighter. I'd like to meet him. A couple of forgeries recently found their way onto the local antiques market, sold through legit galleries. It reminds me of a high-profile case out of New York a decade ago. I bet your brother's familiar with it. I'd love to compare notes. Tell you what, when he arrives, I'll keep him occupied down at the Rabbit long enough for you to spruce up the cottage."

The sudden blast of Tchaikovsky in her head made Gethsemane wince. Why did O'Reilly's offer to talk shop with Jackson set off alarms?

"Something wrong?"

"No, just, um, a cold blast of wind hit me in the ear. Look, I've got some things to do."

"So I should stop jawing and saunter on so you can get to them?" He tipped his hat and winked. "Even a thick guard can take a hint. You'll let me know if you're needing anything?"

Got a ghost handy?

"Thanks, I'll do that."

"Guard! Guard!" A woman's harsh shouts torpedoed Gethsemane and O'Reilly.

Gethsemane, startled, spun around. The inspector's head snapped in the direction of the noise. Gethsemane saw from the corner of her eye how he'd tensed like a wound spring.

A large woman, shoulders hunched, fists clenched, stormed toward them across the green. O'Reilly stepped in front of Gethsemane. The woman stopped in front of O'Reilly, her bright red boots an inch from his toes.

"Guard!"

"Please stop shouting, ma'am. I'm standing right here."

The woman relaxed a bit and stepped back. She didn't look as big without the hunched shoulders.

"What's the trouble?" O'Reilly asked.

"My shop's been burgled, that's the trouble." She pointed at the shop selling stationery and art supplies. She turned back to O'Reilly and wagged her finger under his nose. "And don't you go telling me burglary's not your unit. I want you to come look at my shop right now. See what they've done."

"Of course, ma'am. But first, is anyone injured?"

The woman shook her head. "No. The shop was empty when it happened. I open late, half days only, when school's out. I unlocked the door and found half my stock missing."

"Any idea of what, exactly, they took?"

"You'll have to come see, won't you?"

"If you could give me a hint, ma'am." A muscle twitched in O'Reilly's jaw and his eyes darkened to storm gray. "So I know what I might be getting into."

The woman ticked items off on her fingers. "Paper, ink, and pens."

"Anything missing from the till?" the inspector asked.

The woman cocked her head and said nothing for a moment. Then she replied, "I don't think so. I didn't go all the way inside the shop, mind you. As soon as I saw the empty shelves I went for help, so I can't say for certain. But I don't remember seeing the cash drawer open."

Gethsemane stepped out from behind O'Reilly. "What kind of burglar steals paper and ink but leaves money? Someone planning to print their own?"

The woman puffed up like an offended peacock. "Well, the shelves are easier to get to, aren't they, than the till?" She lowered her voice and leaned toward Gethsemane. "You're that new teacher. This wouldn't be some of your students pulling a prank?"

"No, ma'am." Gethsemane assured her the St. Brennan's roster of acceptable pranks did not include felonies.

"Are you coming, then?" the woman said to O'Reilly. She grabbed him by the elbow.

O'Reilly opened his mouth to say something to Gethsemane, but she waved away his unspoken comment. "You have to go."

"I have to go," he agreed.

She watched the shopkeeper drag O'Reilly toward the other side of the green, then continued to the occult shop.

Two

Arcana Arcanora was one of several shops that occupied the ground floor of a multi-story brick building a few blocks from the pub. A haberdasher hemmed in its door, the same shade of bright blue as Carraigfaire's, on one side, a solicitor's office on the other. The jangle of temple bells announced Gethsemane's arrival as she opened the door. She threaded her way through narrow aisles packed with tarot cards, scrying mirrors, and incense to a wall of books at the back of the store. She scanned the shelves for titles related to summoning ghosts.

"May I help you?" a voice asked. The speaker, a college-aged girl, wore several layers of clothing, the top layer being a flowy chiffon dress. She sported piercings in her lip, ears, and nose and adorned her hair with a variety of ribbons and colorful strings. Tattoos peeked from her neckline and cuffs. Gethsemane felt underdressed in her silk tweed skirt and cardigan.

"Do you, um, have anything on conjuring spirits?" she asked.

The girl stepped around Gethsemane and stopped in front of a bookcase a few feet from the one she had chosen. "All of our selections dealing with ghostly encounters are on these shelves."

"I was looking for something more along the lines of how to summon a ghost."

"You mean like a how-to manual? A grimoire?" The girl's

expression remained as mundane as a grocery store clerk answering which aisle the butter was on. "We don't have anything like that at the moment, I'm afraid. We could order something, or if you need it now, you might want to talk to Father Keating, the parish priest, over at Our Lady of Perpetual Sorrows. He owns a nice collection of occult books, some of them first editions."

Gethsemane masked her surprise. She knew about the books. Father Tim Keating had shown them to her when he'd loaned her his bicycle. His late brother, also a priest, had served the Catholic church as an exorcist. Father Tim had inherited the books from him. Did the whole village know about the collection? No information was secret from Dunmullach's gossip wheel. She thanked the girl for the advice.

Back outside, she retrieved her Pashley Parabike from the rack where she'd secured it and faced the imposing Gothic structure whose spires towered over the village. Time to see a priest about a ghost.

Our Lady of Perpetual Sorrows' rectory stood within the wrought-iron fence that enclosed the churchyard, on the yard's far side, separated from the massive Gothic church by formal gardens and a cemetery. Evergreen topiaries and ornamental grasses provided the priest's two-story Tudor residence a sense of privacy without hiding it from view.

Gethsemane leaned her bike against a statue at the end of the path leading to the front door and rehearsed her speech. Father Timothy Keating knew Eamon's ghost had haunted Carraigfaire cottage, but she wasn't sure he'd approve of her trying to call his spirit back from its eternal rest to stop a real estate deal. Even if it was a deal made in hell.

She climbed the steps and raised her hand to knock when the door swung open and Father Tim rushed out. She jumped back, avoiding collision by an inch.

"Gethsemane," the gray-haired cleric said. "Sorry, I didn't see you there. Just on my way out for a walk." He patted the tiny paunch not quite disguised by his Georgetown University hoodie. "Doctor says I need more exercise."

"I've come at a bad time."

"Never a bad time for good company." Father Tim stepped back inside. "The walk will wait. Come in, I'll wet the tea."

Gethsemane followed him to the kitchen and watched as he brewed a pot of Bewley's. "Plenty of sugar, the way you like it," he said as he handed her a cup. "Tell me what's troubling you."

She sipped the steaming sweet liquid and tried not to remember what almost happened the last time she had tea at the rectory. "Is it that obvious?"

"You get a sense for these things in my line of work."

She bagged the rehearsed speech. "Bottom line up front, if I can't conjure Eamon's ghost to scare off a hotel developer, Carraigfaire cottage ceases to exist."

Father Tim pshawed her. "Billy would never let that happen."

Gethsemane explained Billy's plans to sell to Hank Wayne.

"The divil...Billy must've been ossified to make such a deal. Or maybe he got a bad dose and fever addled his brain. He loves Carraigfaire, has ever since he was a boy."

"Whoever said money can't buy love never dealt with the persuasive power of Hank Wayne's billions."

"What's Eamon's ghost got to do with it?"

"Wayne has a mortal fear of the supernatural. PTSD level. He had a traumatic childhood experience with ghosts."

"Exploiting a man's terror for personal gain is immoral."

"Completely. But I'm desperate. And it's not for personal gain, it's for the good of the community. You'd be better off letting Ronald Crump turn the lighthouse into one of his towers than letting Hank Wayne so much as remodel a bathroom." She named a hotel renowned for its generic chain hotel tackiness. "That's one of Wayne's."

"Jaysus, Mary, and Joseph." Father Tim crossed himself. "But I don't see what can be done. Eamon's passed on."

Gethsemane hid behind her teacup as she spoke. "Maybe some of your brother's books have some ghost conjuring spells."

"What's that? I'm not sure I heard you. Did you say something about spells?"

She put the cup down. "You heard. Your brother left you the biggest collection of occult books I've seen outside of a horror movie. Even the clerk at Arcana Arcanora recommended it. Surely at least one of them contains a spell I can use to conjure spirits."

"Demons, Gethsemane. My brother was an exorcist. He specialized in demons. And he cast them back into hell, not called them up from it. He collected those books, the grimoires in particular, to keep them out of circulation."

"Didn't he also use them as references to distinguish between human and inhuman spirits?" Finally, all those episodes of *Ghost Hunting Adventures* paid off. She almost sounded like she knew what she was talking about. "The psychics and mages and demon hunters who wrote the books would have recorded incantations for calling both types of spirits, wouldn't they? You choose the spell to make sure I don't accidentally raise any demon hordes, and I promise I will only read that one."

"I don't like this."

"Tim, please. It's Carraigfaire."

After several more minutes of pleading—and borrowing his smartphone to pull up a photo of a Wayne Resorts International property—Gethsemane wore the priest down. "All right, enough. I confess, I'd rather see Dublin beat Cork in the All-Ireland than see *that*," he pointed at the image on the phone's screen, "anywhere within a thousand miles of this village. I'll find *one* spell. If it doesn't work, it doesn't work. Give me your word you won't try any others."

She promised. "Will I go to hell if I kiss a priest?"

"I don't think so." He winked. "Though it might be worth the trip."

She kissed him on top of his head. "Let's go save Carraigfaire."

* * *

Gethsemane hummed Eamon's "Etude for Piano in G Major" as she pedaled up Carrick Point Road, Father Tim's grimoire nestled in the Pashley's basket. A thin brass strip marked a single page, a spell to summon a ghost. A ghost to stop Hank Wayne's assault on Carraigfaire. So what if she didn't understand Latin, the spell's language? She didn't have to understand the words to recite them.

Honk!

Startled by the car horn, Gethsemane swerved and almost lost control of the Pashley. Pebbles struck her as the speeding vehicle sprayed gravel while rounding the blind curve. She pulled over to the side of the road and watched as a taxi sped down the hill. "Feckin' eejit!" She started back up the road when it hit her. A taxi. Who'd be arriving by taxi? She raced the rest of the way.

She spied him as she crested the hill: a tall handsome dark-skinned man in a gray fedora, bow tie peeking above the collar of his herringbone overcoat, stood on the porch next to a suitcase and messenger bag.

"Sissy! Hello!" he called, arm raised in a wave.

She parked her bike along the side of the cottage. She peeled off her gloves and laid them in the basket on top of the grimoire before running to the porch. Spellcasting would have to wait.

"Jackson! You're early," she said through hugs and kisses. "You're supposed to arrive tomorrow."

"I know. My apologies for turning up on your doorstep without warning," Jackson said. "I finagled a last-minute invitation to the auction preview tomorrow. It's a chance to get a look at the Hester Creech miniature sampler before the bidding begins. I hopped on the last train from Cork."

"Hester Creech miniature sampler? Is that what you're bidding on?"

Jackson nodded.

"It's a fine example of work from the Kellogg school. It belongs to the McCarthy-Boyle collection of early American needlework.

Rather, it belongs to the collection until after the auctioneer's hammer drops."

O'Reilly guessed right. "You mean Olivia McCarthy-Boyle, the Ballytuam philanthropist."

Jackson arched a brow. "How'd you know about Mrs. McCarthy-Boyle?"

"I have my sources." She winked. "Seriously, compared to the gossip mill in these parts, Bayview's rumor vine feels as slow as the Pony Express. By the time anything hits social media out here the news is already three days old down at the pub. Did you finagle an invitation to Mrs. McCarthy-Boyle's charity ball, too?"

"No. I'm not going to the party. I hate fundraisers, even when they're for the museum. I'm not attending any I don't have to. By the way, I hope I'm not inconveniencing you by showing up a day early."

"Of course not. But," she said as she led the way inside, "no comments about my housekeeping. I didn't get a chance to clean."

"Sissy, I may have married into a Virginia family, but I'm from up north. We don't check the tops of the china cabinets for dust."

"You may not, but I know my sister will ask you when you get home." She hung her brother-in-law's coat on the hall rack and ushered him to the study. "I also haven't done the shopping, so there's not much food in the house. The bar, however, is well-stocked."

"Now *that*," Jackson winked, "is something we northerners check for."

Settled with drinks—Waddell and Dobb for her, Midleton for him—Jackson filled her in on news from home. Her elder sister and her nephew were in Hawaii, combining a vacation with her sister's ethnobotanical chemistry research. Gethsemane in her turn updated Jackson on life in an Irish village after solving two twenty-five-year-old murders.

"You made the news. 'American woman rights injustice after quarter century.' The publicity's prompted the woman who wrote that book—oh, what's her name, you know, the true-crime author?"

"I know the one." Gethsemane detested the book, a piece of bestselling trash based on innuendo and half-truths, full of shoddy writing and assumptions about Eamon's guilt. Assumptions Gethsemane had disproved.

"Anyway, she's releasing a new edition, updated with the results of your investigation."

"I'm sure she won't bother to interview me before she writes more garbage."

"Responsible journalism is hardly her style. But if her new book is as popular as her last, you'd better prepare yourself for a mob of tourists thronging your bright blue door. You'll need to build a hotel."

She sputtered as she choked on her bourbon.

Jackson patted her on the back. "Are you okay?"

"I'm fine. Swallowed wrong. Excuse me for a minute." She rose and waved Jackson back to his seat. "No, don't get up. I just forgot something."

She grabbed her coat and ran outside where she retrieved the grimoire. Too large to hide in her coat pocket, she cradled it in her arm and tried to devise a plausible explanation for why she had it as she walked back to the cottage.

Jackson waited in the doorway. "Is everything all right?"

"Fine." She set the grimoire on the entryway bench while she removed her coat.

"What's this?" Jackson picked up the book.

She grabbed at it. "Nothing. Just something I borrowed—"

Jackson, over six feet tall, studied the book at eye level, out of Gethsemane's five-foot-three reach. "Seventeenth century, gilt spine, intricate head and tail pieces, woodcut page decorations, Latin text. Sissy, this is a rare and valuable book. You were carrying it in a bicycle basket?" He looked mortified.

"I borrowed it from the parish priest. He has a collection of occul—of books stored in his shed and he loaned me this one."

Jackson sank to the bench. "He keeps rare books stored in a *garden shed*?"

"It's a long story."

"And this." Jackson held up the bookmark. "The poor spine."

"No, no, don't do—" Gethsemane grabbed at the book. Too late. Jackson closed it. "I'll never find it." She fought back tears. Crying never helped. Even if it did, she'd have a hard time explaining why she was so upset over a bookmark.

"Find what?"

She took the brass strip. "The page this strip marked."

"Oh, Sissy, I'm so sorry. I didn't think." Jackson held the book up and examined its top and bottom edges. "I'll find it for you."

"How? The book's like a thousand pages long."

"One thousand four hundred twenty-seven pages. Between two of which there is a small gap made by that," he nodded his head toward the bookmark and curled his lip, "thing." He opened the grimoire. "Here it is." He recited the spell. "*Quondam vos eratis quod nunc ego sum, tu es quod ego erit fio. Invoco te. Levate velum inter regna vivos et mortuos. Erunt cum mihi in hoc loco. Quaeso vestra virtutes facere quae oportet fieri. Ut inveniam gratiam in conspecto tuo, meo obsecro.* Why on earth would you need an incantation for summoning spirits?"

"Because..." What could she tell him? Not the truth. Jackson would think she'd gone mad. He was as skeptical as she used to be about the paranormal. "Because I'm composing a danse macabre based on the incantation."

"You're composing? That's wonderful," Jackson said. "You mastered playing the works of others a long time ago. It's about time you created your own music. Past time. Would you play something? I'd love to hear it."

"It's not finished yet." How could it be, since the idea only occurred to her half a minute ago?

"I'd love to hear what you have so far."

She hesitated.

"I'll make you a deal. If you play for me, I'll take you to the auction preview. One of the lots is a 1742 Guarneri Del Gesu from an anonymous seller. Wouldn't you love to see it up close?"

Asking her if she'd like to see a rare violin by a famous violin maker up close was like asking Elizabeth Taylor if she'd like another diamond. She led the way to the music room and shouldered her own violin, a Vuillaume copy of Stradivari's *Le Messie*. "Read the spell again."

Jackson read, "*Quondam vos eratis quod nunc ego sum, tu es quod ego erit fio. Invoco te. Levate velum inter regna vivos et mortuos. Erunt cum mihi in hoc loco. Quaeso vestra virtutes facere quae oportet fieri. Ut inveniam gratiam in conspecto tuo, meo obsecro.*"

Gethsemane improvised an eerily cheerful dance evocative of the allegorical procession to the grave headed by Death personified.

Jackson shuddered. "Spooky. Certainly fits the theme. 'You were what I am now, you are what I will be, lift the veil between the realms of the living and the dead.'"

"Saint-Saëns has nothing to worry about."

"Don't sell yourself short. You have the advantage on Saint-Saëns. You're still alive." Jackson set the grimoire on the piano bench. "I'll leave you to your musical magic. I've got some catalogs to study before the preview. Which is at two thirty tomorrow afternoon, by the way."

"What is it with you art-and-antiquities types and catalogs? Your collection at home's taken over an entire room. Your wife threatens to wall it off if it spreads farther. And remember the time I made the mistake of pulling one from a stack to read? I narrowly escaped burial in a paper avalanche."

"Reference material. Catalogs give you an idea of how much an item's worth so you don't over- or under-bid, and they document provenance. I'd hate to blow the museum's budget on a fake."

"I doubt you'll be taken in by fakes, Mr. Forgery Expert. Which reminds me, I told Niall about your work fighting art crime. He offered to buy you a drink and talk shop."

"Niall?"

"Inspector O'Reilly. He's with the Dunmullach *An Garda Síochana* cold case squad. And before that eyebrow of yours inches up past your hairline, no, he's not my new romance. He's a friend. Sort of." When he wasn't threatening to arrest her. "He has a background in art history."

"I'd love to discuss some cold case art crimes. Like the forgery and theft ring that operated out of New York several years ago. Art galleries would sell forged paintings to buyers, then stage thefts so the buyers could file bogus insurance claims. They never caught the most notorious gallery owners. They fled New York and were spotted in Dublin soon after, but they disappeared."

A ferocious blast of "Pathétique" roared in Gethsemane's head. She winced.

"Are you all right?" Jackson asked.

"Yeah, I'm fine. Sinuses." She shook her head to clear it. "You weren't involved in the investigation, were you?"

"No, paintings aren't my specialty. I did provide the agent in charge with copies of my articles on early eighteenth century pigments and their use in paint versus fabric dye." He excused himself.

Gethsemane tried to forget about art crime as she picked up the grimoire. No time for premonitions. She only had until Epiphany to call Eamon back from wherever. She read the incantation aloud, then waited and listened. Nothing. She sniffed the air. Nothing. What had she expected? Maybe not an instantaneous full-bodied manifestation but—something. She sat at the piano with a sigh and pecked out a C-scale. Another day closer to Twelfth Night and no closer to bringing Eamon back. Time to stop kidding herself. No way she could keep the cottage out of Hank Wayne's clutches.

The C-scale flowed into a melody. She'd always expressed her emotions more easily through music than through open display, so she channeled her frustration and disappointment into the disconsolate notes of Gorecki's "Symphony No. 3." Then, remembering how joyful she'd felt a few weeks ago when she joined the trad music session at the Mad Rabbit, she played "The Lilting Banshee" and "Banish Misfortune." The jigs' spry notes worked their magic on her mood. Spirits lifted, her eyes drifted to the view through the window. The evening sun glinted off the calm blue-gray water of the bay. A ship's horn sounded somewhere distant, and a sea chanty, "Captain Heuston's Lament," popped into her head. She played the ironically named song about a sea captain who spends his shore leave sampling a variety of ways to mend his broken heart through twice. She closed the piano's keyboard cover. Where'd that come from? She picked up jigs, reels, and more than a few drinking songs at her favorite pub while an undergrad at Vassar, but ocean-going songs hadn't been part of the Hudson Valley pub's repertoire. Maybe she'd heard it during the summer she spent in Connecticut with a friend who worked as a historical reenactor at Mystic Seaport.

A tremendous thump reverberated from upstairs, followed by heavy footsteps. Gethsemane ran into the hall, where she met Jackson already halfway up the stairs.

"Stay here," he said.

Gethsemane bounded up after her brother-in-law.

"I thought I told you to—" Jackson said. Footsteps cut him off.

"The back bedroom." Gethsemane pushed past him. She stopped short in the doorway. Jackson plowed into her.

"Empty." He stepped past Gethsemane and searched the room. "No one."

Had the spell worked after all? Disembodied footsteps weren't Eamon's style. He tended toward snarky remarks and swear words.

"Maybe I should search the other rooms," Jackson said.

"There's only the front bedroom, the upstairs parlor, and the bathroom up here. No one could have gotten past us."

"Still..."

Gethsemane waited while her brother-in-law searched the rest of the upstairs. She sniffed. Nothing but sea air and peat. Soap and cologne heralded Eamon's ghost. What, or who, had they heard?

Jackson returned. "No one. And not a thing out of place."

"Probably just the wind." She bit back the urge to call out to Eamon.

"The wind? I'm no meteorologist, but I know the difference between wind and footsteps."

"You searched yourself. No one's here." She tried to sound nonchalant. "What's your explanation? Ghosts?"

"Don't be ridiculous." He made a final circuit of the rooms. "Nothing. The wind, like you said."

"It does sound pretty bizarre coming off the cliffs. Sometimes I swear I hear voices."

Jackson shook his head. "I don't see how you stand it out here, so isolated. I'll stick to big cities and college towns. Hell, even the suburbs beat the back of beyond. At least you have neighbors."

"Oh, I don't know. The wind doesn't ruin your view with ill-placed satellite dishes or let its dog go on your lawn."

"You are truly fearless, Sissy." He kissed her on the cheek. "Back to the auction catalogs." He started downstairs. "Do you want me to sleep on the couch in the study tonight? Between you and the door?"

"No, Jackson, I don't want you to be my bodyguard." He looked hurt, so she softened her tone. "Thanks for the offer, but there's no one out here to protect me from. Another advantage of not having neighbors. Sleep in the back bedroom and be comfortable."

She waited until her brother-in-law returned to the study then circuited the upstairs rooms herself. "Eamon?" she whispered. "Eamon, is that you? Stop screwing around if it is. Eamon?"

Several measures of "Pathétique," but nothing else, answered her. What was it warning her about? Maybe Hank Wayne wasn't her only problem.

Eamon yawned. He'd run out of things to which to compare the dullness of limbo. He'd decided this must be limbo—not as nice as heaven, as perilous as purgatory, or as much fun as hell. He paced. He grew tired of pacing. He looked for a place to sit. He found none. He walked. He missed Dunmullach. He missed Carraigfaire.

He missed his piano. He missed Gethsemane. He especially missed Gethsemane. She aggravated him, but—no, she didn't, not really. Truthfully, he enjoyed their banter. He admired her stubbornness and the way she stood up to him. He found her strong-willed fearlessness appealing. He wished he'd told her.

Three

Gethsemane and Jackson rode the train to Ballytuam past small farms dotted with cottages and cattle. They ended at Ballytuam Station, a quaint stone building with a pitched roof situated at the bottom of a hill. Modern utilitarian stores, boxes constructed of glass and steel, clustered near the train station. An office supply emporium reminded Gethsemane of the odd break-in at the Dunmullach stationers. She described the encounter with the shop's owner.

"And that's all they took?" Jackson asked. "Paper and ink?"

"And pens. As far as I know that's all. Weird, huh? Stealing items of little value and not even trying to get the cash."

"Those items may not be worth much in and of themselves, but in the hands of someone who knows what they're doing, they can be quite valuable."

"Office supplies? How?"

"Pen, paper, and ink. Basic items in a forger's tool kit."

As they walked farther into town, modern architecture yielded to a collection of narrow streets, brick storefronts, and rowhouses with brightly colored doors spreading up the hill away from the station. Glittering tinsel and foil letters hung in several windows to welcome the new year. A mansion built of the same stone as the train depot dominated the hill's summit. Even from the station platform, Gethsemane appreciated the house's massive size. Rife with turrets, towers, and chimneys, the imposing structure loomed over its surroundings from the center of a green expanse of lawn.

She whistled the theme from *The Addams Family*.

"If any place had a ghost or ten, that would be it," Jackson said.

"You don't believe in ghosts."

"A joke. Just kidding." He jerked his head toward the ticket agent's office. "They said the auction house is only a few blocks from the station. Walk or taxi?"

"Let's walk."

They passed various art galleries and antique shops on the way from the station. Jackson pointed out several of the better-quality paintings and objects displayed in the shop windows. He lapsed into lecture-mode—he was an adjunct professor at Bayview University—as he described differences between early- and late-eighteenth century furniture design. Gethsemane stopped short midway through an explanation of French furniture-making guilds.

"C'mon," Jackson said. "The auctioneer's just up at the next corner."

"Look." She stood in front of a store window stenciled with "Perryman Gallery" in a golden arc across the top. A single item held pride of place in the window—a large embroidered tapestry. The bright green panel depicted a tree of life heavily stitched with brilliantly colored fruits, birds, and stylized flowers. "1752" was stitched in a bottom corner. "It's gorgeous."

Jackson leaned close to the window and peered at the tapestry for a moment. "It's modern."

"You looked at that for, like, ten seconds. How can you tell it's a fake?"

"I didn't say it was a fake, I said it was modern. As long as the gallery is selling it as a modern reproduction, they're doing nothing wrong." He peered at it again. "As reproductions go, the stitchwork's lovely. Don't care for the green ground fabric. Light brown or straw colored would've worked better."

"You missed my point, Jackson. How can you tell from less

than half a minute's exam, through a window at that, this wasn't actually stitched in 1752?"

"The colors are wrong. Too bright. Eighteenth-century fabric dyes were mostly plant-based. They produced colors far more muted than chemical dyes. Think indigo blue instead of royal or Mediterranean. Another thing—look at all the light this piece is getting. Sunlight through the window as well as an overhead spot."

"You can tell it's not an antique because the lighting's wrong?"

"No, the lighting's fine. What I meant was, think of how much light exposure a two-hundred-fifty-plus-year-old tapestry must have gotten."

"All those years of light would have faded the colors. The way Grandma's olive green curtains faded to celery green after hanging in the windows for thirty years." She looked at the tapestry again. "I still think it's pretty."

Jackson agreed. "And a modern reproduction would have the advantage of costing somewhat less than my son's future college tuition."

"That much for some embroidery?"

"Snob." Jackson elbowed her playfully.

She elbowed him. "What do you mean, 'snob'?"

"Art snob. You'd never say, 'That much for an old painting?' if we were talking about a Picasso."

"We're not talking about a Picasso."

"Textiles belong in the fine art realm as much as paintings do, even if they don't get nearly the same respect. Did you know one of Queen Elizabeth I's gowns was cut up and turned into an altar cloth at a local church? Creating a magnificent piece of needlework requires as much skill as creating a magnificent painting. People don't appreciate the quality because the stitching was often done on utilitarian items."

"I appreciate textiles. Now," she added *sotto voce*. "I just didn't realize how expensive they could be."

"The needleworker's skill and the textile's rarity factor into the price the piece commands."

"I guess that explains the auction house thefts. Oops!" Gethsemane clamped a hand over her mouth.

"Auction house thefts?"

"I wasn't supposed to say anything. Three auction houses have been robbed. The gardaí expect more thefts, so they're going undercover at auctions and warning auction houses to beef up security."

Jackson frowned.

"It's true. I heard it from one of the cops working on the case."

"I believe you, Sissy. I just hope there's no trouble at Ryan's."

Tchaikovsky sounded in her head. She silently told him to shut up. "I'm sure there won't be. The robberies have been in big cities, like Dublin and Shannon. Ballytuam's a long way from a big city. I'm sure no self-respecting art thief would be caught in it." Jackson didn't laugh at her joke. She leaned close to the gallery window. "A textile thief has an advantage over a painting thief."

"What advantage?"

"You can fold a textile and stick it in your pocket. Hard to do with a Picasso."

They moved on to the next block, a brick row of windowless storefronts punctuated with yellow and red and blue doors. They slowed to read the brass plaques affixed near each door to distinguish one professional office from the next.

"Accountant, solicitor, solicitor, solicitor—they've got as many lawyers here as we do at home," Gethsemane said.

"Where would the art world be without lawyers?"

Gethsemane kept reading. "Here it is." She stopped in front of the next to last office. "M. Ryan, Auctioneer. Smaller than I expected."

"Ryan's specializes in atelier and private collection auctions. Usually only a few lots are offered at a time and there aren't as many bidders." He looked up at the height of the building. "It does have four stories. Not so small."

They rang the bell and followed the young man who admitted them to a reception area. Light reflected off blond wood floors and highlighted gilt-framed pictures hung on dark gray walls. Small statues adorned occasional tables scattered around the room's perimeter. The young man offered them tea or coffee—which they declined—then excused himself.

"Why are we the only ones here?" Gethsemane asked. She'd attended one or two Christeby's presale exhibitions when she lived in New York. They were free and open to the public—two characteristics that made them a viable social outing for a young musician on a fresh-out-of-grad-school budget.

"Ryan's previews are invitation only."

"I don't have an invitation."

"We'll think of something."

She sat in one of the room's few chairs and ran her hands over the beige silk damask upholstery. "Nice setup. I'm not in here five minutes and I want to buy something."

Jackson, attention focused on a petit point cushion, didn't answer.

Several catalogs lay stacked on a marquetry coffee table. Gethsemane sifted through them. "You have some of these same catalogs, Jackson."

"I'm sure I do." He flipped the cushion and studied its back. "Auction houses keep catalogs for the same reasons curators do."

She reached for another stack of periodicals. "Auction houses have their own magazines?" She flipped through the one on top. "*Christeby's Insider*. Glossy pictures of beautiful people. I guess the art world's not so different from the music world. The well-heeled need to memorialize who attended what party and what they wore."

"Those magazines feature some good articles, too."

"That's what they say about *Playboy*."

A door opened and a plump redhead in low-heeled pumps stepped into the room. Her skirt and blazer, the same gray as the walls, fit her perfectly. Bespoke, Gethsemane guessed. She'd learned to distinguish custom tailoring from her grandfather, who'd funded his dream of playing cello professionally with a tailoring and dressmaking business in Washington, D.C.

"Dr. Applethwaite." The redhead shook Jackson's hand. "Sorry to keep you waiting. Michaela Ryan. I've read several of your papers. So good to finally meet such an esteemed antiquarian. I've no doubt you'll find Lot Four exceeds your expectations."

"The Hester Creech miniature sampler. I'm eager to see it. I don't mind telling you adding it to our collection would be a feather in the museum's cap." He leaned closer to Ms. Ryan and lowered his voice. "You couldn't give me a hint on how much competition I'm likely to face?"

"Dr. Applethwaite, you know we maintain strict standards of confidentiality and discretion. It's why so many consigners trust us with their precious objects."

"Of course, Ms. Ryan. That was my unsuccessful attempt at auction humor."

Gethsemane cleared her throat.

Ms. Ryan shook her hand. "You've someone with you," she said to Jackson.

Jackson introduced her. "My associate, Dr. Brown, is a professional musician and expert on antique stringed instruments. I wanted her opinion on Lot Eight. With a favorable report, a colleague at the Bayview Conservatory may phone in a bid."

"The Guarneri del Gesu. An extraordinary violin. Welcome, Dr. Brown. If you'll follow me."

They rode an elevator up a flight to a floor occupied by a gallery space identical to the reception room except in size and furniture. Easels and display cases replaced the chairs and occasional tables. Small white numbered cards provided the only identification for the objects on the easels and in the cases. Ms. Ryan handed Gethsemane and Jackson preview catalogs keyed to the numbered cards. Jackson stopped at the case labeled "Lot Four." Gethsemane went straight to Lot Eight—the Guarneri del Gesu.

Words left her. She closed her eyes and imagined sweet, dark notes rising from its strings.

"Remarkable, isn't it?"

She opened her eyes. Ms. Ryan stood next to her. "Remarkable doesn't begin to describe it." She held her face as close to the violin as the case's glass allowed. Her eyes feasted on its flamed maple wood, the color of rich bourbon, its elongated f-holes, more elegant than any swan's neck, and the "IHS" and cross inscribed on the label.

"You'll need to hear it, I suppose, to make an accurate assessment." Ms. Ryan pulled a keyring from her pocket and opened the case. "Will you be wanting to play it yourself, or shall I call our in-house instrumentalist?"

Gethsemane marshaled all her self-control to keep from flinging her arms around the auctioneer and kissing her. "No need to trouble your in-house person. I'll play."

Ms. Ryan stepped aside as Gethsemane oh-so-gently lifted the violin. "It's shown with an 1850 Dodd bow, but a 1910 Sartory bow is also available from the same seller."

Gethsemane shouldered the violin and bowed a perfectly tuned A. "The Dodd's just fine." She closed her eyes. What could she play worthy of such a prize?

Eamon's "Requiem for a Fallen Angel." Poignant and cathartic, it would serve as both farewell to Carraigfaire Cottage and apology to her spectral friend. She drew the bow across the strings. Dark masculine tones reverberated through the gallery and filled the room with sadness and longing. She played the first movement then lowered the bow.

Ms. Ryan blew her nose into a crumpled handkerchief, then wiped tears from her cheeks.

Jackson looked away and fumbled in his pocket.

Gethsemane turned toward noise near the gallery entrance. A half-dozen people, one of whom she recognized as the young man who'd escorted them in, crowded the doorway. Some swiped at noses with handkerchiefs and shirt cuffs. Everyone bore wet faces.

"Sorry," Gethsemane said. "I didn't mean to—" She imagined Eamon's snarky, "Jaysus, darlin', way to shut down a hooley."

"Captain Heuston's Lament" popped into her head again. She

played the first stanza and alleviated the grief that pervaded the gallery. She replaced the violin and bow in the case. "My report will state that if Jack—Dr. Applethwaite's colleague doesn't bid, he's an eejit."

A staffer's cell phone rang. Everyone jumped. Ms. Ryan and her employees snapped back into business mode. "Dr. Applethwaite, Dr. Brown," Ms. Ryan said. "I trust you gathered all the information you need? I don't mean to rush you, but," she glanced at her watch, "my next appointment arrives at half past."

Their original escort arrived in the entrance as if summoned by some inaudible signal. Ms. Ryan accompanied them as far as the elevator. "I'll see you at the auction, Dr. Applethwaite. You, too, I hope, Dr. Brown. These affairs prove quite exciting, especially if a bidding war starts. Anything might happen."

Back out on the street, Jackson hugged Gethsemane. "Sissy, you are a genius."

"Normally, brother-man, I'd agree with you, but in this case, I have to give at least half the credit to the violin." She winked and nudged him with her elbow. "Wanna grab a bite before we catch the train back to Dunmullach? We passed a fish and chip shop on the way up to Ms. Ryan's."

Jackson made a face.

"Oh, don't even. You eat fried catfish almost every Saturday. This is fried haddock. Close enough."

Eamon sniffed. Fish and chips? Was that what he smelled? Twenty-five years of no eating and the scent of malt vinegar and fry grease still made him hungry. A fish and chip shop in limbo? He peered into the gray mist. Nothing. Absolutely nothing. Did the aroma come from the other side? Was someone trying to reach him?

"Gethsemane?"

Silence.

He shouted. "Gethsemane!" No answer.

He took a deep breath. The aroma had vanished. He was alone

again. No fish and chips, no Gethsemane, no anything. His torrent of curses dissolved into tears.

Gethsemane paused with a forkful of fish halfway to her mouth. "Did you hear something?"

Jackson shook his head. "No."

She twisted in her seat. "I thought I heard someone call me."

"Gastritis-induced hallucinations triggered by fatty food." Jackson ate the last of his fries and licked his fingers.

"No such thing. Trust me, my mother's a doctor." Gethsemane polished off the last of her fish. "I forgot to look at the Creech miniature. What'd you think?"

"The provenance seems in order, workmanship appears exquisite. Assuming I place the winning bid, I've got a spot in the museum's main hall already picked out. After a thorough assessment and authentication, of course."

"You just said it looked fine."

"From the front and on paper. But I'd be an irresponsible curator if I didn't examine the piece from all angles out of the case. I'd hate to make the same mistake the Zaxby made."

"The Zaxby Museum of European Art? The one whose job offer you turned down?"

Jackson nodded. "They purchased—years before they offered me a job—a medieval tapestry collection from the estate of a prominent collector. They independently authenticated two of the pieces, as a formality, and took it on good faith the rest of the collection was genuine. The collector's heirs had hired their own authenticator to certify the tapestries before selling them, and the museum didn't want to insult the heirs. Then the will was contested by some long-lost niece and the probate judge ordered an appraisal. She appointed an authenticator unconnected to either the Zaxby or the heirs."

"Let me guess. The rest were fakes."

"Not all of them. Three were. But three were enough to ruin

the Zaxby's reputation. They never quite recovered from the humiliation."

"What are the chances the Creech sampler's a fake?"

"Low. Not zero, but close to it."

"Less than the chance of it being stolen? I don't think Ryan's got the police's message about beefing up security. I didn't notice anything more high tech than the front door lock. Unless the little guy who showed us in is a secret ninja."

"*Notice* being the key word. The best way to keep thieves from getting past your security system is to not let the thieves know what type of security system you have."

"Good point. How much do you think the sampler will go for?"

"Given its age and condition, I'd estimate somewhere north of twelve, south of twenty."

"Twelve to twenty hundred?"

"Thousand."

"Twenty thousand? For a piece of needlework not much bigger than an index card?"

"For a fine example of nineteenth-century schoolgirl embroidery. Anyway, twenty thousand is less than that violin you played will fetch by an order of ten, at least, if not a hundred."

"Yeah, but I can't put a violin in my pocket." She gathered the trash from the table. "Train leaves in about fifteen minutes."

She whistled as they walked back to the station.

"What's that song?" Jackson asked. "You played it at the cottage and at the auction house."

"'Captain Heuston's Lament,' a sea chanty I picked up somewhere. Can't remember exactly where to save my life. It's been stuck in my head the past couple of days."

"Who've you been hanging out with since you moved over here? Besides policemen."

"Math teachers."

"You probably learned it years ago and forgot it. Living on the bay a few hundred yards from a lighthouse must've resurrected the memory."

"Dearest Jack, always ready with a logical explanation."

"What other type of explanation is there?"

Something behind her caught her attention. She turned and caught a flash of blond hair ducking down a side street.

"Sissy, what is it?"

"I thought—" She shook her head. "Nothing. Let's go before the train leaves us and we have to walk the twenty kilometers back to Dunmullach."

"Walking wouldn't be necessary. I've got money for a taxi."

"Jackson, are all antiquarians as humorless as you? C'mon." She strode toward the station. Her brother-in-law sauntered after her, his long legs easily keeping pace with her quick steps.

Gethsemane stopped short at the corner. She ignored Jackson's apology for tripping over her. "Do you smell that?"

He sniffed.

"Smell what?"

"Something spicy and citrusy. Cloves and nutmeg, oranges and—" She inhaled. "Something else. I know what it is, but I can't think of what it's called." Deep breath. Cologne. But not Eamon's. She stood on tip-toe and sniffed Jackson's neck. "It's not you."

"Because I don't walk around smelling like a pumpkin pie. Maybe you smell dessert. Someone's baking for the holiday. It is almost New Year's."

"Pumpkin pie is not the traditional New Year's dish, alcohol is. And whatever it is doesn't smell like pie. It smells like—" She gasped and pointed in the direction they'd come.

Jackson turned to look.

"Do you see that man?" A blond man stood in a shop doorway, his back to Gethsemane and Jackson. The flash of blond she spied earlier. "I think he's following us."

"He's window shopping." Jackson laid the back of his hand against her forehead the way she saw him do to her nephew whenever the boy sniffled or complained of a sore throat. "Olfactory hallucinations, paranoia. Are you coming down with something?" he asked.

She swatted his hand away.

"I'm not sick, nor am I crazy. Forget I said anything." A train whistle sounded. "Let's go before we get left."

Four

Back at Carraigfaire, Gethsemane left Jackson to his auction catalogs and returned to the music room. She opened the grimoire to the conjuring spell and read aloud.

"*Quondam vos cratis quod nunc ego sum.*" She waited. Silence. "*Tu es quod ego erit fio. Invoco te.*" Nothing. She snapped the book shut and slammed it on the table. "Why can the *Ghost Hunting Adventures* boys rile up full-bodied manifestations with their hokey gadgets and I can't even scare up a lousy orb with a spell from an authentic grimoire? What am I missing?"

"Sissy?" Jackson called from the study. "Who are you talking to?"

"Uh, no one. I mean, myself. I was just trying to decide whether to play Paganini or Ravel." She shouldered her violin and played Paganini's first three "Violin Caprices," then bent to place the instrument back in its case. She stiffened at the sound of a footstep behind her.

"Eamon?" she whispered. "Eamon, if that's you, answer me."

Rattling sounded behind her. She turned in time to see a picture crash from the wall.

"Sissy?" Jackson stepped into the room. "What fell?"

She held up the framed print.

Jackson examined it. "Late nineteenth century—the print, not the brigantine." He pointed at the double-masted sailing ship tossed by waves. "That's eighteenth century. The print's mass-produced, something you might buy at the local bookseller's. It's nice, though."

"Honestly, Jackson." She snatched the frame. "Not every item needs an analysis." She hung the frame back in its previous position.

"You'd do better to use a proper picture hanger. That nail must not be secure. The glass is likely to break if the picture falls again."

"I'll try to remember to stop by the hardware store next time I'm in the village."

"How 'bout tomorrow? Which is my way of asking you to show me around. The auction's not until evening, so we've—I've—got the whole day. You may have plans."

"Nope. The joy of teaching. School holidays."

Jackson grinned. "I thought the joy of teaching came from shaping young minds by imparting wisdom and knowledge."

"Yeah, that, too."

"On that slightly cynical note, I'll bid you good evening. I'm going to take my catalogs upstairs and study myself to sleep."

Gethsemane glanced at the grimoire. "I'm calling it a night, too. I'll turn out the lights. See you in the morning."

Jackson left her. She checked the downstairs rooms. Everything seemed in order. She flipped the hallway light switch and started up the stairs when she caught a hint of the spicy fragrance she smelled earlier, a hint so faint she couldn't be sure she really smelled it.

"Overactive imagination. Wishful thinking." She sighed and went up to bed.

The next morning after breakfast she showed Jackson around the village. They stopped by Our Lady. Gethsemane left Jackson to study the altar frontals while she looked for Father Tim to sneak in a word about the grimoire. The sexton informed her the priest had gone to make sick calls and wasn't expected back soon. A tour with

Jackson through the poison garden earned her a lecture on plant-based fabric dyes. They stopped at the library next.

"Art department's on the sixth floor," she said to her brother-in-law. "I'm headed to music."

"Meet you in the lobby in an hour."

She waited until Jackson disappeared up the stairs then hurried to the information desk. "Do you have an occult section?" she asked the librarian.

"Basement level," the man answered without raising his eyes from his computer screen. "Left at the bottom of the stairs."

Gethsemane tried to ignore the ominous atmosphere created by the lone flickering lightbulb as she descended the narrow stairs. She turned left into a low-ceilinged claustrophobic room, deserted except for dozens of rows of crammed bookshelves. She forced thoughts of a similar scene—the records room of thc abandoned asylum where she narrowly escaped a fiery death—from her mind and found the occult books in a dust-shrouded row at the back. She reached up for a volume on ghost hunting when a hand landed on her shoulder. She screamed.

"Jesus, Sissy." Jackson stood behind her, hand on his chest, looking as frightened as she felt. "It's just me."

"Don't sneak up on people. What're you doing down here, anyway? I thought you were up in the art section."

"I was. The librarian sent me down here for a book on eighteenth-century embroidery techniques." His voice slipped into professor tone. "It's by Malpais. Authoritative but hard to find."

Gethsemane held up a hand. "Jackson, I don't care about rare books on eighteenth-century embroidery."

"It's not actually a *rare* book. It was published in the last—"

She stamped her foot and frowned.

"Sorry." Jackson examined the shelf behind her head. "*Communication Beyond the Veil, Paranormal Invasion*—" He looked down at her. "I thought you went to the music section."

"I, uh, needed a book about an opera I'll be teaching next term." She grabbed the nearest book.

Jackson read the title. "*Hungarian Ghost Stories*?"

"The opera's based on one of the tales. I'm going to have the boys read the story then study the way the composer adapted it." She tucked the volume under her arm. "Find your art book and we'll go. Murphy's got a Bushmills over at the Rabbit with my name on it."

"The Mad Rabbit," Jackson read from the sign hanging over the door. "Charming name. Pubs have such colorful monikers–The Laughing Pig, The Slate and Thimble."

"Let's go in," she said before he launched into a tangent. "The drink selection's more charming than the name."

They had their choice of tables at that time of day. She led the way toward one along the far wall, but as she turned to wave at Murphy, the barman, she spied Francis Grennan seated alone at the end of the bar. The mercurial redhead taught math at St. Brennan's.

Most days he went about in a curmudgeonly funk, swaddled in an oversized tweed jacket and wrinkled khakis, perpetually miffed at the world. On occasion, an amiable, mischievous Frankie emerged. That Frankie held St. Brennan's unofficial title of Master Prankster. That Frankie had helped her break into a dead man's house to search for evidence. That Frankie stayed home today, judging by his hunched shoulders and two-handed grip on his glass.

Jackson sat on a barstool. Frankie scowled. Walking away would be awkward, so Gethsemane climbed onto the barstool between Jackson and Frankie and greeted him. Frankie grunted a response.

She tried again. "Meet my brother-in-law, Dr. Jackson Applethwaite. He's visiting from Virginia."

Frankie raised his glass to Jackson in a silent toast, then drained it.

"Jackson," Gethsemane swiveled on her barstool, "meet

Francis Grennan. His friends call him Frankie. Believe it or not, despite the way he's acting, he has friends."

Jackson leaned across Gethsemane and shook Frankie's hand. "If we're disturbing you, Mr. Grennan, we can find other seats."

"Stay where you are, Brother Jack. You're not what's disturbing me." He signaled Murphy for a refill. "A few more of these and I'll be everybody's friend."

"What's gotten into you?" Gethsemane asked. "You're more morose than usual. Something wrong?"

"Nothing's wrong, fair *maestra*. I'm celebrating. A wedding has been announced."

Gethsemane lost her balance on the barstool. She steadied herself.

"You're getting married? When? To whom? In the months I've known you, I've never seen you go on a date."

"Congratulations." Jackson nudged Gethsemane and frowned at her. "Who's the lucky woman?"

"My ex-wife." Frankie dispatched the contents of his second glass.

Gethsemane goggled. "You're remarrying your ex-wife?"

"No." He signaled for another round. "My ex-wife is marrying someone else. She didn't see fit to tell me who. That's not how she plays the game. She only said, 'It's no one you know,' and left it there. She believes in the importance of maintaining mystery in relationships." He swigged whiskey. "And in messing with my head."

"Sorry," Gethsemane said. "You hoped for a reconciliation? Or for her to die miserable and alone?"

Frankie mumbled into his glass, "Yes."

Jackson tugged at her sleeve. "Perhaps we should find a table, Sissy. I think we're intruding on Mr. Grennan."

"Sissy?" Frankie perked up. A sly twinkle lit his emerald green eyes. "A heretofore unknown sobriquet." She'd never live this down.

"It's a family nickname. Meaning only family can use it." A copy of the local newspaper, the *Dispatch*, laying on the bar offered a change of subject. She reached across Frankie and retrieved it. She pointed to a front page article. "'American hotel magnate expanding empire,'" she read aloud. "'Hospitality mogul, Hank Wayne, visits area. Sources report the billionaire is scouting locations for future hotels.'" She swore and tossed the paper onto the bar. "Is there no way to stop that parasite? No local ordinance to invoke against mauling the landscape or destroying the village's character?" No spell to banish him to hell?

"I didn't peg you for a preservationist," Frankie said.

"He's after Carraigfaire." Gethsemane propped her head on one hand and signaled for a drink with the other. "And I don't know how to stop him."

"Maybe he'll find something more suitable. Maybe he'll realize the cottage is isolated and difficult to reach and choose a different location." Jackson thumped the photo next to the article.

Gethsemane looked over. "An abandoned factory?"

"The old distillery," Frankie said. "On the edge of the village. Sat empty for donkey's years."

Jackson read on. "Says he's 'expressed interest' in purchasing."

"That and everything else in a twenty-mile radius." Gethsemane sipped her drink, Bushmills 21, and waited until the smoky slow burn faded before continuing. "Buying the distillery won't keep him from buying the cottage. He's greedy. He'll snatch up everything."

Jackson, gaze fixed on the paper, didn't respond.

"Jackson?"

"What?" He looked up. "Sorry. I saw this." He pointed to an article on page two. "They're reopening the investigation."

Gethsemane read, "'New leads in Dublin-New York art fraud ring spurs renewed investigation.' Is this the case you mentioned?"

"Looks like it's not so cold anymore," Jackson said.

"This is the third time I've heard about this case. First from O'Reilly, then you, now it's in the paper."

"Not superstitious, are you?" Frankie asked. "Think things happening in threes is significant?"

"No, I am not superstitious." Conjuring ghosts did not make one superstitious.

"What did the inspector say about the case?" Jackson asked. "Did he mention what new leads turned up?"

"Not to me. He said he'd like to discuss the case with you. Are you still in touch with the FBI agent who used your research on historical paint colors to catch the New Haven forger? Maybe you could ask him."

"He retired a few years ago. Not that he'd discuss an ongoing case with anyone without a need to know. But I've no idea who's in charge of the investigation now. Not sure if I could be of any assistance. Of course, if they asked me—"

Gethsemane nudged her brother-in-law. "Look at you. Mild-mannered curator by day, crusading art crime fighter by night."

"Art crime is serious, Sissy. Did you know profits from black market art sales fund—"

Time to head off lecture mode. "We'd better go, Jackson. Frankie wants to drown his sorrows in peace, and we need to get ready for the auction."

"That's not until this evening."

"And if you get to talking about the moral and ethical ramifications of black market art sales, we'll be here until this evening." She tossed money on the bar. "Drinks are on me, Frankie, as long as you promise to cut it off after the next one."

"You're my only man, Sissy."

"You're having a bad day, so I'll let that one slide. That *one*." She placed more money on the bar. "Call a cab home."

"Hey, Jackson," Gethsemane shouted from her bedroom. "What do you wear to an auction?"

"I'm wearing my navy wool gabardine suit."

"Let me rephrase. What should I wear to the auction?"

"Business attire."

Gethsemane shifted hangers in her wardrobe and lifted out a

navy patterned wrap dress. As she held it up in front of the mirror she heard a footstep and saw the reflection of a shadow pass behind her. She spun. "Jackson?"

"Almost ready?" Her brother-in-law's voice carried from the other room.

"Eamon?" she whispered. She poked her head into the hall.

Jackson's head appeared in the back bedroom's doorway. "Taxi'll be here in twenty minutes."

The young man from the previous day escorted them to the top floor of Ryan's auction house. They stepped from the elevator into an auditorium half-filled with folding chairs. Several people sat thumbing through catalogs, checking their smartphones, or fanning themselves with their numbered paddles. A podium stood at the front of the room, near a wall dominated by a large projection screen. Several employees Gethsemane recognized from the preview manned laptops at tables set up behind the chairs. People chatted in scattered clusters. Someone handed Jackson a catalog and a numbered paddle.

Gethsemane surveyed the crowd.

"Do you know anyone?"

"I recognize some," Jackson said. "The white-haired lady in the corner is a distinguished collector of antique furniture. She just donated several pieces to the Winterthur."

"Is that her grandson with her?"

"Sixth husband. See the twins in the opposite corner?"

Gethsemane acknowledged the identical twins wearing identical gray suits.

"They're art dealers. I'll bet they're here to bid on lot twenty-two. And there's—"

"Jackson," a voice called.

Gethsemane and Jackson turned to see an elderly man in a velvet jacket and paisley cravat waving at them.

"That's business attire?" Gethsemane asked.

"It is when you're an eccentric artist. I know him from my days at the Cooper Hewitt. Excuse me while I go say hi."

"Leave me the catalog," she said as he headed toward his friend. "I don't want to stand here empty-handed."

She flipped to the entry for the Guarneri del Gesu violin but only read a few lines before another voice appeared at her elbow.

"Left at the altar?" A handsome red-haired man with remarkably blue eyes smiled down at her.

"My brother-in-law's catching up with an old friend." She nodded in Jackson's direction.

"Ah, the artist. Read slowly." He jerked a thumb at the catalog. "If it's been more than a minute since your brother-in-law last saw the fella, he'll be tied up for a while. The talented gentleman loves nothing more than filling in friend and foe alike on what he's been doing with himself."

"Is this the part where you introduce yourself, or are you so famous I should know who you are?"

He smiled and shook Gethsemane's hand.

"Kenneth O'Connor. I have you at an advantage. I already know who you are."

"How?"

"A bird told me about your virtuoso performance at the preview, so I checked, Dr. Brown. Impressive CV."

She thanked him. "Are you an artist or a distinguished collector?"

"Neither. I'm an agent."

"Agent? Like Secret Squirrel?"

"A buyer's agent. I travel to auctions and sales and make purchases for buyers who can't make the trips themselves."

"Like a personal shopper, except for priceless art instead of clothes."

Kenneth started to answer when a blond man, half a head shorter than Kenneth but stockier, with a scar on his cheek, jostled him. Kenneth stumbled forward and just missed stepping on Gethsemane's foot.

"Sorry," the blond man mumbled. He looked anything but. He kept walking.

"I'm guessing he's not a friend of yours," Gethsemane said. Something about him seemed familiar.

"Ronan Leary. Third-rate art dealer. Owned a gallery in Kilkenny that failed about a year ago. Guess they let anybody into these things these days."

Jackson rejoined them. "Sorry I took so long. The man likes to talk."

Gethsemane introduced him to Kenneth.

"A pleasure to meet you, Dr. Applethwaite. If you'll both please excuse me, there's a woman over there I need to see about a horse. A bronze nineteenth-century horse sculpture, that is."

"Didn't mean to chase him off," Jackson said after he'd gone. "I'll go after him and explain I'm happily married to your sister if you want."

"Don't start." Gethsemane rolled her eyes.

"It's just that—"

"Just nothing. I've been single for barely four months and I'm enjoying it." She sighed with visible relief as Ms. Ryan entered the room. She and Jackson claimed seats mid-row.

The auctioneer took the podium, made a few introductory remarks, then began the auction. An image flashed on the screen behind her. "We have Lot One, a late nineteenth-century mahogany library ladder. We have some interest already." She consulted notes in a binder on the podium. "Three hundred, four hundred, four-fifty from my commissioned bids. Who'll give me five hundred?"

A man in the front row raised his paddle.

'Thank you, sir," Ms. Ryan said. "Do I have five-fifty? Five-fifty?"

A paddle near the window went up.

"Six hundred? Six-fifty?" She fiddled with the gavel in her hand. "Against you, sir. Seven hundred. I'm out. Seven-fifty on the phone. Eight hundred on the internet. Eight-fifty? Do I have eight-fifty? Thank you, madam. Nine hundred. Nine-fifty. The bid is one thousand. Against you. Eleven hundred. Twelve hundred. Thirteen hundred. Well done. Fourteen hundred. Thank you. Fifteen hundred. Any more bids?"

No paddles went up.

"I'm selling at fifteen hundred. Am I bid more? The bid would be sixteen hundred. On the phone? No? Online? Sixteen hundred? Fair warning. Sold." The gavel's rap echoed off the podium's wood. "Bidder number three-eighty-one," she said to a woman taking notes next to her.

Ms. Ryan repeated the process with second and third lots, a painting of a Labrador retriever and a set of architectural prints. Gethsemane watched Jackson. He remained relaxed in his chair, legs crossed, as the bidding for the second lot began. He twirled his paddle in one hand and flipped through the catalog with the other, appearing disinterested in the proceedings. However, he sat straight in his chair, both feet on the floor, by the time Ms. Ryan announced "fair warning" for the third lot. He handed Gethsemane his catalog and held his paddle still.

"Up next, we have Lot Four." An image of the needlework miniature Jackson had studied so intently at the preview, an index card-sized cross-stitched silk on linen alphabet sampler, came onscreen. Tchaikovsky blasted in Gethsemane's head. The young man from reception hurried onto the podium as Ms. Ryan picked up her gavel and whispered in her ear before she could ask for an opening bid.

Ms. Ryan turned off her microphone and huddled with her assistant. He gesticulated and frowned as he cast glances toward the elevator. Ms. Ryan gasped then covered her mouth with her hand as her assistant rushed off. She returned to the podium. "My apologies, ladies and gentlemen. We'll move on to Lot Five, an early nineteenth-century George Three satinwood cheval mirror."

Gethsemane leaned over and whispered to her brother-in-law, seated open-mouthed beside her, "What just happened?"

"I don't know. Maybe the consigner withdrew the lot at the last minute."

The auction proceeded without further incident. Jackson appeared distracted and took no notice when a bidding war over the Guarneri del Gesu violin ended with a bid of five hundred seventy thousand euros. Neither he nor Ms. Ryan gave any clue about the absence of Lot Four.

After the auction, buyers and staff descended in the elevator in groups of three and four. Gethsemane and Jackson got in line. She wanted to ask Jackson about what happened, but his expression said he had no answers and wasn't in the mood to speak.

The elevator doors swished open. The young man from reception stepped off. A squat man with a face as craggy as Dunmullach's cliffs accompanied him. The two blocked Gethsemane and Jackson's path and the young man pointed. Ms. Ryan came up behind them.

The squat man carried a herringbone overcoat. "Dr. Applethwaite," he asked, "is this your coat?" He pulled his identification from his pocket and held it up for them to see—a sergeant with the Ballytuam *Garda an Síochana.*

Why did a policeman have Jackson's coat?

"Yes." Jackson pointed to the monogrammed JTA on the lining. "It's mine."

"Can you tell me, sir, how this got into your coat pocket?" He held up an index-card-sized cross-stitched silk on linen alphabet sampler.

Gethsemane and Jackson spoke simultaneously.

"No, I can't."

"Of course he can't. He didn't put it there."

Gethsemane recognized the look the sergeant gave her. She'd gotten the same look from O'Reilly when he debated between choking her and arresting her. Maybe they taught it in garda school. He addressed his remarks to Jackson. "Perhaps we could continue this conversation over at the station. I do have to caution you that you are not obliged to say anything unless you wish to do so, but whatever you say will be taken down in writing and may be given in evidence."

Gethsemane stepped between her brother-in-law and the officer. "Station? No! You can't arrest him. He didn't do anything. He couldn't have. He's been here in this auditorium since Junior," she nodded at the assistant, "brought us up here. We have a room full of witnesses." She looked around and saw that only she, Jackson, Ms. Ryan, the assistant, and the sergeant remained. "Had a room full of witnesses."

The sergeant exhaled and waited a count of three before speaking to Jackson. "I'd like to ask you a few questions." He looked at Gethsemane. "Someplace where we won't be interrupted."

"Ask Ms. Ryan's staff a few questions," Gethsemane interjected. "Ask them a lot of questions. They had the run of the place. Ask Ms. Ryan some questions while you're at it. She didn't come into the room until a good fifteen, twenty minutes after all the buyers arrived. And she and her staff had access to all the lots. Any one of them could have slipped that thing into Jackson's coat."

Ms. Ryan and her assistant uttered protests.

"Ma'am," the sergeant said to Gethsemane, "if you don't step aside, I will arrest someone—you—for interfering with an investigation."

Jackson put his hand on her arm. "Sissy, it's all right. I'll go with the officer. We'll get this cleared up." He pulled out his wallet. "Here's cab fare. Go back to the cottage—"

She pushed his hand away. "I don't need cab fare, and I'm not going back to Dunmullach without you. You're damned right we'll get this cleared up. This is ridiculous." She appealed to the auctioneer. "Ms. Ryan, c'mon. This is Dr. Jackson Applethwaite. The guy whose papers you read. The esteemed antiquarian you were so honored to meet. He's no thief." Ms. Ryan stared at the floor.

"Dr. Applethwaite." The sergeant motioned to the elevator. Jackson followed him. Gethsemane started after them. The sergeant blocked her. "It's best if you wait for the next car."

"You really should go back to the cottage, Sissy."

"I'm not. Leaving. Ballytuam. Without you. Don't worry." The elevator doors began to close. "Just don't say anything. I'll think of something." She turned to Ms. Ryan. "What are you up to?"

"Dr. Brown, really, I—"

"Really nothing. You and your staff are the only ones who weren't in this auditorium for the entire auction. You're the only ones who know what kind of super-secret security system you have. You're the only ones who had access to all the lots, and you had access to all the coats. One of you planted that sampler on my brother-in-law."

"Obviously you're upset, Dr. Brown. But making unfounded accusations—"

"Ha!"

"I think it's best if we not discuss this situation any further and let the guards handle things from here." The elevator doors swished open. "The elevator's here." Ms. Ryan waved Gethsemane inside. "We'll wait for the next one."

Gethsemane rode down alone. She'd run through her entire repertoire of profanities by the time the elevator reached the ground floor. She kicked a wall just as the doors opened.

"Careful," Kenneth said. "You'll leave a mark." He and four or five others loitered in the reception area. Everyone stared at Gethsemane. Some whispered.

"What are you still doing—never mind. Do you have a phone?"

He handed her his smartphone. "Who are you calling?"

Gethsemane dialed. "Reinforcements." O'Reilly answered on the third ring. Gethsemane identified herself, then asked, "Do you remember telling me to let you know if I needed anything? Well, I know it's out of your jurisdiction, but I need you in Ballytuam."

Five

Gethsemane looked at the clock. Again. Forty-five, forty-six, forty-seven minutes she'd been waiting. O'Reilly couldn't come to Ballytuam, but he'd promised to make a few phone calls on Jackson's behalf. However, no one told her anything about her brother-in-law—not how he was or where he was or whether he'd been formally charged with anything. Frustrated didn't begin to describe how she felt. She got up from the hard wobbly chair to find someone who knew what happened to Jackson when a uniformed police officer called to her from a side door.

"If you'll follow me, please."

The officer led her to a cheerless room with two chairs on either side of a table scarred with doodles, initials, and obscenities. More waiting. Ten minutes passed. She picked up a chair, then took a deep breath and brought her emotions under control. Banging furniture would land her in a cell. It wouldn't help Jackson. She turned the door's handle. Unlocked. She stepped into the deserted hallway. Where was everybody? Where was anybody? Time to make a little noise. She cleared her throat and sang, "Old MacDonald had a farm, ee yi ee yi oh." Her voice echoed off Formica and tile. "And on that farm, he had a cow, ee yi ee yi oh."

A door at the end of the hall opened before she started to moo. A dark-haired Amazon stepped out. Curled tendrils escaped her messy-on-purpose up-do to frame her porcelain face. She wore a tailored dress the same shade of green as her eyes. She towered over Gethsemane, four-inch heels adding to her statuesque demeanor. “Dr. Brown, so sorry to keep you waiting. I’m Yseult Grennan,” she said in a BBC news anchor accent tinged with a hint of brogue.

Grennan. As in Francis Grennan, her favorite curmudgeon. How common was the last name? She must be Frankie’s ex. Less than twenty miles from Dunmullach, yet Frankie hadn’t mentioned it. How bad was the breakup? Gethsemane glanced at her left hand. Nothing on her ring finger. No engagement ring didn’t prove she wasn’t engaged, but...

Yseult ushered Gethsemane back into the room. “Please sit.” She waved at a chair and took the one opposite.

Gethsemane ignored the offer. “Are you one of the gardaí?” She didn’t look like a cop, and she hadn’t introduced herself as one. But she knew Gethsemane’s name and walked in like she owned the place. “Or are you the DA or prosecutor or whatever they’re called over here?”

Yseult hesitated a second before answering. “I’m with an outside agency, on special assignment to the Garda National Economic Crime Bureau.”

Outside agency? An insurance agency? Antiquities carried insurance, loads of it. Jackson said crooks staged thefts so owners could file bogus insurance claims. But an insurance investigator wouldn’t wield the clout Yseult seemed to. Interpol, Military Intelligence, CIA? She tried to picture Frankie married to a spy. The effort gave her a headache. “Where’s my brother-in-law? Jackson Applethwaite. How is he? Do you know? Has he been charged with anything?”

“Dr. Brown, I understand your anxiety.” Gethsemane started to protest, but Yseult’s hand stopped her. “Dr. Applethwaite is fine.”

“So where is he? Is he under arrest?”

“Your brother-in-law is cooperating with the investigation.”

Gethsemane gritted her teeth. This woman had a knack for

giving non-answers. "What investigation? Will you, or someone, anyone, please tell me what the f—" Gethsemane closed her eyes and held her breath for a three-count. "Will you please explain what's happened?"

"Niall said you weren't one for dancing around a subject."

O'Reilly came through on his promise to make calls. But why Yseult? "I'm sorry, Ms. Grennan. I'm worried about Jackson. He has a wife and son. If he's been arrested on theft charges, I need to notify them. I also need to find out about bail and hiring a lawyer or solicitor or whatever they're called."

"As I said, Dr. Brown, I do understand. But your worries are premature. Your brother-in-law hasn't been charged yet." Gethsemane detected a slight emphasis on the word yet. Or had she imagined it? "But he was found with a valuable art object in his coat pocket. The situation needs explaining."

"Your statement needs refining. Jackson was not found with the object. A valuable art object was found in Jackson's coat pocket. A coat he hadn't been anywhere near since he took it off and gave it to one of Ms. Ryan's employees less than five minutes after we arrived at the auction house. A coat pocket that plenty of people, none of whom were Jackson, had access to."

"Point taken. Niall also said nothing slipped past you."

"How do you know Inspector O'Reilly? You know him well enough to call him Niall. You're not a garda, and you're not a prosecutor. You're obviously here in some official capacity. You say you're on 'special assignment,' but what do you do?"

"I'm a forensic document examiner. I'm also a forensic art examiner. I worked with Niall several years ago on one of his cases. Long before he transferred to Dunmullach."

"Forensic examiner. That means you authenticate things. Or expose them as frauds. Jackson's suspected of theft, not fraud, which is out of your lane. You work in a laboratory, not an interrogation room. So why did Niall call you?" If Yseult could refer to him by his given name, so could she. "Because you were in the neighborhood and he thought you'd help in a pinch, or because something about that sampler, which, for the record, was planted in Jackson's coat, interests you?"

"Good again, Dr. Brown. Niall called me because he thought it too much of a coincidence for an attempted art theft in a small town to be unrelated to an ongoing art fraud investigation in the same small town."

"Art fraud? In Ballytuam?" O'Reilly had told her the police were on high alert for theft. He'd also mentioned a couple of fakes turning up on the local market. Were the crimes connected? "How does Ryan's auction house figure into this investigation?" An exclusive, secretive auction house could facilitate the movement of fake art. Could Ryan's be the new information that reopened the New York-Dublin case? Ballytuam was a far cry from Dublin, but maybe the fugitives decided a small town was the perfect cover.

Yseult nodded. "Ryan's is a place of interest, and the Hester Creech miniature is an item of interest."

"An item of interest. You mean a fake? You can't seriously believe Jackson is involved in art fraud. I waited for," she glanced at the clock, "over an hour for someone to come talk to me. Add that to the time Jackson spent here before I arrived, and it adds up to plenty of time for you to do your homework. So I'm sure you know, number one, Jackson's no idiot. If he was going to steal art—which he'd never do—he wouldn't try to walk out of a secure building, or any building, with stolen goods shoved in his pocket. You also must know, number two, Jackson's on your side. He's helped law enforcement more than once in fraud investigations. He's dedicated to stopping art crime, not committing it."

"Yes, I did do my homework. I familiarized myself with Dr. Applethwaite's efforts on behalf of law enforcement, among other things. I also familiarized myself with your career. You're quite the prodigious musician."

What did her musical talent have to do with embroidery, stolen, fake, or otherwise? "We're talking about Jackson."

"Let's talk about parties instead, at least for a moment. Have you ever heard of Olivia McCarthy-Boyle?"

As a matter of fact..."She's an art collector. Lives here in Ballytuam."

"Art collector, philanthropist, renowned hostess. She's hosting a fundraiser the day after tomorrow to benefit the children's hospital. It's possible one or two of the party guests will actually care about children's health."

"Meaning the other guests care about what?"

"Mrs. McCarthy-Boyle's art collection. They'll be there to get a look at it before she sells it off. Which she's been doing bit by bit."

O'Reilly mentioned Olivia's recent auctions. He hadn't seemed to think much of them. Did Yseult? "You're going somewhere with this."

"I'll hurry and get there. We believe an art forgery and theft ring moved from Dublin and now operates out of Ballytuam. They sell art forgeries—paintings, textiles, sculptures, antiquities—to seemingly respectable galleries. The gallery owners are in on the scam; they know they're buying fakes. The galleries then sell the fakes below market value to carefully selected art collectors. These 'special' collectors know they're buying fakes. They're co-conspirators. Now the fakes have passed through the hands of ostensibly reputable galleries into the hands of notable, if unscrupulous, collectors. They have provenance."

"They look legit." Like O'Reilly explained.

Yseult continued. "The collectors wait an amount of time, years in some cases, then sell the fake artworks at auction or in private sales. At or above market value. Sometimes the collectors use an auction house in on the scheme. The auctioneers provide additional completely bogus documentation authenticating the works and steer sales to buyers who won't question the auction house's authentication. Other times, the collectors pretend the objects are genuine. If a collector can't sell the work, it may be conveniently stolen by the same criminal ring who created the fake in the first place and the collector files an insurance claim."

"That's how the scam worked in New York and Dublin? Selling fakes, then stealing them back for the insurance money or pawning them off on dupes at auction? Except in New York and Dublin it was paintings, not textiles."

"You have an interest in art crime, Dr. Brown?"

"I saw an article in the *Dunmullach Dispatch*. Jackson mentioned he'd been consulted about historic paint colors. Of course, since you did your homework, you probably know that."

"I am aware of Dr. Applethwaite's past efforts on behalf of law enforcement. But time passes. People change. They begin to see the world differently after they dedicate years of their lives to doing the right thing with little to show for it while the bad guys go unpunished and reap the wealth."

"Other people change. Not Jackson. Or did you mean Mrs. McCarthy-Boyle? You think she's mixed up in art fraud and theft? That she's become one of the 'special' collectors? I don't know a lot about her, but from the little I've heard, I gathered she's a doyenne of the fine art world."

"Being a respected personage is no elixir against greed."

True. Look at Hank Wayne. And Olivia did own the sampler planted in Jackson's coat pocket. "Do you think she's behind this? The theft was a setup to file a bogus insurance claim?"

Yseult hesitated again. Did she always weigh her words so carefully or was she just holding out? She rubbed Gethsemane the wrong way. Or had Frankie's opinion biased her?

"We're keeping an open mind about the attempted theft of the miniature," Yseult said. "However, my—our—investigation focuses primarily on another piece in Olivia's collection. The star of the show. The Patience Freeman sampler."

"The what?"

"The Patience Freeman sampler, a piece too rare to be believed. Excuse me." Yseult went to the door and spoke to someone in the hall. She came back to the table a moment later with a folder in her hand. She laid it on the table and opened it to a photograph, which she handed Gethsemane.

"What am I looking at?" Gethsemane held up the photo. An embroidered sampler—an alphabet above and a multiplication table below—filled the frame. A flowered border surrounded the letters and numbers and tied the two sections together. Centered at the bottom, below the flowered border, a stitched name and date identified the maker and the year of creation—Patience Freeman, 1764. Someone had written "20 x 24" on the photo's border.

"It's a schoolgirl sampler." She'd learned that much from Jackson.

"Not just any schoolgirl sampler. The Patience Freeman sampler." Yseult took the photo and gazed at it. Almost lovingly, Gethsemane thought.

"Is Patience Freeman someone I should know?" she asked.

"Dr. Applethwaite may have mentioned her?"

Gethsemane shook her head. If he had mentioned her during one of his curbside lectures, she hadn't paid attention.

Yseult explained, "Patience Freeman, the daughter of a free black seamstress and an enslaved silversmith, lived in Williamsburg, Virginia prior to the American War of Independence. She attended the Williamsburg Bray School, one of the schools founded by English philanthropists to provide black children with a Christian education, run by Ann Wager."

Gethsemane nodded at the photo. "Patience Freeman stitched the sampler while a student at the school?"

"Yes, when she was eleven. The photo doesn't do it justice. Patience possessed needle skills as fine as any degree student at the Royal School of Needlework. The quality of the stitching alone would make the sampler worth a fortune. And eighteenth-century schoolgirl samplers are like hen's teeth. A sampler by a less skilled stitcher in such good condition would fetch a huge sum at auction. Plus, samplers by black schoolgirls from any century are practically nonexistent—"

"Meaning this sampler is rarer than rare and you could sell it for more money than what Facebook, Apple, and Samsung combined are worth."

"Precisely. Now you understand why I say the sampler is too rare to be believed. If something sounds too good to be true—"

"It probably is. You think it's a fake," Gethsemane said, "a product of the crime ring you're investigating."

Yseult shrugged. And smiled.

"But you're not sure if Olivia is in on the scam and knows it's a fake, or if she's been duped. But I still don't see what any of this has to do with me. I could understand if you asked Jackson to help, but—"

"Your brother-in-law doesn't play the violin. Olivia's hired an ensemble, a sextet, I believe, to provide the entertainment at her fundraiser. One of the musicians canceled at the last minute. Auditions for a replacement are being held. The last audition is tomorrow."

"And you want me to, what, get the gig? Go to the party?"

"And while you're there, have a look around Olivia's office for the bill of sale for the Freeman sampler."

"I'm a musician, not a detective."

"I hear you're quite the investigator. You found evidence to exonerate a man twenty-five years after he'd been falsely accused of a crime. Don't sell yourself short."

She said she did her homework. "I'm flattered you consider me a first-class snoop, but I'm a civilian. Can't you send a garda or an investigator from the prosecutor's office or one of your 'special' colleagues to look for the receipt?"

"We can't send guards without warrants, and we can't get warrants without cause. We have no evidence—yet—any crime has been committed related to the Freeman sampler. Judges don't issue warrants just so we can look 'round. My 'special' colleagues have other, let's call them *obligations* the night of the party. And you have the best cover. You'll be working at Olivia's house, so you'll have opportunity to search areas not open to party guests without raising eyebrows."

"And if I get caught, you can plausibly deny having anything to do with me." Her mistrust of Yseult had nothing to do with Frankie's opinion.

"You won't get caught, Dr. Brown. I have faith in you. And you won't be completely on your own. Other assets will be present in the arena."

Assets in the arena? Had she stepped into a John Le Carré novel?

"Attending to their other obligations?"

"But available in an emergency."

"I'm not going to steal anything."

"We're not asking you to steal. That would be against the law. We're only asking you to try to find the receipt and to photograph it front and back if you do find it."

"In exchange for which you'll forget the absurd notion Jackson had anything to do with attempted art theft."

"We would certainly take your cooperation in the matter into consideration."

Quid pro quo. Help Yseult, help Jackson. "What if I don't get the gig?"

"Have no fear. With your talent and—what shall we call it—determination, I've no doubt the job is yours for the asking. Especially since the other musicians who auditioned played about as well as my seven-year-old niece."

How could Yseult know what the competition was like, unless..."Lucky break, that musician canceling at the last minute."

"You make your own luck."

"I want to see Jackson."

"You'll help us?"

"Yes, I'll help." Snooping around a fancy party for a receipt couldn't be any harder than snooping around dead men's houses and abandoned asylums for clues to a killer. "I want to see my brother-in-law."

Yseult rose. "One moment. Wait here." She paused in the doorway. "I'd appreciate you not sharing the details of this conversation."

A short while later, Jackson, shirt open at the collar, pants crease wrinkled, sat in the chair vacated by Yseult. The tip of his necktie protruded from his suit jacket pocket.

"How are you?" Gethsemane asked.

"I'm fine, Sissy. How are you? I told you to go home."

"And I told you I wouldn't. Don't worry about anything. It may take me a little while, but I'll find you a lawyer. We'll get you out of here before nightfall."

Jackson put a hand on her arm. "I don't need a lawyer. Not yet, anyway. So far, they've only asked me questions. Lots of questions. Art theft's a serious crime."

"A crime you had nothing to do with."

"I'm sure we'll get things straightened out. I'm not worried."

"Jackson—"

"You shouldn't worry either."

"I swear you'd say don't worry if we were standing in the middle of Main Street during an earthquake with the four horsemen of the apocalypse bearing down on us at full speed. You can't just sit back and trust things will turn out the way they're supposed to." She learned that the hard way. If things had gone as planned, she'd be conducting Mahler in Cork right now. "You have to take action."

"Sissy, it's too early to panic. I haven't been charged with any crime, and I'm voluntarily cooperating with the investigation."

"Can I at least call—"

"No. You know how your sister gets. Please don't call her. She'll only get worked up for no reason."

Her middle sister did tend to overreact to distressing news. "So there's nothing I can do?"

"You can please go home. The one thing I *am* worried about is you hanging around here worrying about me."

Gethsemane acquiesced. She said goodbye to Jackson and promised to come back and fetch him, lawyer in tow, if he didn't return to Dunmullach before midnight. An officer escorted Jackson out and Yseult resumed her chair. She laid a floral pendant on the table.

"Jewelry?"

"Look closer," Yseult said.

Gethsemane examined the pendant. Rose gold petals and pearls concealed a small lens. "A camera."

Yseult bent one of the petals back. Gethsemane barely heard the shutter's soft click. "Remember," Yseult said, "we're only asking you to photograph the bill of sale front and back. Nothing more."

"What will photos of a receipt prove?"

"Prove? Nothing. But they will give us some indication of the legitimacy of the sale. Enough to let us know whether we need to—obtain—the actual document."

"With one of those probable cause warrants you mentioned?"

Yseult shrugged.

"And what if I don't find it? What if no receipt exists?"

"That would tell us something, too. My mother saves receipts for any purchase more expensive than a pair of shoes. You could buy a human life for less than what the Freeman sampler's worth. If you bought something so valuable on the open market, free and clear, wouldn't you save the receipt?"

"Yeah, I guess I would." No further questions. Yseult would only craft another of her non-answer answers. She disliked this woman. She picked up the camera pendant. "I have a train to catch."

"I'll have someone drive you." Yseult rose.

"Don't go to the trouble. The air will do me good." And the wait for a ride would mean another hour sitting in the station.

Preoccupied with her thoughts on the walk to the station, she passed the Perryman gallery without stopping. However, from the corner of her eye she saw the tapestry she'd admired earlier had gone from the window, replaced by a needlepoint fire screen. She backtracked and leaned closer to the window to look. She noticed someone inside the gallery: a well-dressed man with a silver pompadour.

Hank Wayne. In an art gallery. Given his attitude toward classical music, she'd filed him firmly under "Philistine." She couldn't imagine he was buying art. Was he in Ballytuam to buy more properties? She went inside. "Hello, Mr. Wayne."

A practiced smile replaced the developer's annoyed frown. "Dr. Brown, this is a surprise. What brings you to Ballytuam?"

High-end auctions, art crime, family in distress, the usual. "I heard there were a lot of nice galleries here, more than in Dunmullach. I'm looking, uh, for a present for a friend who collects. How about you? Thinking of turning this place into another Wayne Resorts International Star Property?"

The smile dimmed a few watts.

"I'm purchasing a piece or two for my own collection. I think that," he nodded at a tapestry depicting a Roman banquet, "would do nicely at Carraigfaire."

She ignored the gibe. Sort of. "Actually, seascapes are more in keeping with the whole cliffside-cottage-lighthouse-waterfront motif. Kind of like the paintings already hanging. I didn't peg you for an art collector. Seeing as how real estate keeps you too busy for music, I'd have thought it left you no time for any of the finer things in life."

"*Art* is an investment." No trace of smile remained. "Well-chosen, it increases in value. Not this stuff, though." He waved a hand around the gallery. "Strictly for the tourists and yokels. Perryman sources high-value works for me on commission. Don't you, Perry?"

"Yes, sir, Mr. Wayne." A youngish dark-haired man in a mink-brown double-breasted wool suit and wire-rimmed glasses entered from a back room.

"I've known Perry for years, since he was a dealer in New York." He addressed the gallery owner. "You were a kid then. Barely out of short pants."

"Just out of college, anyway."

"You stormed the scene, made the deals, took no prisoners. You were aggressive, hungry. I admired that. Reminded me of me at that age. How long's it been since that auction at Christeby's? What was it called? ContempoPop?"

"Yes, sir, ContempoPop. It's been a while." He turned to Gethsemane. "May I help you with anything?"

"No, thank you. I recognized Mr. Wayne through the window and stepped in to say hello."

"Have you gotten that Jasper Koors for me yet, Perry?"

"Still working on it, sir. The current owner is loath to part with it."

"Offer her more money. Everyone has a price. At some point, she'll decide she'd rather have the cash than the canvas." Wayne's smug smile made Gethsemane want to stomp on his foot. "I've already selected the spot in my New York office where I'm going to hang it, and I want it up before the next board of directors meeting."

Something about the exchange, something other than Hank's attitude, nagged Gethsemane. She spied a copy of *Irish Craft* magazine on a table and it hit her. "You don't have any paintings on display, Mr. Perryman." Needlework hung framed on the walls, lay folded on shelves, and stood incorporated into objects throughout the gallery. But not a single painting.

"I don't deal in that medium anymore." He smiled at Hank. "Of course, I make exceptions for my best clients."

"Can't understand why you got out of the art market, Perry. You were one of the best. You had a gift for finding canvases no one else could. If another gallery told me, 'Impossible,' I'd come to you and you'd say, 'I'll have it for you next week, sir.'"

"I needed a change. Dealers and galleries specializing in paintings are a dime a dozen in New York. The competition is murder. So I came home. I've found my niche here. So, I didn't actually leave the art world, only changed countries and stock."

"You do have some lovely pieces, Mr. Perryman. Like that tapestry that used to be in the window."

"A contemporary piece by a local artist. It sold rather quickly. I expect to have some more of the artist's work next month, if you're interested. And I have a few similar pieces by different artists on hand. I'd be happy to show them to you."

"Sorry, I have to catch a train. Maybe some other time."

As she walked the rest of the way to the train station she wondered what Jasper Koors would think of the lengths a boor like Hank Wayne would go to to get his hands on one of Koors's works.

She arrived home to an envelope slipped under the door. It bore no postage or return address and only her name in neat block letters marched across the front. She removed a single sheet and sank onto the entryway bench as she read its depressing contents:

Gethsemane—

Thank you for looking after Carraigfaire these past few months, and thank you for removing the cloud from Uncle's reputation.

Although I'd planned to turn Carraigfaire into a museum dedicated to my aunt and uncle, recent developments forced a change in plans. As a result, I'm afraid I must ask you to vacate the cottage by—

She crumpled the note. An eviction notice. She cursed Billy for being too chicken to tell her face to face he'd sold out to Hank and for betraying Eamon and Orla's memories for money. Even a lot of money.

She ran to the music room and grabbed the grimoire.

"*Quondam vos eratis quod nunc ego sum, tu es quod ego erit fio. Invoco te. Levate velum inter regna vivos et mortuos. Erunt cum mihi in hoc loco. Quaeso vestra virtutes facere quae oportet fieri. Ut inveniam gratiam in conspecto tuo, meo obsecro,*" she recited at the top of her lungs. Nothing happened. She slammed the book against the piano keyboard. Harsh tones filled the air to match her angry mood.

"Damn it, Eamon, where are you? What's a girl got to do to summon a ghost?"

Six

Jackson arrived back at Carraigfaire before midnight but only just. Despite his haggard appearance—jacket and pants rumpled, shirt collar limp—he assured Gethsemane everything was all right. No amount of coaxing could entice him to divulge details about his interrogation. Guilty over her promise to keep her deal with Yseult secret, she stopped pushing him to talk. She didn't argue when he excused himself to call his wife and son.

She left him sleeping when she arose early the next morning to catch the train back to Ballytuam. She wore a floral dress and a long cardigan. A scarf hid the miniature camera dangling from a chain around her neck. She grabbed her violin and headed for the station.

In Ballytuam, she stood on the station platform as the train pulled out and stared up at the mansion on top of the hill. Olivia lived there. Named Essex House by the English ancestor who purchased it in the seventeenth century, the stone structure had dominated the landscape for over five hundred years.

Gethsemane walked up now familiar streets. She passed the Perryman Gallery. The fire screen remained in the window. She stopped in front of Ryan's auction house. Shades remained drawn, and no people moved about. She wondered if the office had closed. If the art world worked anything like the music world, bad news traveled fast. Word of the attempted theft would have spread and certainly would have been bad for business.

She passed several more galleries, a half dozen solicitors' offices, a tea shop, and a pub before reaching the Essex House gates. Heavy wrought iron and a call box protected the automobile entrance, but the pedestrian entrance consisted of only an arch in a stone wall. She walked through. A stroll past meticulous formal gardens along a path through a green lawn that would have been the envy of any golfer brought her to the mansion's front door. The heavy knocker looked as though it might have rusted in place a hundred years ago. A modern doorbell button had been installed in the ancient doorframe. She rang the bell.

"May I help you?" asked the uniformed maid who answered the door. Her frazzled blonde hair, frown, and cross tone of voice told Gethsemane that she wanted to be anything but helpful.

"I'm Gethsemane Brown. I'm—"

The maid cut her off. "Are you auditioning?"

Gethsemane held up her violin case.

"You'll be wanting to see Mr. Delaney then. This way."

Gethsemane hesitated. Yseult hadn't mentioned a Mr. Delaney. Who was he?

"Step quick." The maid's frown deepened. "Bad enough you lot canceling last minute. Dyspepsia." She snorted. "Out on a drunk's more like it. Sending us scrambling for a replacement right before the missus's hooley. Don't keep us waiting."

Gethsemane hurried to keep up with the maid, a short wiry woman in her mid-twenties. She guessed from the young woman's brisk stride and set of her shoulders questions would be neither acknowledged nor appreciated. She examined her surroundings as best she could while moving at such a quick pace. She followed the maid through high-ceilinged hallways. Their heels echoed off polished wooden floors. The walls hung heavy with framed artwork, both paintings and textiles. Samplers, tapestries, and quilts mingled with watercolors, oils, and sketches from chair rail to crown molding. Any museum would have envied Olivia's collection.

The maid stopped without warning in front of a room off a side hall. Gethsemane avoided colliding into her by an inch. "Wait here," the maid said. She gestured toward the room, then departed as suddenly as she'd stopped without waiting to see if Gethsemane followed her instructions.

She didn't. She ducked into the room and waited until she heard the maid's footsteps fade away. Why not get a jump start on the search for a bill of sale? She poked her head into the hall to verify the maid's absence, then walked back the way she'd come. She didn't get far before she heard other footsteps, heavier and slower than the maid's, approaching.

She scurried back and examined her surroundings. She stood in a music room, much larger than Carraigfaire's. Almost as large as the entire cottage. The cavernous space dwarfed the Steinway grand in the corner. A dozen chairs and music stands clustered near the piano. More than needed for the sextet Yseult said Olivia hired for the party. More like a small orchestra. Yseult didn't know everything.

"Do you play the piano?" a man's voice asked behind her.

"Quite well." She held up her violin case. "And the violin." She greeted the speaker, a man in his early fifties, the hair on his head still dark but a bit of gray visible in the meticulously barbered stubble on his face. Her paternal grandfather, a tailor, would have loved the man's bespoke suit, cut to flatter his broad shoulders and narrow waist. His patterned silk tie complemented both the midnight blue of his suit and the Mediterranean blue of his eyes. His cufflinks matched the suit's mother-of-pearl buttons. The polish on his black leather oxfords rivaled that of the floor.

"I'm Ray Delaney, Mrs. McCarthy-Boyle's estate manager and exclusive personal assistant."

"I'm Gethsemane Brown, a musician from Dunmullach."

"Please play something." He sat in an armchair near the Steinway and slipped a gold-plated cigar lighter from his pocket. Gethsemane eyed it.

"Don't worry, I'm not going to smoke. Mrs. McCarthy-Boyle

forbids it inside Essex House. Doesn't want the fumes to get into the textiles. Please play."

"Which instrument?"

"Your choice." He fidgeted with the lighter, flipping it back and forth, over and under his fingers like a magician about to perform sleight of hand.

"How about both?" She sat at the piano and played Scarlatti's "Sonata in D Minor, K. 141."

Ray rose from his chair to stand near the piano. He kept his eyes on her hands as they flew over the keyboard. He, and the lighter, remained motionless until the last notes faded away. "Brilliant."

She thanked him and removed her violin from its case. "Let's hear something fun." She shouldered the instrument and played "Captain Heuston's Lament."

Ray grinned. He pulled a smartphone from his pocket and slipped the lighter in its place. He scrolled down the screen. "I don't see your name on the list."

"List?" She kept her gaze on her violin as she put it away. He had a list.

"Of auditioning musicians."

Now what? Yseult hadn't mentioned a list. "I'm an add-on." She stepped toward Ray but caught her foot on the piano bench. She stumbled into him and knocked his phone out of his hand. "I am so, so sorry. Good thing I play better than I walk." She scooped up his phone and handed it back to him. But not before she glimpsed the names on the screen. If she could improvise music from magic spells she could improvise a cover story from a list. She borrowed a name. "Lucien Gervais told me about the auditions. It was too late to make an appointment, so I just showed up today and hoped for the best. I guess, technically, that makes me a gate-crasher instead of an add-on."

"How do you know Lucien?"

"Oh, you know, just around, the way one does. We performed together in Moscow, I think it was, or maybe Prague. The cities start to blur after you've been to so many." She leaned close to Ray and lowered her voice. "True confession. Lucien didn't actually *tell* me about the auditions. I eavesdropped. I overheard him mention them to someone else and decided to scoop him. Not strictly ethical, I know, but I couldn't pass up a chance at a gig like this."

Ray slipped the phone back into his pocket and offered Gethsemane his hand. "Congratulations on your scoop. Be here tomorrow, half past ten. That's half past ten sharp. It will be the only time to rehearse with the other musicians. Although, given your demonstrated skill, I doubt you'll have any difficulty." He eyed her outfit. "Do you have something black?"

"Don't all women have at least one black dress?" She didn't, but would have one by tomorrow.

"Brilliant. Until tomorrow, then."

Gethsemane called after him. "When do I meet Mrs. McCarthy-Boyle?"

"Meet her?" Ray's eyes narrowed. "What for?"

"Shouldn't I? It's her shindig. She's hiring me."

"Mrs. McCarthy-Boyle doesn't concern herself with the minutiae of hosting a fundraiser. I handle all the arrangements. You only need to concern yourself with showing up on time and performing well."

"You do all the work and she gets all the credit. Such is the lot of the hired help."

Ray drew himself up to his full height and sniffed down his nose. "I am Mrs. McCarthy-Boyle's confidential personal assistant—"

Glorified hired help with a chip on his shoulder. Gethsemane held up a hand. "I'm not insulting you, Mr. Delaney, I'm empathizing. Most of my ancestors have been the 'help' at some point in their lives. Come to think of it, I'm the entertainment, so I fall into that category, too. I understand what it's like to work hard to make someone else look good."

Ray's expression softened. "Yes, one does what one must."

"At least you get to live in a gorgeous mansion filled with

priceless artworks. Has this place always belonged to Mrs. McCarthy-Boyle's family?"

"Her late husband's family, but, no, not always. The Boyles are Anglo-Irish, descended from the Earl of Cork. They purchased the property during one of the many plantations of Ireland. The original landowners were Irish Catholic nobility."

"Take land away from people you don't like, give it to people you do like. Where've I heard that before?"

"I'll say goodbye again."

"One last thing. May I have a copy of the playlist for the party?"

Ray took out his phone. "Give me your mobile number and I'll text it to you."

"No phone. I, um, lost it and haven't replaced it yet."

Ray pulled a small notebook from another pocket and scribbled. He tore out a sheet and handed it to Gethsemane.

"Thank you. I'll have the pieces ready by ten thirty tomorrow morning. I'll work hard to make Mrs. McCarthy-Boyle look good."

Ray left. Gethsemane followed him into the hall and watched until he disappeared around a corner.

Before she could move, the maid reappeared from the other direction. "I'll show you out."

A lithe elegant woman with thick silver hair worn in a single braid appeared in the hall behind the maid. "Maire, see if the cleaners have delivered my dress yet. If not, tell Ray to call and get after them."

"Yes, Mrs. McCarthy-Boyle." Maire ducked her head and hurried away.

Gethsemane shook Olivia's hand. Olivia's perfect manicure made her self-conscious about her own plain short nails. O'Reilly said this woman could be his grandmother, but only her hair color betrayed any clue to her age. She epitomized timeless beauty with pale blue eyes and a glow to her flawless fair skin.

"Mrs. McCarthy-Boyle. A pleasure to meet you. I'm Gethsemane Brown."

"Yes." Olivia's finishing school voice bore no hint of brogue. "Ray told me you'll be joining my little band."

Told her? When? He'd only been gone a moment before she came in. Gethsemane noticed the slight bulge of a phone in Olivia's pants pocket. Ray must have texted her. So much for not getting involved in the minutiae of party planning.

Olivia continued. "Ray says you're a brilliant instrumentalist. I hope you won't find your talents underutilized by performing in such a small venue."

"Not at all. It's for a good cause. And I'd hardly describe Essex House as a small venue."

"You have an interest in sick children?"

"Who doesn't want to help sick kids?" Did Olivia suspect her of something? Or did she have a generally suspicious nature? She got the feeling Olivia only ever said half of what she knew. Cagey, like Yseult. Capable of palming off a forgery.

"I thought you might have an interest in art. So many people want to come to Essex House to see my pieces. I'm not boasting when I say it's one of the world's premier textile collections. Enthusiasts go to amazing lengths to try to see it."

Olivia's sly smile set Gethsemane on edge. The older woman baited her. She refused to take it. "I'm sure your collection deserves the title of world's premier, but I'm afraid my artistic tastes run to the musical rather than the visual. Not that I failed to notice the lovely pieces you've displayed in your halls. It must have taken decades to amass so many fine things."

"Centuries. My husband's family started collecting art in the 1800s."

Dare she push her luck? Getting bounced from the house wouldn't help Yseult, which meant it wouldn't help Jackson. "With so many artworks, how do you guard against forgeries? It would take a lifetime to research and authenticate every piece. Seems like you could slip a fake into the bunch and no one would ever notice."

Olivia stiffened. "I am not an amateur. I only deal with reputable galleries and auction houses, and each piece is authenticated prior to purchase. My collection has impeccable provenance."

"Right. Of course. I mean, I wouldn't buy a violin labeled Stradivarius without first verifying it was a genuine Strad."

Olivia smiled thinly and turned.

"One more question, Mrs. McCarthy-Boyle?"

"Yes?" Gethsemane noted the exasperation in Olivia's tone. She'd been relegated from party-crashing art fangirl to hired help impinging upon the mistress's time.

"Don't you worry about security? Just the part of your collection I've seen would probably net enough to buy Mars and a rocket ship to shuttle you back and forth. Aren't you afraid someone might steal something? You have so many pieces, a thief could walk out with one and it wouldn't be missed for a week."

"I assure you I'd notice immediately if one of my artworks went missing. And although I haven't placed my security system on public display, I do have one. An excellent one. Simply walking out with stolen art would not be an option."

"But everything's insured?"

Olivia's eyes narrowed. She stepped toward Gethsemane and lowered her voice. "Why do you ask?"

Gethsemane arranged her face into one of the innocent expressions her students used when they explained how the dog ate their homework. "No reason. I read in the paper about that international art theft investigation being reopened. Guess it got me wondering how its victims recouped their losses. Musicians worry about theft." She held up her violin case. "I insured my violin."

"Yes, I can see how you'd be concerned. A rare instrument carries as much value as a rare painting. And you have to worry about loss, too. Much easier to leave a Stradivarius in a taxi than a Picasso."

"True that."

The sly smile returned. "I'm fortunate such a gifted musician came available on short notice. Quite lucky. What are the chances?"

Baited again. Olivia wasn't going to let her off easy. Had Ray repeated her Lucien fib? She stuck to the story, just in case. "I could claim luck rolled my way, but honestly, I overheard an opportunity to earn a little extra income—while helping sick children—so I grabbed it. Can't blame a girl for looking out for her bottom line. Can you?"

"No, I can't." The smile seemed genuine this time. "Mother always said women need a mercenary streak if they wanted to be successful in a man's world. And my husband would have admired your entrepreneurial spirit."

Maire returned. "Your gown's arrived, ma'am. I hung it in your dressing room."

Olivia swept away without another word. Maire remained.

"If you'll follow me," she said to Gethsemane.

Gethsemane followed along the serpentine hallways. She looked at the art as they passed. Were any of them fakes? To her untrained eye, they looked genuine. But tomorrow night's party crowd would include dealers and other collectors. Surely you wouldn't display forgeries where people who knew what they were looking at could see them. Unless you were a gambler with a steel backbone. Or a wealthy imperious widow so sure of her stature in the world you wouldn't dream of anyone questioning them.

The door slammed behind her. Snooping would have to wait. Now she needed to find a black dress.

Gethsemane arrived early for rehearsal the next morning. She rode to Ballytuam in a taxi this time. Jackson rode with her. The gardaí wanted to ask him more questions. The taxi driver's chatter about Cork's chances versus Mayo's chances of advancing to the next All-Ireland final provided the only conversation. Jackson wouldn't tell her why the police were questioning him again, and she couldn't tell him what prompted her to perform at Olivia's party.

A few other musicians arrived early as well, which prevented any opportunity to go off on her own and search. All the musicians arrived by half past ten and rehearsal began. Gethsemane replaced the dyspeptic pianist. The program included works by Saint-Saëns, Prokofiev, Tchaikovsky, and Bratton. Each member of the orchestra was a professional or semi-professional musician. She couldn't imagine anyone less skilled would have auditioned. Unless Yseult's seven-year-old niece was a musical prodigy, her assessment of the orchestra's quality fell wide of the mark. They ran through rehearsal without any significant problems and broke at a quarter past two to give themselves time to rest, eat, and change clothes before the party. The cellist, Ciara Sullivan, invited her to lunch.

Gethsemane admired the view as they descended the hill toward the local pub, Ballytuam's midpoint. "You can see the entire town from here, from Essex House to the train station. I bet I could read the station's timetable board if I tried hard enough." She laughed. "And the sun wasn't in my eyes."

"Or if you used the spyglass in the tower room." Ciara pointed back to Olivia's house. "The late Mr. Boyle used to spend hours up there watching folks' comings and goings. A nosy bugger he was."

"You knew him?"

"Not well enough to be invited for tea, but sure I knew him. Everyone in town knew the laird of the manor." A sneer accompanied the last bit.

"You didn't like him," Gethsemane said. They arrived at the pub and claimed a table near a window looking out at the street.

Ciara continued after they were settled. "No, I didn't particularly like him. 'Tweren't nothing he did, mind you, 'cept spying on people. 'Twas more like who he was."

"Who was he?"

"English. Well, not him directly. His ancestors. Bunch of gobshite undertakers who stole our land. Loads of 'em married Irish women. Half of us hate the women for collaborating with the English, the rest of us love the women for turning the English into Irish." She sipped her Guinness. "You being American, you probably can't understand us holding a grudge for five hundred years."

"I understand quite well how past injustices foster current resentments." She raised her Barry Crockett in a mock toast.

The pub brightened as the door opened to admit someone.

"Mr. Perryman." Gethsemane waved at the gallery owner.

He adjusted his wire-rimmed glasses and studied her face.

"We met at your gallery the other day," Gethsemane reminded him.

"Oh, yes, Mr. Wayne's friend."

"Acquaintance." She shook his hand. "Gethsemane Brown. And this is—"

He shook the cellist's hand. "Ciara Sullivan. We know each other. Small town. Good to see you again."

Ciara invited him to join them for lunch.

"Thank you, but I'm meeting someone."

"Maybe we'll see you at Mrs. McCarthy-Boyle's fundraiser this evening," Gethsemane said.

"I'm afraid my little gallery isn't in that league. Now when I was in New York—never mind, I'm sure you don't want to hear about ancient history." He looked over his shoulder. "I see my friend. Please excuse me. But stop by the gallery again if you have the chance. I just got in a lovely Jacobean-style embroidered wall hanging you might like." He sat at the far end of the bar next to a gray-haired man. Soon the two had their heads bent in close conversation.

"Andrew's always gone for older men," Ciara said. "He told you about New York?"

"Not exactly. Someone mentioned he used to deal art there. Contemporary paintings, I think. He said he left because the market was saturated."

"He left because of a scandal." Ciara lowered her voice. "Haven't sussed all the details, but I gather it had to do with a client's husband and trips to tropical resorts that had nothing to do with buying art."

* * *

The two women finished lunch and returned to Essex House. Several of the musicians lived too far away to return home to change, so they'd been assigned rooms at the mansion to use as dressing rooms. Gethsemane received an assignment in the tower where Olivia's late husband used to keep watch over the town. She looked into several of the rooms she passed on the way to the tower. One held her attention. File cabinets interspersed with bookshelves lined the walls. Art books and auction catalogs crammed the shelves. An oversized desk, its ornately carved cubbyholes stuffed with papers, dominated the center of the room. French windows that led to balconies over an interior courtyard dotted one wall. Statuettes and other tchotchkes—Jackson would cringe at her referring to what were probably priceless artifacts as tchotchkes—decorated the shelves.

However, only a single piece of art adorned the walls. A framed sampler hung opposite the French doors. Gethsemane moved for a closer look. Some of the finest stitching she'd ever seen formed an alphabet on the top half of the twenty by twenty-four-inch piece of ivory linen. A multiplication table done in the same fine stitching filled the bottom. A flowered border surrounded both and tied the sections together. Centered at the bottom, below the flowered border, a stitched name and date identified the maker and the year of creation—Patience Freeman, 1764. Yseult might have been a lousy judge of musical talent, but she'd been right about the photograph. It didn't do the sampler justice.

"Stunning, isn't it?"

Gethsemane gasped, jumped, and nearly fell into a bookcase.

Olivia, her silver hair now in a loose chignon, entered the room. She wore heavily embroidered red Chinese silk pajamas and matching slippers. Ruby and diamond rings graced slim fingers tipped in the same shade of red as the pajamas. A diamond bracelet glittered on a delicate wrist.

Her smile stopped short of her eyes.

"Mrs. McCarthy-Boyle, I'm sorry. I know I shouldn't be in here, but—"

"But you heard about my famous sampler and just had to see it for yourself. Despite your lack of interest in the visual arts."

"But I am interested in history. I'm from Virginia, you see, so when I heard the sampler was stitched in Virginia..." She let the statement trail off. Best not to be too specific. "This," she gestured at the textile, "is absolutely unbelievable."

Olivia moved closer. "It's the star of my collection."

"I can see why. How did you come by such a one-of-a-kind piece? Or is that one of those questions you're not allowed to ask?"

"Right up there with a lady's age and her weight." She held her face inches away from Gethsemane.

Gethsemane stepped back. "Security or no, I'd be afraid to display such a rarity. The temptation to steal it—"

"I don't live my life in fear of maybe." Olivia ran her hand along the frame. "Would you hide a Kandinsky in a vault? Stick a da Vinci in a closet?" She held her face close to Gethsemane's again. "It's not as if I allow hordes of people to troop through my office."

Gethsemane backed up—and bumped into an end table. Papers swirled to the floor as she righted the delicate furniture. "I'm so sorry." She noticed a brochure advertising a golf course as she scooped papers. "Florida? Planning a vacation?"

Olivia snatched the brochure. "Are all musicians this inquisitive?"

"Didn't mean to be nosy. I was just going to recommend a travel agent. My sorority sis—"

"My travel arrangements are taken care of." Olivia held the office door open. "The party's starting soon."

"I was on my way to change." Gethsemane inched past Olivia. "I'll go do that now."

She looked back down the hall when she reached the corner. Olivia stood watching her.

Seven

Gethsemane changed into the black sheath dress she'd purchased in a Dunmullach dress shop after her audition and hurried back to the hall outside Olivia's office. Ray Delaney directed a staggering number of staff members from a position at the head of the stairs. He twirled his cigar lighter through his fingers in time with his barked commands. His presence nixed any hope she had of sneaking into the office for another look.

Maids and kitchen staff and dozens of others she couldn't identify by uniform scurried back and forth carrying trays loaded with drinkware, silverware, and dishes, arranging and rearranging furniture, and checking lists. Several maids, including Maire, dusted and straightened.

Gethsemane excused herself and slipped down the stairs past Ray. She entered the great hall and found most of her fellow musicians gathered. She headed toward them when a commotion broke out in the reception hall. Everyone rushed to see what went on.

"I've every right to be here!" a man shouted from the front doorway. The butler and a man Gethsemane didn't recognize struggled to keep him from coming farther inside.

"I've every right!" he shouted again. He wore an unbuttoned tuxedo jacket with one sleeve pushed up to the elbow. His other shirt sleeve lacked its cufflink. His bowtie hung loose around his open shirt collar and his thinning brown hair stuck out at odd angles. Gethsemane smelled the liquor from where she stood.

Ray pushed through the crowd. He grabbed the man's thumb and bent it back, then twisted the man's arm behind his back before pushing him out the door. The butler slammed the door behind him, and Ray returned to his post without comment.

"Who was that?" Gethsemane asked the person next to her.

"Curtis Boyle, Mrs. McCarthy-Boyle's nephew and heir apparent to the family estate. Assuming she hasn't cut the tosser out of her will."

The crowd dispersed. As guests drifted back to their pre-party small talk, Gethsemane thought she spotted a stocky blond with a scar. The unpleasant man from the auction house. Ronan something. She tried to follow, but a near-collision with a tuxedoed whale derailed her. By the time she and the big man finished their excuses, Ronan had gone. She started toward the reception hall when something caught her eye—an explosion of color on a large canvas, a technicolor riot of word and image fragments. She stepped away. From a distance the seemingly disjointed images formed part of a coherent painting. The massive work occupied most of the wall on which it hung. Gethsemane stepped farther back. The fragments of color coalesced into the shape of a gigantic teddy bear. She leaned in to read the artist's signature. Jasper Koors.

"A provocative piece, no?" Ray stood behind her, flipping his lighter in his fingers. "Bold yet tender. A paean to childhood's innocence but, at the same time, a condemnation of the brutish forces that would destroy that innocence."

Gethsemane frowned and squinted at the painting. "It's—bright."

"Not a fan?"

"Of contemporary art? Not so much. Give me a nice Caravaggio or Reubens over this any day."

"A fan of the Old Masters," Ray said. "Not surprising, I guess. Classical music, classical art."

"Not strictly Old Masters. I admire Kahlo and O'Keefe and wouldn't say no to a Rothko. Just not that into teddy bears." She turned to the pieces hung on the opposite wall: framed silk kimonos, a small Chinese screen, a Japanese fan. "I'm surprised Mrs. McCarthy-Boyle's into Jasper Koors. Kind of out of character with the rest of her collection."

"She made a brief foray into the contemporary art market. She considered expanding her collection in a different direction."

"What changed her mind? The idea of Essex House awash in Day-Glo paintings of children's toys?"

The lighter disappeared into a pocket. Ray's voice took on a hard edge. "Mrs. McCarthy-Boyle doesn't discuss her thought process with—what did you call it?—the hired help." He kept his eyes fixed on the painting. His hand followed the lighter.

Gethsemane watched him for a moment. She imagined the lighter somersaulting in his pocket. "Did Mrs. McCarthy-Boyle acquire this from Andrew Perryman?"

"Andrew Perryman? Doesn't he own one of the galleries here in town? Deals in modern crafts, I believe." He made "modern crafts" sound like a social disease. "I imagine paintings are out of his purview." He locked eyes with Gethsemane. "Why would you think Mrs. McCarthy-Boyle had any dealings with him?"

"He used to sell paintings when he lived in New York. He owned a gallery there years ago; I'm not sure how many. He still sells paintings to some of his more important clients." Hank Wayne counted as an important client, if you considered importance in terms of financial worth instead of worth as a human being.

"You know a good bit about Mr. Perryman. You two are close?"

"Not at all. I really don't know any more about him than what I just told you." Except his taste for older men regardless of marital status. "I know one of his clients, Hank Wayne. I overheard Mr. Wayne discussing a Koors with him and he—Mr. Wayne, I mean—told me Andrew used to own a gallery in New York. I gathered he specialized in contemporary paintings."

"Hank Wayne, the hotel magnate. He's shown interest in

properties in this area. You're one of Mr. Wayne's...?" The question trailed off.

One of Hank's what? Enemies? Antagonists? Or did Ray think—girlfriends? Ick. No. "One of his nothing. I said I knew him, I didn't say I enjoyed sharing air space with him. How do you know he's looking at property—Oh, the newspaper."

"Mrs. McCarthy-Boyle owns the distilleries."

"I'm surprised he hasn't come after Essex House," she said almost to herself. "Much more room for a cocktail bar than at Carraigfaire."

Color rose on Ray's neck. "Mrs. McCarthy-Boyle would never sell Essex House." His voice strained and he stared at the Koors with such intensity Gethsemane half expected flames to burst from the canvas. "This land has been in the family for generations. Generations! She can't sell it." He looked at Gethsemane as though he'd forgotten she stood there and couldn't quite place her. He shook his head and the suave, controlled Ray returned. The lighter reappeared in his hand. "The cocktail hour approaches. I have guests to attend to."

Gethsemane headed back toward Olivia's office. If Olivia wasn't there, she'd snoop for the Freeman sampler's bill of sale. If she found Olivia in her office, she'd ask her about the Jasper Koors, a painting so out of keeping with the rest of her collection and her demeanor.

Everything about Olivia screamed classic. Why had she bought it? When had she bought it? Before or after Andrew left New York? Before or after the fraud investigation went cold? If you bought something knowing it was forged, would you care how ugly it was while you bided your time until you could unload it?

A male voice interrupted her thoughts. "'Scuse me, miss? You Dr. Brown?"

She stopped short in time to avoid a collision with the young man who'd stepped in front of her. She guessed from his shirtsleeves and matching vest and bowtie he was one of the waitstaff. "Yes, I'm Dr. Brown."

"A man out back wants to speak wit ya. Says his name's Jack Apple or something like that."

Jackson? Here?

"Ask him in."

"You'd better speak with him outside, seein' as he ain't got an invite." The young man jerked his head in the direction he'd come. "Through the kitchen."

Gethsemane followed him through a maze of shouting cooks, scurrying waiters, and teeming food service trays to a small courtyard at the rear of the house. Jackson paced in front of a dumpster. He rushed over and hugged her.

"Jackson, are you all right?" He appeared worn out with his shirt collar open and bowtie undone. His eyes were puffy and his lips chapped. "Have you been at the garda station this whole time?"

He nodded. "They seem convinced I'm responsible for the attempted theft, that I have a conspirator who hid the Creech miniature in my pocket so I could walk out with it and meet up later. They've determined the sampler is a fake. They theorize we were trying to get rid of the sampler before the authorities got hold of it."

"That makes no sense, even for the police. You were bidding on the sampler. Why—"

"One of the other bidders was working undercover. He, or she, had no bid limit. They would have outbid anyone."

"It's still ridiculous. Conspirator? Partner? Who? You've been in Ireland for, like, five minutes. Who do they think you know well enough to commit felonies with?"

"They mentioned one name. Ronan Leary. He has connections in the art world and a criminal record. Apparently, he spent time in D.C. They think I met him there."

"Ronan Leary? The guy with the scar from the auction? He's here at the party. I tried to catch up with him, but he gave me the slip. I'll find him—"

"No," Jackson cut her off with a hand on her arm, "you won't. Did I mention he has a criminal record?"

"Yes, you did. Jackson, you worry more than my sister. I'm at a fancy party with hundreds of people around. What could happen?"

"You're at a fancy party in a big house with lots of nooks and crannies. Anything could happen. Leave the investigation to the police."

"Because they're doing such a bang-up job? Jackson, they're trying to pin a crime on you."

"Which they can't do, because I'm innocent."

Famous last words. At least it wasn't a murder case. "Look, Jackson, I don't want to argue with you. You're beat and you need to go back to the cottage and rest. You also don't need the police to find out you've been hanging around Essex House."

"All right, you win. Why don't you come with me? Forget about this party. I don't like the idea of you being here with this Leary character."

"I can't skip out on a performance, Jackson."

He sighed the weight of the world.

"I promise I won't get poisoned, shot, knocked over the head, or set on fire. I'll be careful. Go home, call your wife and son, and then get some sleep."

Jackson kissed Gethsemane on top of her head, then started for the courtyard exit. Gethsemane called after him. "You could do one thing for me. Not now, after you've had some rest."

"What's that?"

"Find out when the original New York-Dublin fraud investigation went cold."

"I don't have to find out. I remember. It's been about nine or ten years."

"Could you find out when someone bought a painting and who they bought it from?"

"Sissy, what are you up to?"

"I'm not up to anything."

Jackson crossed his arms and stared down at her.

"Mrs. McCarthy-Boyle has this big ugly Jasper Koors teddy bear painting hanging on one of her walls."

"Odd. She doesn't collect contemporary art."

"What if she isn't collecting it? What if she's sitting on it? Waiting to sell it because she knows it's a fraud?"

"Olivia McCarthy-Boyle involved in art fraud? Never."

"Why never?"

"She's one of the world's most important collectors. She'd never stoop to such, such..." he sputtered.

"Isn't that how the ring operated? By convincing major collectors to buy fakes cheap, then resell them as genuine? Or allow them to be stolen and claim the insurance?"

"Where did you hear that?"

Oops. From Yseult.

"Just around. You wouldn't believe the gossip going on in there."

"Sissy, I'm not going to help you get mixed up in something—"

"Something dangerous, something I know nothing about, something over my head. I'm not trying to be a hero, Jackson; I'm just trying to throw the guards a bone so they get off their duffs, find the real criminals, and leave us both alone. I have no confidence in their willingness to do the right thing over the expedient thing. They only care about closing the case, not about finding the truth."

He hugged her again.

"I'm sorry I dragged you into this mess."

His coat muffled her voice. "I could do the research myself, but it would save time if you'd do it since you know art people."

"You don't give up, do you?"

"Nope."

"All right, I'll find out when she bought a Jasper Koors and who sold it to her. What's the painting called?"

"Hideous bear? I don't know, it didn't have a label. How many ugly teddy bear paintings could there be?"

"I see you're unfamiliar with Koors' oeuvre. Don't worry, I'll figure it out. Tell me one thing before I go." He looked up at Essex House. "Did you see it?"

"See what?"

"The Freeman sampler."

"For a moment. Until I got caught."

"Is it beautiful?"

"More than you can imagine."

Gethsemane put her brother-in-law in a cab, then tried to clear her mind—of worries about Jackson, doubts about Olivia, suspicions about Andrew and about Yseult. Time to concentrate on music.

The party began with cocktails promptly at six. Olivia swept into the great hall in a cloud of iridescent silver chiffon. Opalescent nail lacquer replaced the red and a diamond solitaire the size of a grape replaced the ruby and diamond rings. The diamond sparkled against her crystal champagne flute. A diamond collar encircled her graceful neck, its center stone a twin of the ring's. Party guests flocked around her like butterflies around Queen Anne's lace. Elbows jostled as guests vied to press her hand. Her laughter bubbled like the fizz in her champagne.

The band opened with Saint-Saëns' "Carnival of the Animals" as uniformed staff served champagne and pink concoctions garnished with colorful plastic monkeys and giraffes, hors d'oeuvres designed to look like lions and elephants, and business card-sized pictures of circus animals drawn, the cellist told her, by the hospitalized children the fundraiser hoped to benefit. Picnic food miniaturized to finger food size accompanied "The Teddy Bears' Picnic," and "The Dance of the Sugar Plum Fairy" came with sugared plums.

"What are they going to serve with 'Peter and the Wolf'?" Gethsemane whispered to the harpist seated next to her. "Fresh kill?"

"Dinner," came the reply.

* * *

The first violin, leading the orchestra in the absence of a maestro, announced a short intermission between Tchaikovsky and Prokofiev. Gethsemane hoped her haste wasn't too obvious as she jumped up from the piano. This could be her only chance to search for the receipt. She reached the stairs to Olivia's office and crashed into Kenneth O'Connor.

He caught her before she fell over. "Apologies. Are you all right?"

"Fine." She straightened her dress and readjusted her shoe. "No harm done." Kenneth had positioned himself between her and the stairs. On purpose? Or was she being paranoid?

"I didn't expect to see you here tonight."

"Last minute thing. The pianist canceled. I figured this was the only way I'd get into this party. Pretty impressive, huh? I love the elephant-shaped hors d'oeuvres."

"No, you don't. You think they're as ridiculous as I do. You don't like the plastic monkey doo-dads on the drinks either."

Either Kenneth was psychic or she needed to brush up her poker face. "Are you here for the children, or did you just want to get a close up of Mrs. McCarthy-Boyle's art? Shopping for a client?"

"A bit of both. Mrs. M-B has been selling pieces off little by little. Figured I'd get a preview of what might be coming on the market while I'm helping the wee ones."

Gethsemane noticed his wristwatch. A Patek Philippe. Personal art shopping paid well. She brought up the one excuse no man ever questioned. "I'd love to chat more, but intermission's short and I need to find a ladies' room. There's a line at the one on this level."

Almost no man. "Ladies' room?"

"What do you call it over here? The jacks? The toilet? I have to pee."

He had the decency to blush as he stepped out of her way. She ran up the stairs. She thanked her luck no one else appeared on her way to Olivia's office as she slipped inside and pulled the door shut after her. No more surprise visits. She tried the file cabinets. Locked. All of them. Shelves came next. Nothing but catalogs. She flipped through some of the catalogs. They formed a travel guide to the world of auctions—New York, London, Paris, Geneva, Hong Kong, Milan. None listed the Patience Freeman sampler as one of their lots. She shook a few. No receipts fluttered to the floor. The desk then. Cubbyholes were ideal places to stuff receipts.

"What're you doing?"

Gethsemane spun with a yelp. She faced a strange man, tall, redheaded, clean-shaven, his brogue a baritone, his expression more puzzled than angry. Staff? Security? "I was looking for, um..." Not the bathroom this time. He'd never believe she'd mistaken the office for the toilet. "I mean, I, uh, I lost..." She stopped. What seemed wrong? She scrutinized the man's clothes. Not the unremarkable suit of a plainclothes security guard or the uniform of a staff member. Not the tuxedo of one of the party guests. Knee breeches. He wore ivory knee breeches. And white hose, a pale quilted vest—silk, it looked like—a white cravat, and a dark blue frock coat. He carried a cocked hat tucked under an arm. His copper-red hair swooped back from his forehead into a ponytail tied with a black ribbon. She knew those clothes. She'd visited Colonial Williamsburg and Mount Vernon often growing up in Virginia. Costumed interpreters in both places wore the same style of dress. So did the male cast of *Hamilton*. Eighteenth century. The man wore eighteenth-century attire. A faint sienna glow surrounded him. She hadn't noticed it at first, in her shock at being discovered. She sniffed. Citrus, cinnamon. Spicy with a hint of sweetness. It reminded her of her grandpa, her mother's father. Bay Rum.

"What is it you've lost, madam?" the man asked. "May I be of assistance?"

At first glance, the man had appeared as solid as the desk she'd been rifling through. On closer look, she discerned the outline of the bookcases near the door through his chest. She squinted. She could almost read the titles on some of the larger books. A ghost. Damn it. She finally found a ghost. In someone else's house, in the middle of a fundraiser, while she was busy snooping. But he wasn't the ghost she wanted. He wasn't Eamon. So much for conjuring spells.

"It's miss, not madam. Miss Brown. Doctor Brown, if you want to get technical." She resumed rifling. "I don't mean to be rude, sir, but you're the wrong ghost and I'm kind of busy right now. So, if you could just, you know, go haunt someone else, I'd appreciate it."

"Wrong ghost?" The man frowned. "What do you mean, wrong ghost?"

"You're not the ghost I ordered."

"Ordered? I am not a pint of ale, Miss Brown. You recited the conjuring spell. Quite a few times, if memory serves."

He'd heard the spell? But she'd recited the incantation back in Dunmullach, not here in Ballytuam. The footsteps and the shadow in the mirror. She groaned inwardly. How had she screwed things up? Conjuring ghosts was like trying to bake a cake using a recipe where the chef left out an ingredient or two. "I meant I intended to bring a different ghost, Eamon McCarthy, back, not you. No offense."

"If you wanted this McCarthy gentleman, why didn't you summon *him*?"

"I did." She mimicked the redhead. "Quite a few times, if memory serves."

"You did not. You summoned me specifically."

"How could I summon you? I don't know you. By the way, who are you?"

"I beg your pardon for my lack of manners. I so seldom talk to humans these days, I've become somewhat neglectful of the niceties of polite conversation. Since there's no one to introduce us, allow me to introduce myself." The ghost bowed. "I'm Daniel Lochlan, Captain of the *Hesperus*. At your service."

"The *Hesperus*?"

"The finest brigantine ever to sail the Atlantic."

"Brigantine? Some kind of ship?"

The man's glow changed from an apologetic magenta to a brilliant blue. Judging by his expression, his blue aura meant the same thing Eamon's blue meant. Anger. "Some kind of ship?" He repeated himself. "Some kind of ship? You say that like 'twas no more than an old pair of shoes or last night's meal. The *Hesperus* wasn't merely 'some kind' of ship. Seventy-five feet, one hundred fifty tons, the finest rigging on two continents. She carried twelve guns and fifty men and could make eleven knots in fair winds. Some kind of ship, indeed."

"Sorry." She'd seen *The Ghost and Mrs. Muir* often enough to know better than to belittle a captain's ship. "I didn't mean to insult you. I'm sure the *Hesperus* was as fine as you say." The blue dimmed. "But you're still the wrong ghost. Why would I summon an eighteenth-century ship's captain?"

"I don't know, Miss. 'Tis my question for you."

"But I didn't call you. I called Eamon McCarthy, a twentieth-century composer. At least I thought I did."

"I don't like to disagree with a woman, but you didn't summon this McCarthy fella. You summoned me. You recited the summoning incantation and played my harmonic likeness and here I am."

"Your harmonic likeness?" She knew about sympathetic resonance in music—passive objects made sounds in response to external vibrations created by other objects with which they shared a harmonic relation. Undamped piano strings vibrated in response to notes played on main strings, windows rattled in response to loud notes played on an organ, sopranos shattered wine glasses when they sang certain notes. None of which had anything to do with ghosts. Did it? "What harmonic likeness?"

"The tune you played. 'Captain Heuston's Lament.'"

Gethsemane's eyes widened. "A sea chanty? You sympathetically resonate to a sea chanty? Seriously?" Captain Lochlan raised an eyebrow. She continued. "Sure, why not? You're a sea captain, so of course you resonate to a song of the seas." The chanty's bawdy lyrics popped into her head. "I hope it's the music and not the words that brought you back."

The captain blushed and his aura turned an embarrassed pink.

"So what song makes Eamon vibrate?"

"I'm sorry, but as I don't know the gentleman, I can't tell you that. It doesn't have to be a song. Could be any sound."

Gethsemane threw up her hands.

"Didn't you ask for his key before you started conjuring?"

"I didn't know I needed to ask. The grimoire left out that tidbit. I'm kind of new at this whole ghost thing. By the way, at the cottage, the footsteps and shadow. You?"

"Aye. I tried to manifest but couldn't manage more. I never entered the cottage while I lived. I was ten years in the grave before 'twas built."

Eamon couldn't appear anywhere he hadn't appeared while he lived either. "So how'd you manage anything?"

"I roamed the cliffs of Dunmullach many a time. No sight's lovelier than the sun rising over the bay. 'Cept for a blue-eyed Dunmullach lass named Molly—"

Gethsemane stopped him with a hand. "Stories about sailors and blue-eyed lasses are seldom fit for mixed company." Maybe he had responded to the lyrics.

The pink aura glowed brighter. "I'll grant you that, Miss."

"How can you materialize here at Essex House? You've been here before?"

"Aye, numerous times. Cornelius Boyle owned an interest in an import-export business in Cork. He brought tobacco from Virginia and linseed from the West Indies and sent linen to Maryland. I sailed as first mate on two of his ships before becoming master of the *Hesperus*. His fourth daughter—"

Another hand. "Stop there."

"My apologies again. I forget myself. I must say, you're quite easy to talk to, and you're handling yourself remarkably well, being face to face with a ghost and all."

"What'd you expect me to do? Scream? Swoon?"

"I've seen grown men do worse."

"Yeah, well, I've gotten used to your type. Ghosts, I mean." She looked at her watch. "Anyway, I don't have time to freak out right now. If you'll excuse me..." She turned back to the desk and opened drawers.

Captain Lochlan rematerialized without warning on the other side of the desk. Gethsemane jumped. Two ghosts or twenty, she'd never get used to *that*. "May I ask what you're looking for?"

"A bill of sale." She slammed a drawer and cursed. The captain stepped back, wide-eyed. "Welcome to the twenty-first century, Captain, where women swear like sailors."

He stiffened. "I'm no hobnail. I've heard such beer-garden jaw used by females." He lowered his gaze and muttered, "Though usually not outside of a fish market."

Gethsemane glanced at her watch again. "I'm aware it's not every day one gets to see a ghost, much less chat with one, and on any other occasion I'd be suitably impressed. However, as fascinating as this conversation is—and I'm not being sarcastic—I've only got a few minutes before we start playing again, and I haven't found anything." She held up a handful of brochures she pulled from a cubby. "Except Orlando, Florida real estate ads. Please, please, please, go haunt somebody else."

"I'm sorry, lass, but you summoned me, so you're stuck with me until my task is complete. If you'll tell me what you're looking for..."

"I told you, I'm looking for a bill of sale."

"I can assist with the search." Captain Lochlan pointed at a file cabinet. A soft click of the lock and the top drawer slid open.

"That is so cool." Gethsemane abandoned the desk and thumbed through files.

"What's this bill of sale for? Tea? Cloth?" He eyed her dress. "If all female attire is so scantily made in this century, a bill for cloth is likely to be a small one."

"This is modest. It goes past my knees. Do that thing with the lock again."

The captain pointed and another cabinet opened.

"I'm looking for a bill of sale for a sampler, eighteenth-century schoolgirl embroidery." She looked at the captain. "You probably know more about it than I do."

"Young girls stitched them to practice their needlework. They displayed their finest as proof of their skill. To help them land husbands. Or work, if they were of those classes."

Gethsemane bit back her twenty-first century feminist retort. "This particular sampler is rarer than weapons-grade plutonium. I know you don't know what that is, but, trust me, it's crazy expensive. You could buy a fleet of brigantines for what that sampler's worth. It was stitched by a free black schoolgirl in Williamsburg, Virginia, in 1764. You can see it for yourself right over—" She froze. The frame—and its contents—she'd admired a few hours ago was gone. Only a forlorn picture hanger remained to mark the space. She put her hand against the wall as if she might be able to feel what she couldn't see. "It can't be gone. It was right here. The Patience Freeman sampler was right here. I saw it with my own eyes. It was. Right. Here." She smacked the wall.

Captain Lochlan paled until the striped pattern of the wallpaper behind him showed plainly visible through his chest. "What was that name you said?"

"Patience Freeman. Why does her name matter? The only thing that matters is that the damn thing's missing."

"Her name matters to me."

"The daughter of a seamstress and a slave in colonial Virginia? Why? It's not like you knew her."

"I knew her. I knew her quite well. I ought to." He dematerialized. "I'm the man who killed her."

Gethsemane gasped. Her eyes darted about for something heavy to throw. Then she remembered objects tended to pass through ghosts without harming them. Damn.

Why hadn't she listened to Father Tim and left the ghost conjuring alone? Bad enough she failed to summon Eamon. Worse, she called up the ghost of a child murderer. Probably from hell where he deserved to spend eternity. "You murdered an eleven-year-old?"

Captain Lochlan rematerialized full force. The blast of Bay Rum knocked Gethsemane back. The captain blazed bright cerulean blue. Sparks popped and sizzled around his head. Gethsemane ducked and waited for orbs.

"Murdered?" the captain yelled. Gethsemane glanced at the door, hopeful no one else could hear him. "You think so little of me? You think me so low I'd murder a child, an innocent girl? Am I a highwayman, a fiend, an agent of Satan himself?"

"I'm sorry. I retract the question. Stop with the pyrotechnics before you set the house on fire." She made a mental note: don't accuse ghosts of murder. They don't take it well. "You said you killed her."

"I didn't murder her." The captain leaned against the file cabinet, dejected. A drawer protruded through his stomach as he dissolved partway into it. Gethsemane flinched and reminded herself Eamon said it didn't hurt. "But I'm no less responsible for her death than if I'd squeezed the life from her with my own two hands." He held them out in front of him and stared, lost in some distant painful memory.

"I'm confused. You didn't murder her, but you're responsible for her death? What happened?" The faint cacophony of violins being tuned floated up from downstairs before the captain could answer. She looked at her watch. Seven minutes until show time. She'd be missed. The story and the search would have to wait. She closed the file cabinet.

Captain Lochlan started as the drawer passed through him. He vanished, then reappeared next to the French windows and stepped onto the balcony. He leaned into the railing. Gethsemane thought he might speak, but he only peered down toward the patio below. He swore, then leaned so far over the railing it passed through his midsection. "Get help, lass," he said without taking his eyes off whatever he saw.

"Help? Why?" Gethsemane moved toward the balcony.

"Stay back."

She leaned over the rail next to him. "Damn. Not again."

Olivia lay prone on the patio's slate tiles, arms and legs akimbo, head and neck twisted at an awkward angle. Even if her mother hadn't been a physician, and even if she hadn't seen more dead bodies in the past three months than any musician should ever have to see, she would know that Olivia was now the late Mrs. McCarthy-Boyle.

Eight

Had Olivia fallen? Gethsemane gripped the balcony's stone railing. Couldn't be any sturdier. The handrail came up past her waist. But Olivia stood several inches taller than her. The handrail would've stopped at her hips. Gethsemane craned forward and scanned the courtyard. She forced herself not to stare at the crumpled figure of her hostess. Except for the dead woman, the yard was deserted. No lights in any of the windows opposite. She swallowed nausea and looked down again. Moonlight sparkled off something near Olivia's hand. Shattered glass. Had she gone out onto the balcony to sip champagne in the night air? She'd had at least one drink downstairs. Maybe she got dizzy and stumbled. Or maybe—did she imagine it—maybe something below caught Olivia's eye. Gethsemane leaned out farther over the rail. There *was* something, something caught in the bushes. Something light-colored. She could see it better if she just leaned out a little bit more...

Gethsemane felt the back of her dress jerk upward. She gagged as the front neckline caught her in the throat. A yank and she fell back into the room, where she landed hard on the floor. "Ow." She scrambled to her feet and glared at Captain Lochlan. "That hurt." She rubbed her dignity. "Throw me across the room next time. What's wrong with you?"

"Are you touched in the head?" The captain nodded toward the balcony. "Do you want to end up down there like the poor woman?"

The office door flew open before she could answer. Ray huffed in. A vein pulsed in his temple and a muscle twitched in his jaw. "Where the hell've you been? You're due to start again in five—" He checked his watch. "Make that two minutes. Damned unreliable temperamental musicians." He gave no sign he noticed Captain Lochlan.

"I hate to interrupt your tirade, Mr. Delaney, but I think you better call the gardaí."

"Why? What's happened?"

Gethsemane pointed to the French windows. Ray rushed onto the balcony and looked over the rail. "What have you done? You've killed her."

"I didn't kill anybody," Gethsemane said to the sour-faced female sergeant who interrogated her in the courtyard. She tried not to think of Olivia's crumpled body covered with a sheet a few yards away. She shivered in the cold and longed for her coat, out of reach in her tower room. The sergeant, who'd introduced herself as Heaney, bundled in a parka and gloves, didn't seem to notice the temperature or Gethsemane's shivering as she asked the same questions again and again.

"No," Gethsemane said. "Mrs. McCarthy-Boyle wasn't in her office when I went in. No, I didn't see anyone else in the room." She assumed the sergeant meant anyone corporeal and omitted mention of Captain Lochlan. "I went to the office to look at the Freeman sampler. Everyone knew Mrs. McCarthy-Boyle displayed it in her office." She didn't know who in the garda knew about Yseult's investigation. If she told the sergeant what she was doing and Yseult denied it...

"This interest in antique textiles." The sergeant scribbled in her notebook. "It's a new hobby? Music not fulfilling enough anymore?"

Captain Lochlan's disembodied voice whispered in her ear, "Is sarcasm a standard part of modern law enforcement?"

Gethsemane flicked her fingers to shoo him away. Sergeant Heaney noticed.

"Something wrong, Dr. Brown?"

"A bug. And my music is plenty fulfilling, thanks."

"Textiles are a family thing then?"

"Meaning?"

"Meaning your brother-in-law is suspected of trying to steal an antique sampler from an auction just a couple of days ago." She consulted her notes. "A quite valuable piece of embroidery."

"That sampler was planted in my brother-in-law's coat. He traveled all the way from Virginia to Ballytuam to bid on the piece with the full knowledge of the entire museum staff and approval of the museum board. He could hardly return home with the miniature and no proof of purchase. Jackson had no reason to steal it."

"And you had no reason to help the victim over the balcony?"

"Of course I didn't!" A stream of curse words streamed through her head. She closed her eyes and counted to five before speaking. "I hardly knew the woman. Why would I kill her?"

"To derail the investigation into your brother-in-law's crime."

"My brother-in-law hasn't committed any crime. Your accusations are false. *All* of them." Gethsemane balled her fist. She'd never wanted to hit anyone as badly as she wanted to hit the sergeant right in her thin-lipped mouth. "What is it with you people? You pin a crime on the first person you see and cook up some cockamamie explanation to avoid actually investigating. Investigations seem too much like real work?"

A tingle shot from her elbow to her shoulder as a ghostly hand materialized on her arm. The scent of Bay Rum tickled her nose as the captain's voice filled her ear. "Easy, lass."

Gethsemane took a deep breath and tried to relax. "You don't know me, Sergeant, but please believe me when I tell you I'm not stuck on stupid. Even if Jackson had stolen that sampler, which he didn't, I wouldn't kill someone to cover it up. Murder is a far more serious crime than theft."

"The twenty-first century has a gift for understatement," Captain Lochlan whispered.

Gethsemane hissed at him to shut up.

Sergeant Heaney shot her a strange look as she tried to hide her admonishment under a cough. "Did you say something, Dr. Brown?"

"No. The, uh, night air dries my throat." She coughed again. "I was just clearing it. Isn't it more likely that Mrs. McCarthy-Boyle just leaned too far out over the rail and lost her balance than someone pushed her?"

"Leaned out to do what? Catch some night air?"

The captain asked Gethsemane, "Do you think she was born a bitch or is it a technique she's perfected through years of practice?"

Gethsemane stifled a laugh. "Maybe she leaned out to see something."

"Such as?"

"When I was standing on the balcony I saw something caught in one of the bushes. Something light-colored."

"What did you see?"

"I don't know. I couldn't tell. It was way down in the bushes. If I'd leaned any farther I would have ended up on the patio next to Mrs. McCarthy-Boyle."

"This, perhaps?"

Gethsemane and Sergeant Heaney faced the newcomer as she walked across the courtyard. Yseult. One gloved hand grasped a light-colored object.

"Could be." As Yseult came closer, Gethsemane saw she carried a rolled ivory-colored fabric. Embroidery threads showed around Yseult's glove. Surely it wasn't—"What is it?"

"I'll ask the questions," Heaney said. She stood at attention. Yseult didn't try to suppress a grin. The sergeant didn't seem to notice. Gethsemane wondered at the sergeant's deference. Yseult's assignment must be quite "special" for her to pull rank on the local guards. "What's that, ma'am?"

"Something I found caught in a bush." She took care not to let the cloth touch the ground as she unrolled it in front of her. The now familiar embroidered alphabet marched in neat rows across the upper half of the large linen rectangle and the embroidered grid filled the lower half of the fabric. The missing sampler. With the fabric out of its frame, Gethsemane saw just how perfect the letters were, how precise the numbers were. The exquisite stitching resembled printer's ink.

"You found it," Gethsemane said.

"Is that the missing textile, ma'am?" Heaney asked.

"No, Sergeant, it isn't." She reconsidered her words. "Strictly speaking, it may be the missing textile. But it's not the genuine Patience Freeman sampler. *This* sampler is a modern fake."

"A fake?" Gethsemane and the sergeant exclaimed simultaneously.

Captain Lochlan said something Gethsemane was glad only she could hear.

"How can you tell, ma'am?" Heaney asked. "I mean I know how *you* can tell, but how can you tell?"

"May I borrow your torch?" Heaney handed her a pocket flashlight. Yseult flipped the sampler to its reverse and shone the flashlight beam on the embroidery threads. Gethsemane noted the stitching was almost as neat as that on the front. "See how the stiches on the back of the sampler are faded?"

Gethsemane and the sergeant nodded.

Yseult flipped the sampler to its face. "See how the stitches on the front are also faded, exactly as much as they are on the back?"

"Shouldn't they be?" Gethsemane asked. She remembered what Jackson told her about light exposure on color. "The embroidery thread's almost two hundred fifty years old."

"A sampler this fine would have represented the culmination of Patience's training, her best work, meant for display. It would have been framed on a wall for a good part of that two hundred fifty years."

Captain Lochlan confirmed Yseult's statement.

"Light would have fallen on the front of the piece and faded the threads, but the frame," she turned the sampler again, "would have protected the back."

"So the back should have faded less than the front. The colors should be brighter," Gethsemane said.

"A common forger's mistake. But one they often get away with until someone takes the piece out of its frame and examines it closely. If they ever do. By then the sale is often made, the money's stashed in an offshore account, and the forger's laying low in a country with no extradition treaty."

"Why would someone hide a fake antique in a bush, ma'am?" Heaney asked. "And what's it got to do with Mrs. McCarthy-Boyle's death?"

"As to your first question, I have my suspicions, but I don't know why for certain. Yet. As to your second question, maybe nothing. Or maybe everything. We don't know whether Mrs. McCarthy-Boyle died from misadventure or homicide."

The sergeant opened her mouth to speak when Ronan Leary burst into the courtyard.

He pointed at Gethsemane. "You! You were at the auction the night of the theft. You're no musician. What're you doing here? Casing the house?" He turned to the police officer who'd followed him out. "It's her. She's the thief. She's the one you should be questioning."

Kenneth sauntered up behind the officer. "Shut it, Leary. Of course she's a musician. You heard her play. And so what if she was at the auction? So were you."

Leary turned on Kenneth. "So were you, for that matter. Maybe you're the one. Maybe you're in it together. I saw the two of you talking inside. You didn't know that, did you? I saw you plotting."

"Are you delusional or just ossified? Sure, I was talking to her. I always talk to beautiful women. The only thing I was plotting was how to get her phone number. Which I failed to get, I'm sorry to say." He shrugged and winked. "Best laid plans..."

"A friend of yours, Dr. Brown?" Yseult asked.

"A recent acquaintance."

"A lifelong flirt," Yseult said.

"Perhaps an alibi," Kenneth said. "No one saw Mrs. McCarthy-Boyle after 'The Teddy Bears' Picnic.' Dr. Brown remained seated at the Steinway in front of three hundred people through the end of 'The Dance of the Sugar Plum Fairy.'"

"Do you know what he's on about?" Yseult asked Gethsemane.

"The music. Those were two of the pieces we performed. Children-themed music, since the event benefitted a children's hospital."

"Sorry I missed it."

"I'm not one to call a lady a liar," Captain Lochlan whispered to Gethsemane, "but I don't think she's sorry at all."

"All right, Leary," the officer standing next to Ronan said. "C'mon. I've some more questions for you. You, too, O'Connor. The guard waiting over there is all yours. Sorry he's not a beautiful woman, but he'll be sure to get your phone number."

Yseult addressed the sergeant after the men left. "I'm going to bring Dr. Brown to the station with me. I need to ask her more about this." She held up the sampler. "You can finish taking her statement about the deceased there after I'm done with her. In the meantime, one of the guests, Mr. Fitz-something-or-other, Fitzpatrick, Fitzwilliam, I don't remember, corralled me to tell me he saw someone crawling into one of the windows from the courtyard. He's adamant. Would you talk to him and see if you can make some sense out of his story?"

The sergeant snapped her notebook shut, shoved it into her pocket, glared at Gethsemane and Yseult, and stomped off in search of the adamant Mr. Fitz.

Someone called out to Yseult and motioned her over toward the bushes where she'd recovered the sampler.

"A moment please, Dr. Brown. I'll be right back and then we can go."

Gethsemane rubbed her arms to try and warm herself. Captain Lochlan offered her his coat. "Thanks, but I don't think it'll work."

She stamped her feet and paced around the patio. She stepped off the edge of the slate on her second pass. She expected to step down into soft grass, but the toe of her shoe landed on something hard. After making sure no one watched her, she picked it up.

"A button," Captain Lochlan said over her shoulder.

"Not just any button." She turned the silver shank button over in her hand. "This is custom, like a tailor would use on your bespoke suit."

"Aren't all suits bespoke?"

"Remind me to explain ready-to-wear." She turned away as Yseult approached and slipped the button into her cleavage. She wished she'd bought a dress with pockets. Much easier to hide things from people you don't trust.

"Dr. Brown?" Yseult asked.

"Just trying to warm up." She held her hands close to her chest and blew on them.

"We can go now. I sent a uniform for your coat. It'll be waiting in the car."

Nine

Gethsemane sat in the Ballytuam garda station in the same windowless interview room in the same chair at the same graffiti-scarred table and waited for Yseult. She ran through the first three verses of "Bingo Was His Name-oh" before Yseult entered the room with two Styrofoam cups.

"Tea?" She placed a cup in front of Gethsemane.

"Thanks." Gethsemane pushed the cup aside. "Where do we start?"

"Down to brass tacks? All right." Yseult set her cup aside, too. "The bill of sale."

Not the dead body on the patio. Interesting. "I didn't find it."

"Where'd you look?"

"In Olivia's office—her desk, bookshelves, filing cabinets."

"You looked in the filing cabinets? They weren't locked?"

"I, um, managed to open a few." She wished Captain Lochlan had come with her, if only for moral support, but the garda station only dated back to 1932.

"And you found nothing at all?"

"Florida real estate brochures and auction catalogs. No bill of sale."

"Damn." Yseult seemed to be speaking to herself. "Where the hell is it?"

Gethsemane repeated Sergeant Heaney's question. "Does the

attempted theft of the Freeman sampler, excuse me, the fake Freeman sampler, have anything to do with Olivia's death?"

"Sorry, what?"

"The Patience Freeman sampler, Olivia's death? Are they connected?"

"As I said—"

"I know, until the medical examiner rules on the cause of death you can't say for certain. But if you had to hazard a professional guess?"

"Unofficially, yes. I believe someone pushed Mrs. McCarthy-Boyle over that balcony. She probably interrupted the thief. Maybe that's why the thief stashed the sampler in the bush. They'd just murdered a woman, needed to escape quickly, and couldn't risk taking the sampler with them."

"At least you don't think I killed her."

"Nor do I think your brother-in-law did."

Why would she, or anyone, suspect Jackson of murdering Olivia? Did they know he'd stopped by Essex House? Had one of the staff mentioned seeing him?

"However," Yseult continued, "Ballytuam's finest would just as soon pin the blame on the most convenient suspects and close their case."

She'd said those same words to Jackson, but she had reason to mistrust the police. Yseult was supposed to be on their team. Did Yseult feign disdain for her colleagues to trick her into thinking she found an ally? Or did the forensic examiner who spent more time in the field than the lab really hold the guards in contempt?

"I'm afraid," Yseult said, "things may become—complicated—for you and Dr. Applethwaite."

Complicated how? What did Yseult know? And what did she want in exchange for simplifying things? A tip about a possibly fake Jasper Koors teddy bear painting?

Sergeant Heaney burst into the room. "Gethsemane Brown, I'm arresting you on suspicion of the attempted theft of the antique embroidery known as the Patience Freeman sampler. I caution you that you are not obliged to say anything unless you wish to, but whatever you say will be taken down in writing and may be given in evidence. Please stand."

"Arrested?" Gethsemane looked back and forth between Yseult and the sergeant. "You must be joking. Or out of your fu—I've done nothing wrong. You've no cause to arrest me. No, I won't stand. And I want a lawyer." Welcome to complicated.

Yseult stood next to Sergeant Heaney, close enough for the police officer to notice Yseult's height advantage. "Sergeant, don't you think your charges are premature?"

Heaney, some of her bravado gone, stepped back. "Preliminary, ma'am, not premature. Once the medical examiner's ruled on Mrs. McCarthy-Boyle's cause of death we'll be amending the charge to homicide."

"The hell you will!" Gethsemane slammed her palm on the table. "I didn't kill anyone. I didn't steal anything. I played piano at a fundraiser, that's all."

"That's for a jury to decide." The sergeant smirked.

"You're getting ahead of yourself, Sergeant. You've already brought Dr. Brown to trial for a crime that may not have been committed. We don't know there's been a murder."

"Well, no, not yet, but—"

"Witnesses who can account for Dr. Brown's movements? At least one has already come forward. Have you completed your interviews yet?"

"Not all, no, but—"

"I appreciate your eagerness to close this case, but we mustn't let enthusiasm lead to cutting corners."

Gethsemane emerged from her fog of anger long enough to pay attention to Yseult and Sergeant Heaney's interaction. Yseult reprimanded a garda sergeant, practically ordered her to undo her arrest. Who gave her such authority? She admitted being loaned to the garda's fraud bureau but never said who loaned her. It had to be Interpol or some government alphabet agency if she could pull rank on the locals. Was this art crime ring that big of a deal? Or were

Yseult and the sergeant blowing smoke, trying to trick her into incriminating herself or her brother-in-law? Maybe this was the Irish version of good cop/bad cop. She decided not to mention her theory about the Koors painting. If Jackson came up with anything, she'd tell O'Reilly. Him, she trusted.

"Sergeant," Yseult said, "I'm still questioning Dr. Brown. In the meantime, why don't you pursue some of your other lines of inquiry? When I've finished with Dr. Brown, we'll see about resolving this situation to everyone's satisfaction."

Sergeant Heaney reddened. "Yes, ma'am. I'll ask her brother-in-law what he was doing at Essex House tonight. In the meantime." She drew out the last word.

Yseult said nothing.

The sergeant brightened. "Did you know Jackson Applethwaite went to Essex House? He went looking for Dr. Brown. The kitchen staff saw them talking."

So the house staff squealed. Gethsemane glared at Heaney. "And he got in a cab and left Essex House to go back to Dunmullach while Olivia was still alive. Why don't you pursue that?"

"I'm sure Sergeant Heaney will interview the taxi driver as well as anyone else with relevant information. Now, if you'll excuse us, Sergeant, we must be keeping you from your work."

Sergeant Heaney turned on her heel and left.

Yseult resumed her seat. "You didn't mention Dr. Applethwaite's visit to Essex House."

She didn't mention a lot of things. "He didn't go into the house, and Olivia was alive when he left. I didn't want to further complicate things."

"I appreciate your wanting to protect your brother-in-law, but I expect candor if I'm going to help you."

Candor. A funny demand from a woman anything but candid. Gethsemane crossed her arms over her chest and felt the button dig into her flesh. Relevant? Maybe, maybe not. One more thing not to share with Yseult.

"I apologize." She dropped her arms. "I'm not used to being a suspect. I'm not sure how to act." She added the button to the list of things to eventually tell O'Reilly. After she checked it out. Assuming she ever got out of the garda station.

"Understood." Yseult stood. "If you'll excuse me for a moment, I'm sure the guards are bringing Dr. Applethwaite back to the station, if he isn't here already. I want to speak to him myself rather than rely on Sergeant Heaney's interpretation of events. I also want to speak to her superiors about her aggressive handling of the case." Yseult paused at the door. "You should drink your tea before it cools. It's quite good. Bewley's."

A moment turned into an hour, then two. All law enforcement officers must use the same broken timepiece. Gethsemane put her head on the table and closed her eyes. Footsteps awoke her. Yseult stood in the doorway with Jackson and a surprise visitor.

"Niall?"

"Dr. Brown. How are you holding up?"

Titles and last names. An official visit. "I'm hanging in there, Inspector. You know me. Takes more than a multiple-hour garda interrogation to wear me down."

"Sissy." Jackson pushed past Yseult and O'Reilly and wrapped her in a bear hug. The soft wool of his coat tickled her face. "Ms. Grennan explained what happened. Don't worry, she's taken care of everything."

The phrase "deal with the devil" popped into Gethsemane's head. She forced it out.

"Please, Dr. Applethwaite, be seated." Yseult waved at chairs. She sat opposite and waited until Gethsemane and her brother-in-law settled into chairs. O'Reilly remained standing.

"Does 'taken care of' mean not under arrest anymore?" Gethsemane asked.

"Sort of," O'Reilly said.

"Sort of? Isn't being under arrest an either-or kind of thing? You're either under arrest or you're not."

"Sergeant Heaney's pushing to send the file to the DPP."

"The what?"

"DPP. Director of Public Prosecutions. The DA, you call her. Ms. Grennan's pushing back, pointing out the holes in Heaney's case. The DPP could take weeks to review the file, then decide not to prosecute for lack of evidence."

"Weeks?" Gethsemane turned to Yseult. "You could keep me in a cell for weeks?" She felt lightheaded.

"Not to panic, Dr. Brown," Yseult said. "I discussed the situation with the sergeant's superiors. It boils down to this. Please don't take this the wrong way. You and your brother-in-law are, relatively speaking, unimportant. We're investigating a crime ring we suspect of moving multiple millions of euros in forged and stolen art. We've been after these bastards for over a decade now. Even if you and Dr. Applethwaite were involved in it, which I don't think you are, but if you were, it wouldn't have been for very long and you'd be small fish in the criminal pond. We want the sharks."

"I can guess how this works," Gethsemane said. "Either Jackson or I or both of us can do something for you. If we agree to help, you'll let us little fish swim through the net."

"Anything," Jackson said. "Anything either of us can do to assist your investigation. You have our fullest cooperation."

"Fullest" might overstate things. Gethsemane looked at O'Reilly. "What's the catch?"

"I guaranteed you wouldn't leave the county and you'd check in with me once a week. And you'd surrender your passports."

"Reasonable requests, Inspector," Jackson said.

"So, Ms. Grennan," Gethsemane leaned toward Yseult, "what do you want?"

"The recovery of the Patience Freeman sampler, due to its value, has become our top priority. Mrs. McCarthy-Boyle's death is, of course, tragic, but we don't know yet if her demise resulted from criminal activity. If she was murdered, one can assume whoever stole the sampler bears responsibility for her death. If we apprehend the thief we may solve two crimes. Dr. Applethwaite has numerous contacts in the antiques trade: curators, dealers, textile conservationists. People who know the best market for the sampler. People our thief may contact about selling it."

"And you want me to provide you with these contacts," Jackson said. "Put them on the alert, perhaps even set up a sting operation. Naturally, I'll do whatever I can. I detest those who abuse art for illicit gain. Art is meant to enlighten and uplift, not line criminals' pockets and fund degenerate activities. Give me a phone and a computer with internet access and I'll start right away."

"After first light will be soon enough, Dr. Applethwaite," O'Reilly said. "I'll drive you both home. You look beat."

Jackson had gone out by the time Gethsemane woke up. He left a note telling her to expect him around lunchtime propped against a full pot of coffee. She drank half the pot, then went to the music room with the grimoire. She recited the conjuring spell, then sat at the piano.

"Harmonic likeness. What is Eamon's harmonic likeness?"

She played "Requiem for a Fallen Angel," "Jewel of Carraigfaire," "*An Fhuaim Agus An Fury*," and half a dozen more of Eamon's compositions. Nothing happened. She played Debussy, Hayden, Satie, Tchaikovsky, and a dozen other composers. Her fingers cramped, but no Eamon. She played drinking songs, patriotic songs, Broadway show tunes. Her fingers swelled. She even played "The Wheels on the Bus" and "The Itsy, Bitsy Spider." Nada. Zilch. Zip. No ghost. She slammed the keyboard cover. What the hell sympathetically vibrated with a snarky dead Irish composer?

She held a pencil in fingers too sore to push the telephone buttons and called Father Tim.

"Gethsemane, how are you?" Concern filled the cleric's voice. "I heard about your troubles in Ballytuam. What can I do to help? Tell me what you need."

"The answer to a question. You knew Eamon well. If you had to name a piece of music that most reminded you of him, what would it be?"

"A single piece of music? I don't know as I could narrow it down to one. Any of his own compositions."

"I tried those. They don't work."

"Don't work? What do you mean?"

She explained the spell, harmonic likenesses, and Captain Lochlan.

"Good Lord, deliver us. What if you'd inadvertently conjured up something not as benign as the helpful Captain Lochlan? What if you'd called up some foul fiend from the depths of Hell?"

"But I didn't. And now I understand how the spell works. I'll be careful."

"Careful? How many songs did you run through before you called me, not knowing who'd answer to any of them?"

She glanced at her bruised fingers and recited her playlist.

"Oh, Jaysus," Father Tim said once she'd finished. "Thank God none of them worked. Who knows what awful creature might have vibrated to 'The Wheels on the Bus.'"

"Okay, point taken. I'll be careful from here on out. But I need to figure out what music to play."

"No, Gethsemane."

"But, Tim—"

"But nothing. We had a deal, remember? One spell only. If it didn't work, it didn't work."

"It is only one spell, and it did work. It just didn't work out the way I planned. We're talking about saving Carraigfaire. I have to keep trying."

"I know you love the cottage, but this isn't the way to go about saving it. I'll talk to Billy and I'll talk to a solicitor. Our Lady's got one on retainer. He's experienced in historic property preservation. I'll see what can be done through mundane means. But no more spell-casting. It's not safe."

She sat unmoving at the kitchen table for a long while after hanging up. She felt lost. Carraigfaire's fate was out of her hands. She needed to do something. Sitting still and letting events run their course wasn't in her nature. She showered and dressed, then retrieved the button she found in Olivia's courtyard from her bedside stand and examined it. The hallmarks on the button back identified it as sterling silver. The front bore a coat of arms incised into the metal.

She debated turning the button over to the Ballytuam gardaí but thought of having to deal with that sergeant again. She shuddered. Besides, she couldn't be sure the button had anything to do with Olivia's death. She didn't find it on or under her body. It could have lain in the grass for—Gethsemane recalled the last rainstorm. If the button had been lost before then, it would have been embedded in the ground, covered in mud, not lying clean on the surface of the grass. It might have been lost anytime in the past couple of days, anyway. She needed to find out who it belonged to. She'd passed a tailor's shop tucked in amongst the galleries and solicitors in Ballytuam. She'd start there, but she'd need a cover. And she knew just the man to provide it.

Gethsemane parked her bike in front of Erasmus Hall, a red brick Georgian building on the east end of St. Brennan's campus. Bachelor teachers who lived on campus boarded in one of its two wings. Their number included Francis Grennan.

Most of the faculty had gone away for the holidays, but a few, Frankie among them, chose to celebrate the season on campus and remained in the hall. Gethsemane's footsteps echoed along the empty corridor as she approached Apartment 1B. She knocked and held her breath while saying a silent prayer. What if Frankie wasn't in? Would he be at the pub this time of day? How much time would she spend tracking him down? He was the only one who could help her with her plan.

Luck worked with her for a change. Frankie answered the door. He wore an oversized t-shirt emblazoned with a picture of

Miles Davis in place of his usual Oxford button-down, but his wrinkled khakis and wire-rimmed glasses hadn't changed. He hadn't shaved since she last saw him, and he sported facial hair somewhere between five o'clock shadow and a sparse beard. She ran a still-puffy finger along his jaw.

"Going hipster?"

"Good morning. Or afternoon." He grabbed her hand. "What happened to your fingers?"

"Morning to you, too. Piano accident, nothing serious."

"What's wrong?"

"Nothing's wrong. Can't I just stop by for a visit, see how you're doing? You were in bad shape the other day."

"Come for the craic? Gethsemane Brown, this is me you're talking to. The only reasons you'd stop by unannounced are something's wrong or you're up to something."

"I told you nothing's wrong." Frankie's cynicism was matched only by his perspicacity.

"Then what're you up to?"

She pulled the button from her pocket and held it up. "May I come in? Or are you hiding a girl in there?"

"I like women, not girls." He took the button. "Where'd this come from?"

He backed up to let her pass into his tidy living room. Wall shelves held a collection of books and vinyl records. They flanked a wall-mounted flat-screen television and a record player on a console. A leather couch stood opposite. A stack of jazz magazines, edges perfectly aligned, sat on the coffee table. Nothing seemed out of place. The only thing rumpled about Frankie Grennan was his wardrobe. She'd fix that.

He repeated the question. "Where'd you get this? It looks expensive. Real sterling."

"I stepped on it at a crime scene."

"And you immediately turned it over to the gardaí as possible evidence of whatever crime occurred at the scene."

She took the button back. "The gardaí were preoccupied

collecting other evidence and wouldn't see the significance of this button." Never mind she didn't trust his ex any more than he did. "I secured it and brought it to you, because you're going to help me track down its owner."

"What is it you're about to get me into?"

"That sounds like a yes."

"There's no point in saying no to you. You either talk me into going along with you or you go off on your own and nearly get yourself killed. What're we doing?"

"You're my Captain Hastings, Frankie. Grab your coat and your car keys. I'll explain on the way."

She filled him in on the events of the auction and Olivia's fundraiser, including the thefts, Olivia's murder, and both the Creech miniature and the Patience Freeman sampler turning out to be fakes as they drove to Ballytuam. She omitted the details of her and Jackson's deals with Yseult.

"So did Olivia fall or was she pushed?" he asked.

"I don't know. The police haven't released any statements yet. The autopsy's pending." As was her potential murder charge, if Sergeant Heaney had her way. "Seeing as Olivia was involved in art crime, I vote for pushed."

"Involved in as a conspirator or as a victim? And they're called gardaí, not police."

Gethsemane rolled her eyes. "It's hard to imagine anyone victimizing Olivia McCarthy-Boyle. She seemed like a high-class force to be reckoned with, one of those women who can smile sweetly at you while crushing your hopes and dreams. I don't have as much trouble imagining her conspiring in art fraud." She explained her theory about the Koors teddy bear painting.

"A giant teddy bear? You're codding."

"I'm not."

"Some folks are lucky poor taste isn't an art crime."

"This is serious, Frankie. A woman's dead." She stared through the car window at the countryside roaring past. "Conspirator or not, however you look at it, she ended up a victim."

"One question: who put the fake sampler in the bushes and why?"

"That's two questions." Frankie returned the eye roll. "I have no idea who hid the fake. As for why, most likely Olivia's death interrupted them. They probably planned to put the fake sampler in the frame and replace it in Olivia's office. The evidence of forgery was hidden on the back of the piece. In a frame on a wall..."

"You wouldn't be able to tell what the back looked like."

"And the substitution might have gone undetected for years. Yseult said the crime ring would sometimes substitute fakes for originals and resell the originals."

Frankie didn't respond. Gethsemane kept her eyes forward but watched him in her peripheral vision. His knuckles whitened as he gripped the wheel tighter.

"Yseult Grennan. She's your ex-wife, isn't she?"

Frankie nodded, eyes fixed on the road.

"She seems..." Not nice. No reason to use euphemisms to herself. To Frankie, on the other hand..."Intense? Dedicated to her profession?" Borderline sociopathic? No response. "She's beautiful."

Frankie lowered his voice to just above a whisper. "Aye, she is that." He drove silent for a while then added in his normal voice, "Smart, too. A feckin' genius." The car buzzed past the Ballytuam town limit sign. "Would you mind telling me where we're going? It's customary to let the driver know where he's driving to."

Gethsemane plucked at his t-shirt. "Frankie, I think it's time you upgraded your wardrobe."

"This is ridiculous."

They stood in the doorway of Walsh and Sons Men's Tailor and Haberdashery. Frankie crossed his arms and mimicked the expression of a schoolboy told there'd be a pop quiz.

"It's not." Gethsemane tugged at his arm. "Tailors keep records. My grandfather kept a record of every detail about every suit and dress he ever made. Color, cut, size, fabric, price. He even kept fabric swatches and sketches of the finished piece."

"So you're just going to walk in there, hand the proprietor your 'appropriated' button, and ask him who he made it for. *If* he made it. It could've come from anywhere."

"Not *any*where. Custom-made sterling silver buttons engraved with coats of arms don't come from the local superstore."

"Walsh and his sons aren't the only tailors around."

"They're the only ones in Ballytuam." She pulled him into the shop. "Come on."

"If it is his button, he's not going to volunteer the name of the person he sold it to. Don't high-end shops pride themselves on keeping their clients' details confidential?"

"Yes, they do. Which is why you're going to distract the Messrs. Walsh while I have a peek in the office."

A cheerful "Hallo!" cut Frankie's sputtered protest short. A slim gray-haired man in the most exquisite double-breasted pin-striped suit Gethsemane had ever seen stepped out from behind a display shelf filled with neckties. "May I help you?"

Gethsemane nudged Frankie forward. The other man ran his eyes over him from head to foot, then spun him around and did the same over his back. "Yes, well, everyone loves a challenge."

"Loves a—" Frankie flushed as red as his hair. "Why, of all the—"

Gethsemane squeezed his elbow, hard. "Francis, dear, we've discussed this. I simply can't take you to meet Mother wearing t-shirt and jeans." She rolled her eyes and sighed a deep sigh any Southern belle would have envied. "Men. Whatever can you do with them?"

"You can trust this one," the gray-haired gent took Gethsemane's hand in his, "to me."

"Thank you, Mr.—Walsh, is it? Are you the eponymous proprietor? Or one of the sons?"

"The original Mr. Walsh passed on about one hundred thirty years ago, I'm afraid. I'm currently the senior Mr. Walsh. Both of my boys are away in London at the moment, attending a Savile Row design conference. And may I know your names?"

"I'm Miss Brown and this is Mr. Grennan. And my mother is a very particular woman." Which was true, even if the rest of what she told the tailor was a fable.

"Don't worry. I'll make your fella a suit fit for an audience with the Taoiseach."

"I adore *your* suit. Such a magnificent wool flannel. Vitale Barberis Canonico?"

"You have an eye for fabrics, Miss Brown."

"My grandfather was a tailor. He taught me few things make a man feel more vital than an expertly crafted bespoke suit: his first love, the birth of his first child, and his daughter's wedding."

"A wise man, your grandfather. I'll do my best to honor a brother of the cloth and to please his granddaughter. And his granddaughter's ma." Mr. Walsh winked as he steered Frankie toward a corner crowded with jacket-wearing mannequins, sample books, and bolts of fabric. "Perhaps a Merino-wool flannel in navy to highlight those green eyes? Double-breasted, of course. Or something in a silk-linen blend. Judging from the lady's accent, you'll be needing a wardrobe for warmer climes."

Gethsemane called after them. "Excuse me, Mr. Walsh. Do you custom-make buttons?" She kept her tone casual and flirtatious. "My brother lost a button from his favorite jacket—something to do with a party, an alpaca, and the ambassador's daughter, he really doesn't like to talk about it—and he hasn't been able to replace it. He's devastated. It was sterling, hand-engraved."

"I don't make them myself, no, but I use a reliable manufacturer who can create any button to order. He does monograms, coats of arms. I've several samples displayed over there in the rear of the shop."

'Thank you. Oh, and take your time with my fella. Some things shouldn't be rushed."

She strolled to the rear of the store, pausing every now and then to admire a shirt or a necktie and to make sure the tailor's attention stayed focused on Frankie. She reached a row of display cases filled with dozens of buttons of every hue, size, and material, including sterling silver. She pulled out the button she found at Olivia's and compared it to the samples on display. She spotted three or four similar ones. Then she spotted something else a few feet away from the display cases—an office with an open door. Binders filled floor-to-ceiling shelves and a massive card catalog occupied an entire wall.

She checked on Frankie and Mr. Walsh. "How's it going?"

Frankie shot her a look that would have been censored had he verbalized it. Mr. Walsh assured her everything was just fine, no need to worry, he'd suited clients much more difficult than her fella. He'd once outfitted an entire Gaelic football squad for an awards ceremony.

She'd have plenty of time to search for her button. She started toward the rear of the store but paused near the suspenders. She spoke over her shoulder. "Francis, while you're here, why not get something to wear to Nia's Valentine's party? Maybe a sports coat and slacks? You know Patsy will be there with that stuffy prince of hers. I want to show her up." She hurried off before he could wrap Mr. Walsh's tape measure around her neck.

Gethsemane slipped into the office. Convinced Frankie's sartorial challenges would occupy the tailor for the foreseeable future, she risked turning on a desk lamp. She scanned the binders. They were sample books, an archive of fabrics and finishings like the ones her grandfather kept. A label affixed to each listed a year, the contents, and a Dewey-decimal-like code. The earliest book dated to 1902. The card catalog went back even further, to 1812. She pulled open a drawer in the nearest one. Each card listed not a book but a name, an address, and vital statistics: waist, collar, sleeve length, hat band. The cataloger had annotated a code in a lower corner of each card. Another look at the binders confirmed the codes on the cards corresponded to those on the labels.

She examined her found button. Still shiny, no trace of tarnish, few scratches, no dents or nicks. A new, or at least new-ish, button. She pulled the current year's button binder from the shelf and skimmed its illustrated pages. She found what she wanted about two-thirds of the way through. Schematics for a sterling silver shank button with a hand-engraved coat of arms. She held her button next to the illustration. A match. The same coat of arms graced its front. She noted the button's code and turned to the card catalog.

Finding the card took longer. Two forays to the showroom floor reassured her she needn't rush. Mr. Walsh was in his shirt sleeves, Frankie wore a jacket borrowed from a mannequin, and half the bolts of fabric had migrated from the shelves to the table and floor. She concentrated on the catalog.

She opened the "P" drawer and located this year's cards. She stopped at the thirteenth card and bit her lip to keep from shouting. A name printed in block lettering as neat as that of the Freeman sampler paraded above the code for the silver button. A name she recognized. Andrew Perryman.

Ten

"This is what happens when I let you talk me into things."

Gethsemane and Frankie walked the three blocks to Andrew's gallery, Gethsemane in the lead.

"Stop complaining," she said. "It's going to be a beautiful suit. The midnight blue flannel was an excellent choice."

"It's going to cost me a month's pay."

"But it will be oh so worth it. An investment. That suit will last you thirty years. You'll more than get your money out of it. Would you please hurry?"

"Where'm I going to wear a suit, anyway?"

"That cute new chemistry teacher's throwing a housewarming party next month."

"Don't start, Sissy."

"Don't call me Sissy."

"Why are you walking so fast? Nothing's on fire."

"I want to catch Andrew at his gallery before closing time. Which is in forty-five minutes. Come on."

The gallery seemed deserted.

"Hello," Gethsemane called. "Anyone here?" She whispered to Frankie. "Think he closed early?"

"And left the door off the latch?"

"I'm so sorry." Andrew hurried from a back room, glasses

perched on top of his head, brochure in one hand. Today's suit was a navy single-breasted pin-stripe. He laid the brochure on the counter as he dabbed at his lips with his pocket square. "How may I help you? Have you come about the Jacobean-style embroidery? The wall-hanging I mentioned at the pub?"

"We're not interrupting your dinner, are we?"

"No, no, of course not. Just having a little snack to keep the wolves from the door, as they say."

"And doing some vacation planning?" Gethsemane picked up the brochure. "Spain, is it? Everyone's going on trips. Olivia was headed to Florida."

Andrew took the brochure and folded it into a pocket. "I detest Florida. I'm thinking of Barcelona. Ibiza has too much of a party atmosphere. Guess I've outgrown that scene. But you don't really want to know about my travel plans. Perhaps I can show you something?"

Frankie chimed in. "We'd love to see the wall-hanging. She can't stop talking about it. Sight unseen, she's ready to buy." Gethsemane pinched him.

Andrew didn't appear to notice. "Wonderful. Such an exquisite piece. And at a surprisingly affordable price point." He gestured to chairs. "Make yourselves comfortable. I'll go get it."

Gethsemane hissed at Frankie as soon as Andrew was out of earshot, "What are you doing?"

"I bet 'affordable price point' means less expensive than a bespoke suit." He settled in an overstuffed chair and lifted a magazine from a stack on a nearby end table. "*Art Quilt Review*. Quilts are meant to keep you warm in the dead of winter, not to be hung on the walls. Basquiat is meant to hang on your walls."

Gethsemane picked up another magazine. "*Christeby's*. Wonder what Andrew's doing with this? He said he didn't deal in paintings anymore."

"They handle more than just paintings." Frankie reached for the magazine. "It's old; look at the date. A souvenir of a former life."

"This issue's about the ContempoPop auction. The one where

he met Hank Wayne. Jackson said the New York-Dublin art crime investigation folded about nine years ago. This magazine's eleven years old."

"Does that mean something?"

Andrew returned before she could answer. He carried a rolled fabric tube. Gethsemane held it while he cleared the table. Then he unrolled the fabric.

"Isn't it gorgeous?"

A riot of bright-hued pomegranates and flowers and vines and birds and fantastical creatures spilled across the linen square. "Yes," Gethsemane said. "It is."

"Nia would just die if she saw that." Frankie draped an arm across the back of his chair. "It's twice as nice as the one her stuffy prince gave her."

Andrew frowned, puzzled, and looked back and forth between the two.

"Ignore him," Gethsemane said. "He thinks he's being witty."

"I do think you should get it," Frankie said. "Hang it in the music room to inspire the boys when you start the Jacobean music unit."

"It's definitely more my style than that ghastly painting at Olivia's. You know the one I mean? The Jasper Koors, with the bear?" She shuddered.

"You were at Essex House?" Andrew used his pocket square on his neck.

"I was there the night, you know, *it* happened. Dreadful business. Dreadful evening. For no one more so than Olivia, of course."

"Of course," Frankie said.

Gethsemane pinched him. "I hate to speak ill of the dead, but I *cannot* imagine why Olivia would display a painting as awful as that Koors thing."

"Jasper Koors is highly sought after by collectors. One of his most recent works sold for over thirty million."

"Some folks have more money than taste." Frankie thumbed a

magazine. He stopped at a photo of a Banksy mural. "I'd spend thirty million on that. Well, maybe fifteen."

"Aren't you looking for a Koors for Mr. Wayne?" Gethsemane asked.

"You remembered," Andrew said.

"Between you and me—"

Frankie interjected. "And me."

Gethsemane ignored him. "I bet you could snag Olivia's Koors for a bargain. She has no use for it anymore, and it doesn't go with the rest of her collection. Her estate would probably be happy to sell. Which would mean a handsome commission for you."

Andrew fiddled with his pocket square's hem. "I'll certainly pass the word on to Mr. Wayne."

"Maybe you're familiar with the work? A giant teddy bear. Lots of garish colors."

"Mr. Koors has painted several teddy bear portraits. He's known for them."

"A guy who sells paintings for thirty million should be able to afford a life model," Frankie said.

"He's making a statement." Andrew sounded offended.

"He certainly is."

Gethsemane refocused Andrew's attention. "This canvas is massive. Takes up almost an entire wall. Are you sure you don't know it? I thought with your experience in contemporary art..."

"I'd have to see the piece to be certain." He looked at his watch. "I do hate to rush you, but..."

"It's almost closing time and you'd like to get home. Forgive me. I'm so—distraught—over what happened to Olivia, I haven't been able to get her or her collection out of my head." She laid a hand on the tapestry. "I'm going to get this. Frankie's right, it will go nicely in the music room."

Andrew's shoulders relaxed. "I'll be happy to wrap it up for you."

"Mr. Perryman—"

"Andrew, please."

"Andrew, I almost forgot. I think I found something that belongs to you." She held out the button.

"What's that?"

She held it closer.

Andrew paled. He started to reach for it but pulled his hand back. "Not mine, I'm afraid. Too bad, it's lovely."

"Are you sure it isn't yours? I found it at Mrs. McCarthy-Boyle's." No need to mention finding it near her body.

"In that case, I'm certain it's not mine. I've never been to Essex House."

"Not once, not even on the grounds?"

He shook his head. "I deal in contemporary textiles. The late Mrs. McCarthy-Boyle collected strictly antiques. We orbited different spheres."

Gethsemane tossed the button on her palm. "I could have sworn this came from you."

He held up his arms so she could see the sleeves of his suit jacket.

"All buttons present and accounted for. None missing."

"My mistake." She put the button away. "I'll turn it in at the police station—"

"Garda station," Frankie mumbled.

Gethsemane elbowed him. "It looks like real silver. Someone's bound to claim it."

"No doubt." Andrew's hands shook as he rolled up the embroidery.

Gethsemane paid in cash. She hadn't gotten around to replacing the stolen card she canceled. Andrew took the money and disappeared with the embroidery. A few moments later he returned with a brown paper package and a handwritten receipt.

"You have such nice handwriting, Andrew." Gethsemane read the receipt. "Mine bears a strong resemblance to the deranged scratching of a drunken chicken." She held the slip of paper up for another look. "This reminds me of someone else's handwriting. I can't think of who." Where had she seen similar writing?

"Must've been someone who studied penmanship, like I did," he said. "Gives your handwriting a characteristic style."

Gethsemane accepted the package from the gallery owner. She turned toward the display window and let out a staccato scream. A face glared at her from the other side of the glass, a face with a scar.

"Ronan Leary. What's he want?"

Andrew brushed past her and burst out onto the street. Ronan had gone.

"Feckin' gowl," Andrew muttered as he came back into the gallery.

Gethsemane fidgeted with the button on the drive back to Dunmullach. "I'm sure this belongs to Andrew. I saw his expression when I showed it to him. His heart practically stopped. So why'd he deny owning it?"

"He didn't want you to know he'd been to Olivia's."

"But he denied it even before I told him where I found it."

"He knew where you found it because he knew where he lost it."

"Why didn't he want me to know he'd been to Essex House? Tons of people go there. He's an art dealer, regardless of whether he deals antiques or not. He could have a hundred legitimate reasons for visiting Olivia. And why didn't he ask me how I knew the button was his?"

"You're like a four-year-old with the why, why, why."

"Here's another. Why was Ronan Leary lurking outside the gallery? Guy gives me the creeps."

She dropped the button. She twisted in her seat and rummaged on the floorboard to find it.

"What are you going to do with that? I doubt Andrew will follow up on your suggestion to claim it from the gardaí."

"I guess I'll give it to O'Reilly, tell him where I found it and what we learned from it." She paused. "I could give it to Yseult."

Frankie stiffened. "If you do decide to confide in my ex, I'll thank you not to mention my name to her. But you should give it to O'Reilly."

"May I ask what happened between you and Yseult?"

"No, you may not."

"C'mon, Frankie, talk to me. This woman holds my life in her hands."

"I know the feeling."

"At least tell me if I can trust her. Answer as a logical mathematician, not a burned ex."

"Answering as a logical mathematician—trust O'Reilly."

Gethsemane watched the passing landscape as they neared Dunmullach. "How drunk would you have to be to tell me the entire story?"

"Murphy's not got enough liquor in the whole of the Rabbit."

"How 'bout Bunratty's Off License?"

Frankie didn't laugh.

"All right. No more questions about sketchy ex-wives. Drop me off at the garda station, please. You reminded me I have to check in with Niall."

The station's front-desk officer informed her O'Reilly had gone to lunch. Lunch meant the Mad Rabbit, as they had the best food in Dunmullach.

She chuckled when she saw him sitting in the same booth he'd sat in the last time she interrupted his meal. Had it only been a month? It felt like a lifetime.

She slid into the seat across from him. "How's my favorite cop? Garda?"

"Guard." He finished a bite of fish and washed it down with a swig of Guinness. "Fine, thanks. How's my favorite felon?"

"Not funny." Her eyes narrowed and her face grew hot. "You know damn well I had nothing to do with stealing that sampler or with Olivia's death. Neither did Jackson."

"You're right. I apologize. You had nothing to do with any of this. You're no criminal." He raised his glass to her. "A pain in the arse from time to time, but no criminal."

"You say *I* had nothing to do with any of this. Does that mean you think Jackson's involved?"

"Can't picture it. Your brother-in-law seems too—what's the word?—earnest about fighting art crime to perpetrate it."

"Apology accepted. But you owe me a drink and half your fries." She snatched a crispy golden potato wedge from the pile on O'Reilly's plate.

"When will ya learn to speak English? They're chips." He pushed the plate toward her and signaled the barmaid. "Have 'em all."

"All of them? You really are sorry." She ordered a Bushmills, helped herself to the fries, and watched O'Reilly read his newspaper. She really ought to hand him Andrew's button. She ought to hand it over, leave art crime to the gardaí and Jackson, forget about wealthy widows falling over balconies and stalkers with scarred faces, and concentrate on calling Eamon back in time to save Carraigfaire. She reached into her pocket. Her fingers closed around the cold metal.

Without warning, a twenty-something woman wearing a hipster hat and holding her smartphone like a tape recorder pushed her way onto the seat next to Gethsemane. "Finn Conklin, *Dunmullach Dispatch*."

Gethsemane froze with her hand half out of her pocket. She let the button go and rested her hand on the table.

The reporter held her phone an inch from O'Reilly's face. "Is it true, Inspector, that Olivia McCarthy-Boyle, late of Ballytuam, was mixed up in an art fraud scheme?"

O'Reilly muttered a string of unprintable words. His eyes darkened to storm gray.

"Where the devil did you hear that?"

"Confidential sources close to the investigation." Finn persisted. "Is it true that most of her world-renowned textile collection is fake?"

Gethsemane offered O'Reilly her Bushmills. "You look like you need this."

He shook his head and glared at Finn. "I wouldn't want tomorrow's *Dispatch* headline to read, 'Guard Drinks on Duty.'"

"Give me a break, O'Reilly. I'm just doing my job." She tried again. "Did one of Mrs. McCarthy-Boyle's accomplices push her off the balcony to keep her from giving evidence?"

O'Reilly closed his eyes and massaged the bridge of his nose. Gethsemane counted ten seconds before he spoke. "Where the hell did you get this information, Conklin? Who are your," his hand balled into a fist as he practically snarled the word, "*confidential* sources?"

The reported sniffed and looked hurt. "Do you think I'd give them up?"

"I think you'd better go away from me in the next twenty seconds or I'll arrest you for interfering with a guard."

Gethsemane hid a smile behind a sip of whiskey.

"Give me one comment and I'll saunter on," Finn said.

"All right." O'Reilly held her phone near his lips. "For the record, may the cat eat you, and may the devil eat the cat."

She snatched her phone and stood. "Maybe I'll do a story on lax security and loose lips at the garda station." She stomped to the door.

O'Reilly stood and tossed euros on the table. "Hate to cut this short, but the fellas in Ballytuam need to know they've got a leak that needs plugging. I'll tell 'em you checked in like you were supposed to." He winked and smiled his dimple. "That is why you came to have lunch with me?"

"Nope." Gethsemane held up a potato wedge and returned the wink. "I came for the chips."

She watched the door close behind O'Reilly and remembered the button. She wouldn't chase after him. He'd be too preoccupied with Finn Conklin and the news leak to be anything other than annoyed with her for disturbing a crime scene.

She raised a hand to signal for a refill, when her empty glass refilled itself. A Bay Rum-scented breeze brushed her cheek. "That has to be the coolest ghost trick ever," she said. "Thank you, Captain Lochlan."

She found the ghost waiting for her outside the Rabbit. "May I carry your parcel?" he offered.

Gethsemane glanced around. None of the few people on the street noticed her. "Thanks, but a bag floating in mid-air would probably attract unwanted attention."

"You're right, of course." He walked beside her, his appearance as solid as Eamon's when the spectral composer was in a good mood.

"Thanks, again, for the drink."

"You're welcome."

"Why didn't you come inside? O'Reilly wouldn't have noticed. He doesn't see ghosts."

"Not because I would have minded the company, I assure you," the captain said. "Alas, your fine tavern is too new. I died long before the Rabbit poured its first libation."

"How'd you manage the trick with the whiskey and the," she leaned toward Captain Lochlan and took a deep breath full of orange, clove, and bay leaf, "Bay Rum breeze?"

"I patronized the establishment that preceded the Rabbit on occasion. Or two. Certainly, no more than a half dozen times."

"I'm going to regret asking what type of establishment, aren't I?"

A wistful smile played across the captain's lips. "Mrs. Rourke's, the finest school of Venus—" His aura darkened to a shade of pink that matched the flush on his cheeks. He bowed his head. "Apologies, Miss Brown. I forget myself. A testament to the ease I feel in your presence."

"How are you holding up?" Gethsemane asked.

"Holding up what?"

"I mean, how are you doing? Finding out the supposed Patience Freeman sampler was a fake upset you."

A sad yellow aura surrounded him. "I remember the day

Patience finished it. I'd got to chatting with a fella named Jefferson at the Market House—"

Gethsemane interrupted him. "Jefferson? As in Thomas?"

"Aye, that's him. He boarded at the tavern while he read law. Do you know him?"

"Heard of him. But go on. You were telling me about Patience."

"She was so excited. School had just let out, she hadn't even been home yet. She stood off to the side, near the magazine, bobbing from foot to foot, doing her best to wait until Mr. Jefferson and I finished jawing. I thought she was like to burst, so I called her over. You should have seen her smile when she showed us. She was rightly proud of her work. Some of the finest stitching I ever saw. Most women twice her age couldn't sew half as well. She impressed Mr. Jefferson, too. He wrote her a letter recommending her for an apprenticeship with a mantua maker." The captain's aura dimmed to yellow and he dematerialized until the bricks of the buildings they passed showed through his chest. "She never got the chance to use it."

"Sissy." Frankie's voice carried across the village green.

Gethsemane cringed at the nickname.

"A certain math teacher is damn lucky I'm in enough trouble with the law or I might be tempted to commit the crime I'm suspected of."

"Easy, lass." Captain Lochlan solidified again. His green aura, as well as the grin fighting for control of his lips, belied his stern voice.

She called across the green, "What, Francis?"

"It's Francis, now, is it? After all I've done for you."

"Consider yourself fortunate we're not back to a last-name basis."

Frankie relaxed into a lean against his car. His lopsided grin brought out the dimple in his left cheek. Was every man in Dunmullach intent on teasing her?

"You haven't done enough to call me Sissy," she said.

"What if I drive you up to the cottage? May I call you Sissy then?"

Captain Lochlan's full throaty laugh sounded in her ear. "I'll bid you good day and leave you to the gentleman's care." He vanished before she could comment on whether he handed her over to a gentleman.

She looked back and forth between Frankie standing by his open passenger door and her boot-clad feet. Carraigfaire meant a long walk, even in comfortable footwear. "Yes, Frankie, you may drive me home. No, you may not call me Sissy. Move a mountain for me, and I'll think about it."

Jackson met her at the door as soon as she returned to Carraigfaire. "Sissy, where've you been? Are you all right? I was worried. You really need to get a cell phone."

Caught off guard, Gethsemane stalled by taking extra care hanging up her coat. What could she say? Not that she'd run off with a possible piece of evidence in a criminal investigation and launched her own investigation by trespassing in someone's private files. Jackson fell into the law and order camp. He would not be okay with her actions. She groped for words, then seized upon the first thing that offered a plausible explanation. She held up her package from the Perryman gallery. "Shopping."

"Shopping? Now?"

"Sure. Why not now?" Shop 'til you drop had never been her mantra, but she enjoyed a good sale as much as anyone and often took her nieces and Jackson's son out on mini-sprees when she visited. "What's wrong with shopping?"

"With everything that's going on, the auction, and the Freeman sampler, and Olivia's death..."

"Retail therapy. I needed to get out and do something to take my mind off things. You know me, I'm no good at moping around feeling sorry for myself or huddling in a corner to ruminate. I need to *do* something. In this case, there's not much I can do—" she uttered a mental prayer for forgiveness for lying, "—so I shopped." She handed Jackson her purchase and led the way to the study.

"I've been uncommunicative the past few days, wrapped up in my own issues. Finding Olivia like that, it can't have been pleasant. I'm sorry I haven't been much of a shoulder to lean on."

"Honest, Jackson, I'm fine. I'm not going to wilt like a delicate flower or have a nervous breakdown or anything." Her tone sounded harsher than she'd intended. Her brother-in-law dropped his gaze and toyed with the wrapping on her wall-hanging. She'd hurt his feelings. "I didn't mean to snap. I know you're worried and trying to help." She hugged him. "But I'm hanging in." She hated to admit it, but after what she'd been through in recent weeks, finding dead bodies and ghosts no longer made her list of life's strangest events. "How about you? How're you doing? You come all the way over here to purchase a piece for the museum and end up wrapped up in theft, fraud, and death under suspicious circumstances."

"Nothing's gone as expected, has it? But I'm managing. I—" His voice cracked. He sank into the couch.

She sat next to him. "Just remember if *you* ever need a shoulder to lean on, I've got two. You'll just have to bend way, way down to reach them." She clasped his shoulder on the way to the bar. "I'll pour. Laphroaig?"

"Oh, the reason I was waiting for you." He pulled a folded note from his pocket. "A messenger delivered this while you were out."

"For me?" She took the sheet of paper.

"For me. A summons—" Jackson shook his head. "Let's call it a request. Summons sounds too much like it involves a trip to the police station."

"'Your presence has been requested' sounds too much like an invitation to a garden party." She read the note. "Olivia's will? Isn't it too early to read her will? I thought they waited until after the funeral to do that."

"Maybe the police asked for the reading to be moved up. Maybe they're hoping to find out who benefits from Olivia's demise."

"You mean find out who had a motive to help her over that balcony rail. But why are you invited?"

"Apparently, I'm a beneficiary. Olivia left me something in her will."

Half of Ballytuam crowded into the solicitor's office for the reading of Olivia's will. Gethsemane stopped counting at twenty-two. She recognized Curtis Boyle, several of Olivia's staff, including Ray and Maire, and a few of the party guests. She also recognized Sergeant Heaney, as surly as ever. Heaney skulked the crowd's periphery and signaled occasionally to three men in uninspired suits. Fellow gardaí, Gethsemane assumed. Maybe the police *were* behind the early reading of the will.

The solicitor's bird-like secretary flitted among the crowd and fretted about the size of the conference room and the number of available chairs. Another assistant, a man in his mid-twenties with stringy hair and bad skin, trotted in the opposite direction, making notes. The solicitor, an intense woman with close-cropped hair, steel gray eyes, and a take-no-prisoners suit, held a hushed conference with the parish priest (who Gethsemane overheard confide to Olivia's cook that he expected to be able to repair the steeple after the will had been read), then announced the meeting's relocation to the church a few doors down.

Once at the church, several people headed straight into the nave to claim pews down front. Others mingled in the narthex. Gethsemane convinced—begged—Jackson to go in without her and find seats. She stood to one side, partially hidden behind a statute of Saint Jude, and watched. Everyone gathered profited from Olivia's death in some way. "Would any of them profit enough to kill her?" she asked aloud.

"Put money on that one." A whiff of Bay Rum accompanied Captain Lochlan's voice. He materialized and pointed at Curtis Boyle. "A bacon-fed belly-gut if ever I laid eyes on one."

Gethsemane looked at the portly man, now sober, his brown

hair styled in a comb-over that drew attention to its thinness. He'd caused a scene at the party, but she'd taken him more for a man of bluster than action. She couldn't imagine him being involved in art forgery or theft. Or in anything to do with art unless the art featured poker-playing dogs painted on velvet. "You really think Curtis Boyle would push his aunt off a balcony?"

"I saw his behavior the night of the party. Disgraceful. Any man who goes about in public in a drunken rage is a reprobate, capable of any sort of perfidy. And I've known men to do far worse than push a woman from a balcony for far less than Essex House."

"You've got a nerve, coming here after the trouble you've caused."

Gethsemane turned toward the angry voice and faced Maire, her cheeks flushed and eyes narrowed. Wisps of hair framed her head in a wiry halo that reminded Gethsemane of the sparks Eamon and the captain gave off during rages.

Gethsemane stepped back. A buzz shot through her as she passed through Captain Lochlan's chest. Maire held her ground and kept her eyes locked on Gethsemane. If she saw the ghost, she didn't let on.

"Trouble I've caused?" Gethsemane asked. "I haven't done anything."

"You call lyin' about being a musician to worm your way into Essex House not doin' anything? The whole town knows your brother-in-law was caught stealing. What were you doing? Looking to add to his take? Did she catch you at it? Is that why you pushed her?"

"I've never raised my hand to a woman," Captain Lochlan said, "but in her case—"

"Maire! That's enough." Ray came up behind her.

Maire stared at her feet. "Sorry, Mr. Delaney."

"I know you were fond of Mrs. McCarthy-Boyle, we all were, but hurling careless accusations helps no one."

"It's my grief talking, Mr. Delaney. 'Tis a terrible thing what happened. Mrs. M-B wasn't always the easiest woman to work for—

she knew how she wanted things done, and she weren't afraid to say so—but she was a decent person. She didn't deserve to—for someone to—" Maire's voice caught.

Ray laid a hand on her shoulder. "Be brave, girl. We don't know for sure foul play occurred. Mrs. McCarthy-Boyle may have fallen off the balcony, a tragic accident. Nothing official's been determined yet."

Maire glared at Gethsemane. "'Tweren't no accident. Someone pushed her." She shook Ray's hand off and walked away. The solicitor's pock-marked assistant tried to put an arm around her, but she brushed him off, too.

"You'll have to forgive her. She was one of Olivia's favorites. She's taking her death particularly hard."

"How're you holding up?" Gethsemane asked. "You must have been close to your employer, being her personal assistant."

"I'm devastated, of course." His hand disappeared into his pocket and reappeared with his cigar lighter. "But, unlike young Maire, I came up in an era when emotions were kept under wraps. Appearances mattered." He flipped the lighter back and forth.

"The famous British stiff upper lip."

Ray's ears flushed bright red. He pursed his lips, then pulled out his pocket square and passed it over his face.

"Sorry. I forgot where I was. My gram would rise from her grave to beat me shite-less if I spat in church. I'm Irish, not English. Named Raymond after Redmond O'Hanlon, fearless leader of the Rapparees."

"I meant no offense."

"You weren't to know. The complexities of Anglo-Irish relations are probably as of much interest to you as American football is to me."

"Don't tell anyone because they might not let me back in the States, but I can't stand American football."

Ray refolded his pocket square, slipped it back into his breast pocket, and straightened his jacket. "Will you tell me something? Why did you crash the party? Surely you weren't desperate to play songs about teddy bears while grown men and women sipped pink cocktails and nibbled animal crackers."

How close could she come to the truth without exposing Yseult's investigation? Or herself? "I heard Ronan Leary would be at the party. I don't trust him. He acted shifty at the auction. I thought he might have had something to do with planting that miniature in my brother-in-law's coat pocket. The police were more interested in Jackson, so I decided to check out Leary myself. I thought—hoped—maybe I could catch him up to no good. I know I should have left it to the police, but..." She shrugged.

"That's the only reason? To spy on Leary?"

"And I did want to see the Patience Freeman sampler. It's kind of like the Mona Lisa of the antique textile world." She shifted the discussion. "Do you know who inherits it? Who would have inherited it?" She nodded at Curtis. "The nephew, I suppose."

"That bollix? Olivia would no sooner have left such a rare and beautiful specimen to that gobshite than she'd have left dynamite to a baby. He'd have lost it to a bookie before the frame came down from the wall," Ray said. "Olivia left the Freeman sampler to your brother-in-law."

"To Jackson? You're sure?"

"I know the will's contents. Damned difficult to keep a secret in Ballytuam, let alone Essex House."

Gethsemane felt giddy. She swallowed a giggle. Olivia left Jackson the Patience Freeman sampler. If she'd left him the Holy Grail or the Shroud of Turin, he wouldn't be more over the moon. Alarm replaced excitement. If Jackson inherited it, he'd have motive to kill. That's what the police would think. That's what anyone who'd ever read an Agatha Christie novel would think.

Ray touched one elbow, Captain Lochlan the other. Electric shocks ran up that one. "Are you all right?" they asked simultaneously.

She directed her reply to Ray. "I just don't understand why she'd will something so valuable to a man she never met."

"Technically, she left it to his museum along with several other pieces in her collection. Dr. Applethwaite's made quite a name for himself over the past decade. Olivia may not have known him, but she knew his reputation. She followed his career for the past four or five years and liked what he'd done with the museum. She believed he'd earn needlework the respect as an art form it deserved, and she hoped the Freeman sampler would be a catalyst. And, between you and me, she relished the thought of being remembered for such a generous legacy."

Which meant she couldn't have known the Freeman sampler was a fake. She'd never risk giving a fake to a museum where it was sure to be examined for authentication and ruin her reputation when the fraud was discovered. But what about the Creech miniature? Would she sell a fake at auction to get rid of it before any museum curators had a chance to look too closely? And where did the Koors painting fit in?

Eleven

The church bell pealed. Ray looked at his watch. "We're running late. Not like Cecily."

"Who?"

"Cecily Dowling, Olivia's solicitor." He headed for the nave.

The priest shepherded the remaining crowd in after him. Captain Lochlan followed Gethsemane.

"You're allowed in there?" she whispered.

"I set foot inside once or twice while I lived. I'm no heathen. Well, not a complete one, anyway."

Gethsemane found Jackson and slipped into the pew next to him. She debated telling him about Olivia's bequest to the museum but decided to let Ms. Dowling break the news. The captain perched on the altar. The frontal's embroidered pattern shown through his legs. Gethsemane said a prayer and held her breath. No lightning bolts struck.

Ms. Dowling moved to the pulpit once the crowd settled down. "Ladies and gentlemen, I apologize for the delay, and I thank you for your patience. I realize this is a trying time for many of you. Reading the deceased's will before the funeral is an unusual occurrence, but the guards felt—" She broke off at a motion from her secretary. The little woman hopped up to the pulpit and whispered in her boss's ear.

"Are you sure?" the solicitor asked.

The secretary nodded.

The solicitor addressed the crowd, "Ladies and gentlemen, I'm sorry, but," she looked at her secretary again, "there seems to have been some sort of mishap. Olivia McCarthy-Boyle's will has gone missing."

Gethsemane stretched out on a pew in the rear of the narthex and watched Jackson pace. The police refused to let anyone leave and they'd waited an hour.

"Sorry you gave up smoking?"

"Right about now, for the first time in twelve years, yes."

Jackson stopped pacing and Gethsemane sat up as two police officers approached them. She groaned as she recognized Sergeant Heaney's approach.

The passage of time had done nothing to improve Heaney's demeanor. "Why is it that every time something goes missing I turn 'round and find you in the midst of it?"

"Luck? Skillful plotting?"

"Make fun if you like but know that I'm handling this one. Yseult Grennan won't be coming to your rescue."

"Is that tone necessary, Sergeant?" Jackson looked down on her. "My sister-in-law and I have waited patiently—"

"Why is she even here?" Sergeant Heaney turned to Gethsemane. "Did you convince the deceased to leave you a party favor in her will before you pushed her over the rail?"

Jackson protested. "Sergeant, really, that's uncalled for. I'll be reporting your behavior to your superiors. I'm the one named in Mrs. McCarthy-Boyle's will. Sissy just came with me for..." He faltered.

Gethsemane jumped in. She looked past the sergeant at the other officer. "I came because I had a hunch Sergeant Heaney would be here, and I wanted to make sure she got a chance to practice her people skills today."

The second garda unsuccessfully hid a grin behind her

notebook and stepped forward. "Were you aware, Dr. Applethwaite, that Mrs. McCarthy-Boyle left several items in her collection, including the missing textile known as," she checked her notebook, "the Patience Freeman sampler, to your museum?"

"What?" Jackson sank into a pew. "She left—she—the Freeman sampler? To my museum? I had no idea. No idea."

"Mrs. McCarthy-Boyle's solicitor," the garda read her notes again, "Ms. Dowling, gave us the names of the will's major beneficiaries. Your museum's on the list."

"I don't understand," Jackson said. "I never met Mrs. McCarthy-Boyle. She'd never been to the museum. Why would she—"

"That's what we're asking you." Heaney snapped open her notebook and pushed past her colleague.

"I can't answer that, Sergeant."

"You could answer," Captain Lochlan said to Gethsemane. She wished he had ribs to elbow.

"And you can't tell us anything about the will's disappearance?"

"Of course not. I didn't know of the will's existence until last night. And why would I steal the will if it benefitted me?"

"So we wouldn't think you had motive to do away with Mrs. McCarthy-Boyle. If we didn't know you were a beneficiary, we'd be less likely to suspect you of involvement in her death."

"If you think I'd destroy that will and sacrifice the Patience Freeman sampler just to avoid prison," Jackson said, "you know nothing about museum curators, Sergeant."

Both officers' eyebrows shot up. Gethsemane cringed and waited to hear, "You're under arrest." She exhaled audibly when a commotion on the opposite side of the church distracted them.

"I am Olivia's rightful heir!" Her nephew, Curtis, pounded a pudgy fist on a pew. "I am her husband's next of kin. If she's died without a will, Essex House—"

"There is a will, Mr. Boyle," Ms. Dowling said. "It's just been misplaced."

"Don't you have a duplicate copy of the will, Cecily?" Ray asked.

The solicitor reddened. "Er, that seems to have been misplaced as well."

"Stolen, you mean." Maire shook her finger under Curtis's nose. "Him's the one that took it. He knew Mrs. M-B wouldn't leave a Euro to his manky self so he stole the will. Probably burnt it up."

"Why, you little—" Curtis huffed out his chest. "You're the hired help. How dare you accuse me? You may consider yourself unemployed when I claim what's mine by rights."

"You won't be claiming nothing but de social. There's another copy of the will up at the house. I've seen it. Mrs. M-B always kept copies of important papers at the house."

"You're right, Maire, she did." Ray twirled his lighter. "There should be a copy of the will somewhere at Essex House."

Gethsemane leaned toward the pleasant garda. "Say the original will isn't found and there are no copies. What's at stake? Aside from the artworks?" No harm in planting the suggestion someone other than Jackson had motive to get rid of the will. And Olivia.

"Essex House, of course. Quite a large sum of money. The distilleries, one here in Ballytuam and one over in Dunmullach. The land may be valuable, but the buildings aren't worth shite. They're both abandoned, derelict. The only spirits you'll find in them now are the kind that go boo."

Captain Lochlan stood behind the sergeant and shouted "boo" in her ear. Gethsemane forced herself to look away from him.

The officer continued. "I hear there's some American developer been asking 'round about buying them. Maybe he can get them cheap."

Gethsemane and Jackson stepped out onto the church's porch. They'd given their statements and avoided arrest. Jackson went down to the street to hail a taxi. Gethsemane leaned against one of the columns supporting the portico. Captain Lochlan leaned into an adjacent one.

Gethsemane made sure no one could see her—who knew what Sergeant Heaney would do with reports of her talking to herself. Then she asked the captain, "What did you mean when you said you killed Patience Freeman?"

A faint blue glow appeared around his edges. "I never said such a thing."

"You did. When we met, you said you were as responsible for Patience Freeman's death as if you'd killed her with your own two hands."

The captain's glow morphed into a despondent yellow. "I sailed into Jamestown and Yorktown on my regular route. While I waited to collect my full load of tobacco, I'd travel up to Williamsburg to attend to legal matters."

"Did you get sued a lot?" She meant it as a joke.

The captain answered in a serious tone, "Planters were a contentious lot. I availed myself of what the town offered during my stays. I confess a weakness for Raleigh's ginger cakes. The coffee at Charlton's did me no harm, although I can't say the same for Williamsburg's many excellent taverns." He stopped, lost in a two-hundred-fifty-year-old memory. A faint happy red edged the yellow in his aura.

Gethsemane nudged him back to the present. "You didn't meet Patience in a tavern."

"No, but I met her mother, Constance Freeman, in front of one. A discussion with another ship's captain over the relative speeds of our vessels devolved into fisticuffs. The tavern's proprietor threw me out bodily onto the street. I landed at Constance's feet. Specifically, on her left foot. I tore my coat and she offered to repair it for me. She worked for one of the milliners."

"That's how you met Patience? Through her mother?"

"Aye." The captain nodded. "Constance and I got to talking when I went to the shop to claim my coat. She had a sharp mind, a quick wit, and more sense than any man I knew. I visited her whenever I came up to Williamsburg. I bought more neckerchiefs and shoe buckles than any man had need of just to have an excuse to stop at the milliner's shop."

"You grew fond of her," Gethsemane said.

"It's not what you're thinking, Miss Brown. I'd be a dishonest man if I denied Constance was a great beauty, but she was also a respectable woman. She was with Cicero."

"Cicero?" Gethsemane recalled Yseult mentioned Patience being the daughter of an enslaved silversmith. "Patience's father?"

"His owner hired him out to the silversmith. Cicero was a brilliant artist. The things he did with a silver ingot made angels weep. He lived in town with Constance and Patience."

"When did you meet Patience?"

"She was eight. Her first day at the Bray school, she runs into the milliner's excited to see her mother, runs smack into a table, and upsets a box of pins. I helped her pick them up. We remained friends ever after. She reminded me of my sister's child back home in Cork." Captain Lochlan smiled. "I'd walk Patience to school sometimes. She'd babble at me about disguising herself as a boy so she could go to sea. She was pretty and sweet and smart as her mother. A wee bit mischievous. She'd draw caricatures of the town's more colorful residents and slip 'em in my coat pocket for me to find later. I called her my little imp."

"What happened?"

All trace of red disappeared from his aura. Bright blue threaded itself through the yellow. "We heard rumors Cicero's owner planned to sell him out of state. The family would have been torn apart. We found some people, abolitionists, who could help Constance and Cicero get away over land. But they were afraid the journey would be too dangerous for Patience. She was fourteen by then but still too young for such an arduous journey. So I agreed to take her on my ship. I'd bring her to her parents later, when they were safe."

"But that never happened."

Captain Lochlan's aura deepened to a mustard yellow.

"There was a storm. I lost her. She sacrificed—it should have been me."

A man's voice interrupted. "Gethsemane Brown?" The captain vanished. A bald man climbed the steps and showed Gethsemane his identification. Another garda. An inspector this time. "May I ask you some questions?"

"You have got to be kidding—what happened? Did everyone else in town invoke their right to remain silent and I'm the only one left to interrogate? What is it this time? A missing grand piano? Did someone steal the Guinness Brewery?"

"Someone murdered Andrew Perryman."

"Dr. Brown has nothing to say until after I've had a chance to consult with her." Cecily stood between Gethsemane and the inspector.

"Dr. Brown has nothing to hide." Gethsemane turned to her brother-in-law beside her on the church steps. "Jackson, I don't need a solicitor."

"She's here to help, Sissy."

"I don't need help. I didn't kill anyone, including Andrew Perryman."

"You're not a suspect, Dr. Brown," the bald garda said.

"I'm not?"

"She's not?"

He shook his head.

"You may be a witness, though. We found a receipt with your name on it at Mr. Perryman's gallery. He was seen alive at a bookshop about thirty minutes after the time on the receipt. He wasn't seen alive again. Early this morning, the boy who delivers his newspaper found him stabbed to death."

Gethsemane, Jackson, and Cecily all chorused, "My God," "That's awful," "Poor Andrew."

"When you were at the gallery, Dr. Brown," the inspector asked, "did you see anything or hear anything unusual? Anything at all you remember. It may not have seemed that unusual at the time. Did anyone call? Was anyone else in the gallery?"

"I was there with a friend, Frankie Grennan, but—wait, I remember, I did see someone."

"Go on." The inspector readied his pen.

"Just before I left, I noticed a man looking through the gallery window. Andrew ran out into the street after him, but he'd gone."

"Can you describe the man?"

"I can do better than that. I can tell you his name. Ronan Leary."

Twelve

"Are you sure you saw Ronan Leary through the window?" Yseult asked Gethsemane at the Ballytuam garda station. Yseult tracked her down after she gave her statement to the homicide investigator. They sat in the now familiar interview room.

"I'm positive. The scar's hard to miss. Who is Ronan Leary? He keeps turning up in weird places then vanishing. Like a stalker. I heard he has a criminal record."

"He's no one you need concern yourself with." Yseult waved a dismissive hand.

"Jackson said you think Ronan's his partner. That does concern me."

Yseult's eyes widened and her hand flew to her chest. "I think they're partners? Have you heard me make that claim?"

"No, not you, specifically. The Ballytuam constabulary in general."

"Ronan Leary co-owned a gallery in New York with Andrew Perryman. They closed the gallery and Andrew left New York. Ronan left soon after. And, yes, Ronan has a criminal history, which is why you shouldn't concern yourself with him."

"When did they close their gallery?"

"Nine, ten years ago? Why?"

"Didn't the FBI suspend their investigation into the New York-Dublin art crime ring about nine or ten years ago? Is it coincidence

Andrew and Ronan closed their gallery around the same time? Were they involved? Or was Ronan involved in the scandal that sent Andrew packing from New York?"

"Scandal?"

"Involving a client's husband."

"Who have you been talking to, Dr. Brown?"

"No one. Just party gossip."

"You shouldn't listen to gossip, Dr. Brown. It can mislead you."

She'd done well by it so far.

"Speaking of the party," Yseult extended a hand, "I'll have to ask for the camera back."

Gethsemane still wore the pendant. She'd forgotten it was anything other than jewelry. She handed it over to Yseult. "If Olivia really did will the Freeman sampler to Jackson's museum, no way she knew it was a fake."

"You're right. She most likely owned the genuine sampler at some point. Someone with access to her house switched it for the fake, careful to place the fake in the frame and replace the frame on the wall. The fake was unlikely to be detected as long as it remained in Olivia's collection. The real sampler went straight to the black-market."

"But if the fake went to a museum, it would be removed from the frame and authenticated." At least it would be if it went to a museum with a conscientious curator who consulted with the FBI on art crimes.

"The thief must have known, or suspected, as much. He or she attempted to get rid of the fake before that happened. If we hadn't discovered it in the bushes, whoever hid it there would have retrieved it and destroyed it."

"Do you think Ronan Leary brokered the black-market sale of the original?"

Another dismissive hand wave. "Leary is one of those sad little men doomed to always be on the outside looking in. Don't concern yourself about him. Really." It sounded more like an order than a suggestion.

* * *

She ran into Kenneth O'Connor on the way out of the station. The redhead smiled and spoke before she could ask him why he was there. "Did the guards run you in, too? I'll tell you a secret. The number of folks they haul down for questioning is directly proportionate to their level of cluelessness."

"I gave a statement about seeing Ronan Leary outside Andrew's gallery. They seemed to know each other."

"You're sure you saw Leary?"

She traced the pattern of his scar on her cheek.

"Yeah, well, you'd do well to stay clear of that one. He's a bad bit."

Maybe Kenneth knew something. Time to play dumb. "I heard he was just a small-time gallery owner."

"Small-time gallery owner, big time hood. Rumor is, he fled the Big Apple late at night one step ahead of the Feds. Mixed up in theft and forgery."

"The New York-Dublin art crime ring I read about in the paper?"

Kenneth shrugged. "Nothing ever proven. Just rumor running through the art world like a trophy wife through money."

"If art gossip's like village gossip, there's usually some truth to it. And it can ruin you."

"Can't argue with that."

"What's Ronan's connection to Andrew? They didn't seem to be friends."

"The Ronan Learys of the world don't have friends. He and Andrew probably had an old business rivalry. The art world is scary competitive."

She wasn't the only one playing dumb. Andrew and Ronan's gallery partnership was no secret. She knew, law enforcement knew. A savvy buyer's agent, an art world insider, should know as much as a musician-turned-schoolteacher and the country cops. Why was he holding out? Who was he protecting? Andrew? Ronan?

Himself? "What's your connection to Leary? He doesn't like you."

"Leary doesn't like anyone. And the feeling's mutual. He hates me because he claims I cheated him out of a Caravaggio. Truth is, I got there first. Leary's a sore loser."

"Do you think he'd get sore enough to stab someone?"

"I don't know about that. Seems extreme, even for him," Kenneth said. "Still, you never can be too sure about people. The ones you least expect to cross the line are often the ones who commit the worst crimes."

"What about you? Would you ever get sore enough to kill someone? Or kill someone over a priceless piece of art? Did you kill Andrew Perryman?"

"Bottom line up front, huh? You don't pull punches. No, I didn't kill Andrew. Or Olivia, in case you were wondering."

"Sorry, had to ask."

"Be dog wide when you go around asking such bold questions. Not everyone is as easygoing as I am. They might take it the wrong way."

Gethsemane left the Ballytuam garda station and headed up the hill toward Essex House. She'd sent Jackson home. She needed to return to retrieve the change of clothes she'd left in the tower room the night of the party. An ominous air had settled over the place since then. The night of the party was the night of Olivia's death. Of her murder. She felt sure Olivia had help going over that deep balcony with its sturdy stone railing. She didn't simply stumble or lean out too far and fall. But was her murder connected to art crime or to the missing will? Or were those things somehow related?

A newsstand caught her eye. A headline sprawled across the front page of the *Ballytuam Bugle* announced, "Dead Heiress Involved in Art Fraud Scam." She squinted at the byline: "Finn Conklin, special to the *Bugle*." Apparently, the fellas in Ballytuam hadn't plugged their leak.

* * *

The somber mood of the house hit her as soon as the butler, black band around his arm, admitted her. Party decorations had been removed. The grand piano and music stands no longer occupied the great hall. Black crepe hung over mirrors. Gethsemane sniffed. She hoped to catch a whiff of Captain Lochlan's Bay Rum, but she only smelled the cloying sweetness of flowers. Floral arrangements dotted the house. All wore black or white or deep purple ribbons labeled "With Sympathy." She caught a glimpse of crime scene tape on the patio as she followed the butler past.

They reached the tower. The butler excused himself to attend to his other duties and left Gethsemane to gather her things. Nothing was where she left it. Her dress, which she'd hung in the wardrobe, lay bunched on the bed. Her shoes had been neatly lined up next to the dresser. Now one lay on its side. The safety pin and ballpoint on the floor next to her bag meant someone upended and shook it.

Who searched her things? And why? What could they have hoped to find?

Maire appeared in the doorway as Gethsemane finished repacking. Did she ever smile? "'Bout done? I'll show you out."

Gethsemane pulled the zipper on her bag closed. The maid was either psychic or she spied. Gethsemane didn't believe in psychics. "I understand you and your late employer were very close. I'm sorry for your loss."

Maire narrowed her eyes. "Are you?"

"Of course I am. A dreadful thing happened to Mrs. McCarthy-Boyle. It was a terrible, tragic end to a remarkable life. And, for the record, I had nothing to do with her death. I didn't push her. What reason would I have to kill your employer? I'd just met her the night she—the night of the party."

"What reason would you have for poking around her office?"

Aside from being put up to it by a forensic examiner with secrets of her own on special assignment from some unnamed agency? "I wasn't poking around. I, um, wanted to see the Freeman sampler."

"Which went missing the same time you turned up."

"I had nothing to do with that either."

"All I know is, everything was fine 'til you got here. You show up and bad things start happening. Things disappear. People die."

"Like Andrew Perryman? I suppose you suspect I'm involved in his murder, too."

"Are you? Word around town is you were at his gallery."

Ballytuam's gossip mill rivaled Dunmullach's. "I did go to his gallery. I shopped there. I didn't kill him. He was alive when I left him." Maire didn't miss much. Maybe she'd seen Andrew at Essex House. Gethsemane feigned interest in straightening the bed covers. "Did you know Andrew?"

"Let me do that." Maire jostled Gethsemane out of the way. "Why would I know him? What have I got to do with art galleries?"

Gethsemane shrugged. "Small town. You might have run into him at the pub. Or seen him here."

Maire let the bed cover fall and stared at Gethsemane. "What would Andrew Perryman be doing at Essex House?"

"Attending one of Mrs. McCarthy-Boyle's affairs. Lots of gallery owners attended. Auctioneers and collectors, too."

"Antique dealers, important gallery owners, not small-time locals dealing that modern crap like Andrew. He'd never be invited to one of Mrs. M-B's parties."

"It's just that I found something here that I think belonged to him."

"What could you possibly have found of his?"

"A silver button. Quite unique."

"Can't be his, 'cause he's never been here." She went back to making the bed and spoke with her back to Gethsemane. "Why don't you give me the button? I'll ask around, see if I can find who it belonged to."

"I don't have it with me. And you needn't trouble yourself. You've got enough to deal with. I'll turn it over to the gardaí. It looks quite valuable, so I'm sure someone will report it missing."

"You do that." Maire finished with the bed. "If you're ready, the exit's this way."

"Is Mr. Delaney in?"

"What do you want to see him for?"

What was she, his wife? How did she get away with being this rude and keep her job? "I want to offer him my sympathies."

Maire hesitated, then admitted he was in the library. "Cataloging books."

"Not searching for a copy of Mrs. McCarthy-Boyle's will? Wouldn't finding it be priority number one?"

"The will'll turn up, I'm sure of it. I'll find it myself. I know where the missus kept all her things."

No doubt because she'd snooped through all of them. "If you'll take me to Mr. Delaney, I won't be but a minute."

"This way." Maire scowled.

Gethsemane shouldered her bag. "Out of curiosity, how do you know what kind of art Andrew sold through his gallery?"

"What?"

"You said Andrew sold modern crap."

"He did."

"But you said you didn't know anything about art galleries."

Maire reddened. "Small town, ain't it? Everybody knows everybody's business. C'mon if you're coming. Ain't got all day."

Gethsemane followed the maid back to the main part of the house. Maire led her through a formal dining room with space for two dozen and several parlors, each filled with a different style of antique. Staff, the men wearing black armbands, passed them going back and forth. None of them took notice of Gethsemane or Maire. Except for the dour atmosphere and the funerary flora, Essex House didn't seem like a place whose mistress had just died unexpectedly and violently. Business appeared to be running as usual.

Maire stopped as they crossed the main hallway. The solicitor's assistant lingered by the front door like a lost puppy.

He stepped forward. "Maire—"

The maid cut him off. "What're you doing here?" She called to the butler. "Who let him in? He's got no business here."

"I came to see how you were." He clasped his hands and pleaded with Maire with his eyes. "You're not returning my calls. I was worried."

"I didn't return your calls because I have nothing to say to you. Why can't you get that through your thick head? We're done. We're over." She yanked the door open. "Goodbye."

The solicitor's assistant shuffled out. On the porch, he turned back toward Maire. She shut the door in his face. "Maggot," she mumbled. She gestured across the hall. "Library's through there." She left Gethsemane to find her own way.

Gethsemane crossed the hall and stepped through an arch into a bibliophile's paradise. Books filled shelves from floor to ceiling in a room the size of a small city. Ladders of various heights stood ready to be rolled into position and scaled to reach books far above the arm span of even the tallest man. A delicate wrought-iron spiral staircase led to a catwalk around the upper edge of the room to allow access to the uppermost volumes. Ray looked down at her from the top of the spiral stair.

"Dr. Brown." He set down the stack of books in his arm and descended. They shook hands. "How are you?"

"That's what I came to ask you. I know everyone at Essex House is having a rough go of it."

"Yes, thank you. We're soldiering on. The world doesn't stop in the face of tragedy, even if one sometimes wishes it would."

"You've been dealt bad news on top of bad news. Olivia's death, then the theft of the sampler. Then Andrew Perryman's murder coming so soon after all that. Did you know him?"

"Not at all, I'm afraid. But what a ghastly way for him to go. Stabbed, I hear. Oh, and allow me to apologize."

"Apologize for what?"

"For accusing you of pushing Olivia over the balcony rail. The night of the party? When I came looking for you and found you in her office? It was the shock of discovering her. I didn't mean it."

"Apology accepted. People say all kinds of things when they're upset, most of which they don't mean."

"By the way, what were you doing in Olivia's office? Have I asked you?"

Everyone's favorite question. She gave her now stock answer. "I wanted to see the Freeman sampler. Such a rarity and from near where I grew up in Virginia. It's not every day you get the chance to see such a thing. I'm disheartened by its theft."

"As are we all. We launched an immediate review of our security system. We can't imagine how someone got in. Perhaps in all the confusion of the party."

"You don't think it was a member of the household? It took time to study the sampler and make a copy. Hard to imagine a stranger coming in and doing that. Maybe one of the maids? They certainly would have had time alone in the office to study the original while they were cleaning."

"Impossible. Every member of Essex House's staff underwent a vigorous security screening before they were hired. A necessary precaution with so many valuables around. Their backgrounds are impeccable. I'd vouch for every one of them. They are all completely trustworthy."

"What's your explanation for the switch?"

"I'm not convinced there was one." Ray slipped his lighter from his pocket and twirled it through his fingers. "Olivia purchased a fake. Unknowingly, of course."

"Wouldn't she have had the piece authenticated?"

"I must confess we were a bit lax in our due diligence with the Freeman sampler. Olivia was ecstatic when she acquired it. Wanted to put it on display immediately. She bought it from a dealer with an impeccable reputation. The dealer performed the authentication and we accepted his word all was in order. We didn't have it independently authenticated. We should have."

"I can't believe you'd let anything slide. I see how well this house is run, even now, under horrible circumstances."

"Thank you for your vote of confidence in my management skills."

"Speaking of which, what happens now? With the will being missing and all. Is everything in a holding pattern until a copy of the will turns up or the estate is probated?"

"No, things will go on as usual for now. I'll continue to manage Olivia's affairs until the court decides otherwise. Or until the will names an executor."

"You haven't found the copy yet?"

"No, not yet."

"Any idea where it might be?"

"Essex House is a huge house. Lots of places left to search. It'll turn up."

"Well, I don't want to keep you from your search. I just wanted to pay my respects." She held up her bag. "And get my things. I'll get out of your way."

"Allow me to walk you to the door."

"Don't bother. I'll see myself out."

Ray called after her. "Oh, I'll be out your way soon."

"My way?"

"Dunmullach. In the next day or two. I'm showing one of Olivia's properties, the old distillery. An American hotel developer is interested in buying it."

He didn't need to tell her it was Hank Wayne. She knew.

"Perhaps when I'm out that way we might have a drink at the pub," he said.

"I'll look forward to it." As she headed for the front hall, her gaze landed on a small painting tucked into a corner. She stopped to admire it. The five-by-seven canvas depicted a tropical beach scene. "Where's this?"

"Ibiza," Ray said. "Do you know it?"

"Never been there. Have you?"

"I used to summer there. Haven't been in ages."

"Looks like a nice place." She continued out the door. "I'll hold you to that drink."

* * *

The scent hit her by the front door. Bay Rum. Captain Lochlan materialized next to her. "Morning, Miss Brown. Paying our respects to the bereaved?"

"Something like that. And trying to connect Andrew Perryman to someone in this house. Unsuccessfully."

"I heard what the gentleman said about having a drink at the pub at a later date. Perhaps you'd rather have one now."

"Why would I want to do that?"

"Because the pub's where you'll find Mr. Curtis Boyle. Charity leads me to say he's drowning his sorrows. But truth encourages me to say he's celebrating his fortune."

"Seems a shame to have to celebrate alone. I'm kind of an old pro at crashing parties. Maybe we should invite ourselves to share in Mr. Boyle's good news."

Gethsemane walked the short distance from Essex House to the pub. Captain Lochlan walked beside her. None of the people they passed saw him, but a few heads turned in his direction as if they'd heard something or smelled something or caught a glimpse of something out of the corner of their eye. One or two passersby walked through him.

"Careful, ya blasted beef-head!" he yelled after the second one, a corpulent man with spiked hair and a ring in his nose. He apologized to Gethsemane. "Please forgive my appalling lack of manners. It's been so long since I've been in the company of a lady, I forget myself."

"It's okay, Captain. I don't mind if a sailor cusses like a sailor."

"Don't mind me saying, but methinks you'd have made a fine captain's wife."

"I noticed you didn't call out the first person who walked through you."

The captain blushed and glowed pink.

"Well, one makes allowances for ladies."

"Especially when the ladies are petite pretty blondes with cornflower blue eyes."

"As I said, a fine captain's wife."

"Were you ever married?"

"Get myself a load of mischief? No. Not for lack of trying. On the ladies' part, not mine. Constance Freeman came closest."

"She had a husband."

"Closest to marrying me off, not closest to marrying me herself—although if she had chased me, I'm not sure I would have run. Cicero was a fortunate man. Constance sewed dresses for a wealthy widow with an eye out for husband number four. She tried to make a match between us."

"What happened?"

"I did mention the widow was after husband number *four*?" He held up four fingers. "I couldn't keep my mind off of what might have happened to husbands number one through three."

"This is it," Gethsemane said. They stopped in front of the pub and peered through the window. Few patrons filled the seats at that hour. Olivia's dissolute nephew, Curtis Boyle, numbered among them. His brown hair stood out at the same odd angles it had when he'd been thrown out of Olivia's party. He wore his shirt unbuttoned halfway down his chest, his jacket collar half turned up, and his untied necktie draped around his neck. He leaned back in a chair at a table littered with empty pint glasses. His eyes were closed and his mouth open. "You think he's asleep?"

Captain Lochlan curled his lip. "A beau-nasty gundiguts if ever there was one. If a member of my crew conducted himself as shamefully, I'd have him keel-hauled and flogged."

"The twenty-first century's a bit more lax in standards of public deportment." Gethsemane squinted. "He's not dead, is he?"

"When you go in, poke him in the eye and see if he moves."

"Can you go in with me?"

"Nay. This one's even younger than the Rabbit. I'll wait out here for you."

Gethsemane entered the pub and walked over to Curtis's table. "Mr. Boyle?" She leaned close to him, but his beer breath drove her back. She tapped his shoulder. "Mr. Boyle, are you all right?"

Curtis sat bolt upright, eyes wide. "Whooza, whatza? What's happening?" He looked around the room a few times before fixing his gaze on Gethsemane. "Who're you?" He gestured to the pint glasses. "Bring me another."

"I'm not the barmaid, Mr. Boyle."

"Who are you then?" He looked past her. "Where's the barmaid?"

"She's on break." Gethsemane cleared a space on the table as best she could and sat across from Curtis. "I'm Gethsemane Brown. I'm a musician. I played at your aunt's party the night she—had her accident."

"Accident? Was it an accident?"

"Wasn't it?" She tried to picture Curtis sneaking up behind his aunt and shoving her over the balcony rail. He'd been this drunk when he tried to crash the party. From the looks of him in his apparently semi-perpetual drunken state, she imagined he'd be more likely to end up falling over the rail himself. Which didn't mean he couldn't hire someone to do his dirty work for him. Like a maid. "I'm sorry for your loss."

"Loss?" He laughed, a noise somewhere between a snort and a guffaw. "My gain, you mean. Or hadn't you heard? Dear departed auntie's will's gone missing, which means I get everything." He drained the last few drops from the nearest pint glass.

"You and your aunt weren't close?"

"That stuck-up old bitch? Prancing around Essex House, lording it over everyone. Don't know why Uncle married her. She's Irish. Should have found himself a nice English girl."

"Didn't your uncle love her?"

"Love's for movies and romance novels. We're talking about family legacy. Land ownership. That land's been in the Boyle family, in English hands, going on five hundred years."

"Didn't the land belong to an Irish family before the Boyles owned it? I thought lands that ended up under English ownership had been confiscated from Irish Catholics."

Curtis sneered at her. "What are you, some sort of confederate? Whose side are you on?"

"I'm not on anyone's side. I'm just expressing my sympathy for your aunt. And for you."

"Keep your sympathy. Olivia doesn't deserve it. With her high and mighty ways, always going on about her precious antiques. She didn't start that collection; Boyles started it, long before Olivia McCarthy married into it."

"But Olivia added to the collection."

"Those embroidered things, what do you call 'em, samplers. And some tapestries." He snorted. "She told me I couldn't have 'em. Said I didn't appreciate them. Said I'd sell them off cheap and waste the money on this." He raised an empty glass. "Well, maybe I would've. So what? 'S what she did in the end."

"Olivia sold her collection cheap? What do you mean?"

"Well, not cheap maybe, but sold it. Or was selling it. Bit by bit, so's it wouldn't be noticed. All managed by that assistant of hers, Little Lord Foy-de-doy or whatever his name is."

"Ray Delaney."

"Yeah, Delaney. Moved in on Aunt Olivia like a hungry babe on its ma's teat. Managing her estate, he says."

"He does seem incredibly organized and efficient. The house practically runs itself."

"My house. I should be running that house, not that old busted boot Delaney."

"If your aunt's will isn't found, you will be running Essex House. Unless they can locate the copy your aunt's supposed to have kept in the house."

"Even if they do find it, I'll challenge it. I'll get what's mine. Mine by birthright." He signaled to the barmaid.

"One more question. Why was your aunt selling off her collection?"

Curtis took his time with his fresh pint before answering.

"Don't know for certain. Said she needed to lighten her load. I think she was planning to travel. Some old ladies do that, you know. Hit a certain age, sell off some assets, and spend their last years taking theme cruises with their entourage in tow. Though, from what I hear, Aunt Olivia's collection might not have been worth the price of a ticket on the Portlaoise ferry. They were all fakes."

"All fakes? Where'd you hear that? Finn Conklin?"

"You said one more question. Now you're up to four. I'll answer one. All of 'em fakes, some of 'em." Curtis shrugged. "Makes no difference. One fake is enough to tarnish that shiny reputation of hers. Silly cow with all of her supposed expertise didn't recognize the phonies right under her nose."

"Did you know Andrew Perryman?"

"Too many questions. You said one more. You asked about Olivia selling. Now you're asking about Perryman. That's the fifth one."

"Can you answer it? Did you know Andrew Perryman?"

"Nah. Poufty Perry wasn't my type."

"So you wouldn't have had any reason to invite him to visit Essex House."

"Didn't have any reason to get myself invited to visit Essex House. Why the interest?"

"I found something at Essex House that belonged to him, and I can't figure out how it got there. Everyone I ask says he's never been to Essex House."

"Maybe he snuck in. Heard he was involved in some dodgy business when he lived in the States, had to hightail it back home. He's probably good at sneaking around."

"I heard he had to leave because of romantic problems. Something to do with a client's husband."

"Maybe he snuck into Essex House to meet a date. Plenty of handsome young men on Aunt Olivia's staff." Curtis went back to his drink.

Gethsemane went back to Captain Lochlan. "What did you think?" he asked.

"I think Curtis Boyle spends most of his life ossified," she said. "Can't picture him putting his clothes on straight without help, much less plotting murder, fraud, and theft."

Gethsemane pressed her hand against the perimeter wall and let the cool stone numb her fingers. She looked up at Essex House. Its towers and turrets and chimneys challenged her, dared her to uncover secrets hidden within. She shivered as the house's shadow fell on her.

"Cold?" Captain Lochlan started to remove his coat.

"Thanks, but—"

"I forgot."

She pointed at the house. "What's going on up there, Captain? Olivia's death, fake antique textiles, missing wills, an ugly painting worth millions. Andrew's death, is it connected? Then there's Ronan Leary, who shows up everywhere and may or may not have had reason to kill Andrew. Maire, who knows more about Andrew's gallery than she lets on. Why? I doubt she earns enough to buy from Andrew or any other gallery. Maybe her angry maid routine is just an act. And what about Kenneth O'Connor? Calls himself a buyer's agent but doesn't know things someone who works in the art world should know. At least he claims not to know. And why does he show up everywhere Leary appears? Are they connected? What about Yseult and her special assignment? I don't trust her for a minute. Wants everyone to keep her secrets, then demands full disclosure from others. How about Ms. Ryan? Is she part of the fraud ring, using her auction house to move fakes? Was Olivia really auctioning her collection for travel money, or was she selling to unload her fakes before her collection went to a museum? And how do I keep Jackson and myself from landing in prison? Every day I expect O'Reilly to show up at my door and tell us the deal's off, we're under arrest, and we're going to jail."

"So many questions. I wish I had some answers." His aura changed to a deep melancholy yellow.

"You're thinking about Patience."

Captain Lochlan nodded. "I promised Constance and Cicero I'd keep her safe. I gave them my solemn word. I failed them. I let them down in the most unforgivable manner." He stared at his boots. "You must think I'm overreacting."

"No, I don't. I've got this thing about not ever being a disappointment to anyone. I can relate."

"It was such a dangerous time. Constance and Cicero had to flee in the middle of the night with only what they could carry on their backs. I hid Patience onboard the *Hesperus*. I planned to sail to Mystic, Connecticut, then on to New Bedford, Massachusetts. Constance and Cicero would meet us there." The captain dimmed. Gethsemane saw through him to the stone wall. "We never made it to Connecticut. A storm hit. I told Patience to stay below decks, but she was as headstrong as her mother. As headstrong as you. The *Hesperus*'s main mast broke." His voice wavered. "Patience pushed me..." He dematerialized.

Gethsemane waited to see if he would come back. When he didn't, she started for the train station.

He reappeared in front of her on the sidewalk outside Andrew's gallery. She jumped and swore. "Sorry. I just can't get used to that."

"What's going on in there?" Captain Lochlan nodded toward the window.

Gethsemane peered into the well-lit showroom. Several uniformed gardaí and the bald inspector who'd questioned her about Andrew's murder moved around inside. "Searching for clues, I guess. Maybe Ronan Leary's name scrawled on a mirror in Andrew's blood."

"He was killed at home, not in his shop. Are your thoughts always so gruesome?"

"Only when my life's falling apart. Say, you haven't seen anything going on inside Essex House, have you? Anything that would answer any of my questions?"

"I wish I had, but I wasn't at the house until you called me.

And now I seem to be able to manifest only when you're in the vicinity."

"The ghost business is tricky. I remember."

"Your other ghost? Eamon McCarthy?"

She nodded.

"I promise, if I ever cross back to the other side, I'll try and find him and tell him you need him."

"Thank you, Captain Lochlan. You're a good man. I don't think for a minute Constance, Cicero, or Patience blamed you for what happened."

The captain dematerialized again. Gethsemane thought she saw a tear fall before he winked out.

She turned back to the window. Yseult stepped out of the back room and spoke to a garda. She moved and Gethsemane ducked to avoid being seen. Ronan Leary wasn't the only one who popped up in unexpected places. Why was Yseult involved in a murder investigation unconnected to her case? Or was it connected? Her head hurt trying to figure that woman out. How had Frankie ever married her?

Thirteen

Gethsemane arrived home to an empty house. Jackson's note pinned to the door stated he'd gone to check in with O'Reilly and for a walk along Carrick Point. She hung her coat on the hall rack and stood in the entryway as she debated between a hot shower and a bourbon. Bourbon won. She took her drink to the music room and sat at the piano. Eamon's piano. His beautiful Steinway that would soon be auctioned off at someplace like Ryan's.

The phone rang in the kitchen. Gethsemane answered on the third ring. Tchaikovsky's "Pathétique" sounded as soon as she lifted the receiver. She thought back to another unexpected phone call she'd answered. One that made her an ear-witness to murder. She spoke cautiously. "Hello?"

"Is that Dr. Brown?" The woman's voice sounded familiar.

"Who am I speaking to?"

"Have you forgotten already? Can't blame you, I guess. No one really pays attention to what the hired help sounds like."

Maire, of course. She of the frizzy hair and bad attitude. "How can I help you, Maire?"

"It's me what can help you. After you finished snooping and left with all your questions, I got to thinking. Maybe I know more about that will than I let on. I bet you'd like to know what happened to it. I bet you'd like to know where the copy is. I bet that will would clear up all the confusion around you and your brother-in-law. Stop people from thinking you had anything to do with murder or fraud or theft."

"The gardaí would also love to know what happened to the will. Why don't you go to them?"

"Thought about it, but the blue bottles don't pay so well. Department rates."

Blackmail. She'd seen this before. It didn't end well. Just hang up the phone.

"Dr. Brown, you still there?"

"Still here." Hang. Up. The. Phone. "Waiting to hear your offer."

"There's a fella would pay to make sure no one ever learns the truth. But I like you better than I like him, so I thought I'd give you first dibs."

Maire didn't like her that much. She must detest the other guy. Curtis? He was detestable. "How much?"

"Five hundred euros. But I need the money today."

"I'm not sure I have that much on hand."

"This fella—"

"But I can get it." She told Tchaikovsky to shut up. "I might need a couple of hours." She might be rushing out on a fool's errand, but if Maire really had the will...True, the maid hadn't come right out and said so, but from the way she talked, if she didn't have it in hand, she knew where to find it. She couldn't let this chance slip away.

"Half past five. The old distillery, the one out by you. That'll leave you plenty of time to get the cash and get there. But if you're late, Dr. Brown—"

"I won't be."

"And it goes without saying you should come alone. No guards."

"It goes without saying."

The line went dead.

* * *

Five thirty. Gethsemane checked the clock. She had to hurry. Jackson might come back at any time. She only had about three hundred euros on hand, plus another one hundred she borrowed from Jackson's emergency reserve, the one her Nervous Nelly sister hid in the lining of his suitcase. She'd pay him back later. If getting hold of the will meant they were both cleared of suspicion, and he got the Freeman sampler as a bonus, he might not even care if she repaid him. One hundred euros short. Maire wasn't likely to give her a discount. Where could she make up the rest of the money? And find a car? Pedaling the Pashley out to the distillery would take too long. Besides, she didn't relish being out at some creepy ruin on a bicycle. She had enough of that at St. Dymphna's. At least in a car she'd have some protection and means of escape if—she shook her head to clear it of the memory and the Tchaikovsky. She picked up the phone and dialed.

"Father Tim," she greeted the cleric after he answered. "I need a favor. Two favors."

"If you're calling about ghosts—"

"I do need to talk to you about that incantation but some other time. What I'm calling about now is urgent."

"Are you all right? Is Jackson all right? Is anyone injured?"

"No one's hurt and Jackson and I are both fine. I need—I can't tell you why I need them—but I need one hundred euros and your car. To borrow. I promise I'll return the car tomorrow, and I'll pay you back the money with my next paycheck."

"Gethsemane—"

"Please, Tim. I'm begging you to trust me. I swear I wouldn't have called if it wasn't extremely urgent. I can't tell you what it's about. I wish I could, but I promised I wouldn't. All I can say is I'm trying to make sure Olivia's final wishes are honored."

Father Tim sighed on the other end. "When do you need the money and the car?"

"Now. Five minutes ago."

"I don't like this, but...all right, I'll be over there. I don't know how I let you talk me into these things."

"Thank you, thank you, thank you, a thousand times thank you."

"Anything else yourself will be needing?"

"I'd appreciate it if you could spare a prayer or two."

The Dunmullach Distillery sat abandoned at the edge of the village, untouched for fifty years. The glorious reds and oranges of the sunset only made the derelict building appear more ominous in contrast with its crumbling ivy-choked walls and caved-in roof. Gethsemane couldn't imagine Hank Wayne renovating this place. If he bought it, it could only be to finish nature's demolition and use the property for something else. The distillery made St. Dymphna's look like Disney. She patted the money on the seat next to her, glad she'd convinced Father Tim to loan her his vehicle. Being out here on her bicycle would have been even worse than she imagined. Even locked inside a three-thousand-pound car with the windows rolled up, it took all of her willpower to keep from turning around and going back to the cottage.

She parked the car a few yards away from the building. She scanned the surroundings as she walked the final distance, searching for figures lurking in the untamed growth. The distillery's front door had rotted away at some indeterminate time past. She stepped over its remains on her way inside. Bits of slate tiles still showed through the brush that had taken over the floor. A broken down still and a row of monstrous mash tuns lined up beneath an iron catwalk provided the only clues to the building's former purpose. A manila envelope sat propped at one end of the catwalk, accessible by an iron ladder bolted to the wall.

"You've got to be kidding me," Gethsemane muttered. She called for the maid. "Maire, where are you? Come on out." She pulled a roll of bills from her coat pocket and held it up. "I kept my end of the bargain, you keep yours. Where are you?"

No answer. She called again and waited five minutes. Still no answer. She sighed. Obviously, Maire expected her to climb to the catwalk, take the envelope, and leave the cash in its place. She probably watched from some secure remote area. Nothing to be done for it.

She slipped the money back into her pocket and grabbed the ladder with both hands. She shook it as hard as she could. It didn't move. She climbed up to the catwalk.

She knew she was in trouble as soon as she put her weight on the platform. A terrifying metallic groan filled the air as the railing tilted down toward the mash tuns. She looked down and saw empty holes where bolts used to secure the deck plates and railing to the wall should have been.

The manila envelope slipped from the platform and tumbled down to a mash tun. It sank into the murky black liquid that had filled the vessel over half a century of rainstorms. Gethsemane flailed her arms as she slid in the same direction. She managed to hook a section of railing as her feet left the platform. That section of catwalk now swung free from the wall. It remained attached to a neighboring section of catwalk by a cross beam. It swung back and forth on this tenuous hinge, dangling its terrified passenger first over the mash tuns, then over the slate floor, then back over the mash tuns. A hysterical laugh escaped her lips when she realized the creaks and groans of the fatiguing iron had a musical quality. At least she'd have a funeral dirge.

The cross beam gave way with a final blood-freezing crack. Gethsemane lost her grip on the railing as she and the catwalk plunged. She closed her eyes...

And hit something wet. She sank slowly but steadily as though falling through glycerin instead of water. She thrashed her arms and legs, desperate to find something to halt her descent. She opened her eyes but saw only darkness above her. She heard a distant echo of something metallic hitting the side of the tun, then clattering away. She closed her eyes again, ready to give up for the first and last time in her life, when she felt a hand grab her by the arm. A sizzling charge coursed to her shoulder as the hand pulled her upward. She broke the surface of the water with a lung-restoring gasp. Momentum carried her halfway out of the mash tun. She draped herself over the container's side, head toward the floor, and swallowed air in great gulps. She looked up to see Captain Lochlan floating above her.

"It's done now," he said. "I've redeemed myself." He began to dematerialize.

"Patience drowned. She drowned, didn't she, and you couldn't save her? You tried but you couldn't save her."

"I've saved you. And she's forgiven me."

"I doubt she ever blamed you in the first place."

"I blamed me." Gethsemane saw the remaining ceiling beams through his chest. "I promised her ma I'd look after her. I've never gone back on my word to a woman."

"Have you forgiven yourself?" Now she saw trees silhouetted against the twilight. She could no longer make out the details of his clothes.

"Aye, I have." He smiled. "You'll be all right now. When you're rested, there's a ladder on the side of the tun. Use it to climb down."

"I won't see you again, will I?"

"I'm afraid not. At least not on this side of the veil. So I hope I won't be seeing you for a good long time."

"Not even if I sing that awful song?" She hummed a few bars of "Captain Heuston's Lament."

His eyes and his smile were the last things to go.

Gethsemane pulled herself around to the side of the mash tun where the ladder was attached. She heard voices. She ducked down, careful not to submerge her face in the muck, and listened.

Male voices. "Are you sure we haven't met somewhere before? I don't forget faces and yours is familiar to me. I swear I've seen you someplace."

"Perhaps you've confused me with someone else."

Voices she recognized. One American, one Irish.

"Don't collect art, by any chance? Maybe I've run into you at an auction. ContempoPop, maybe, at Christeby's? In New York."

"The only things even resembling art I've ever collected have been pinups I clipped from magazines, and I've never been to New York."

"You say you've never been to New York? Everyone's been to New York."

"It's on my bucket list."

She hoisted herself up and grabbed the ladder. "Mr. Wayne, Mr. Delaney, can you give me a hand?"

The two men rushed into the distillery.

"Dr. Brown." Hank stared up at her from the base of the mash tun. "What the hell? How'd you get up there?"

Ray climbed the ladder. "Don't move." He grabbed her by the hand and helped her down. "Sit here." He eased her to the ground as her legs gave out.

She propped her back against the tun. "Thank you."

"What's going on?" Hank asked. "What're you doing out here?"

Gethsemane countered. "What are *you* doing out here?" She said to Ray, "Not that I'm not glad to see you."

"Delaney's showing me around. I'm thinking of buying the property. He's executor of that woman's estate, or will be if they ever find her will, so I asked him to give me a tour."

Ray had told her he'd bring Hank to tour the distillery, even offered to meet her for a drink after. But a tour at night? She assumed he'd give Hank the tour during normal business hours. Why so late? "I forgot Ray mentioned you'd be coming. Please forgive me. Near-drowning has me a little fuzzy."

"You didn't answer my question, Dr. Brown," Hank said, "about what you're doing out here. If this is an attempt to sabotage my purchase of Carraigfaire—"

"Maire tried to kill me."

Ray sputtered. "Mrs. McCarthy-Boyle's Maire? Surely, you're coddin'. Why would she—"

"She called me and told me she had the will. Or, strongly implied she did. She offered to sell it to me for five hundred euros.

She lured me out here, but she never showed up."

"But how'd you end up in the tub?" Hank asked.

"I saw an envelope on the catwalk. I assumed it contained the will and Maire meant for me to take the envelope and leave the cash for her to collect later. So I climbed up. What I didn't know was she'd removed the bolts that secured the catwalk to the wall. I fell."

"You're lucky you landed in one of the tuns instead of the floor," Ray said. "We'd have come upon a tragic scene if you had."

Lucky she didn't hit the floor and lucky a ghost saved her from drowning. "Tell me about it."

"I'll call an ambulance." Ray pulled out his phone.

"No need for that," Gethsemane said. "I'm not hurt, just wet. I have a car."

"We didn't see it," Hank said.

"I left it a little way down the road. I'd appreciate an escort." Maire was probably long gone but no point taking chances.

Ray walked her back to her car. "Will you be all right to drive?"

"I'll be okay. I don't have far to go. Thank you again."

"Dr. Brown, are you sure the will was in the envelope Maire left here?"

"Well, no, I'm not sure. I never opened it. It could have been a blank piece of paper or the envelope might have been empty. Whatever it was, or wasn't, it's at the bottom of a mash tun now."

"If it was a decoy, Maire might have kept the will."

"If she did, she'll probably try to sell it again. She mentioned a man who wanted it. Maybe Curtis. If the will disinherits him, he'd pay to make sure it disappeared forever."

"You should report this to the gardaí, Dr. Brown."

"I will. As soon as I get home." She sniffed her coat sleeve. "Almost as soon as I get home. First, I'm going to wash the sludge off before it eats through my skin, then I'm going to burn these clothes. I'll call the police after that."

Fourteen

Gethsemane eased open the cottage door and tiptoed to the stairs. She hoped to slip up to her room unnoticed. However, she only made it to the second stair before the stench of the mash tun's foulness gave her away.

"What's that smell?" Jackson called from the study. He stepped into the hall and wrinkled his nose. One glance at her wet clothes and slime-flecked hair and he phoned the gardaí. She jumped to grab the receiver from his hand, a futile effort thanks to his foot's height advantage. She succeeded in splashing some of the distillery's filth onto his sweater.

"At least give me the phone," she said when she heard the annoyed "hello, hello" on the other end of the line. "I'll talk to them."

"Who is this? I'm warning you, wasting gardaí time—"

"This is Gethsemane Brown. I need to speak with Inspector O'Reilly."

"The Inspector's not available," the voice said in far less time than it would have taken to actually check.

"When will he be available?" She hunched over the receiver to keep it away from Jackson, who tried to grab it. "Did I mention this was urgent?"

"Urgent, eh? What's this about then?"

The truth would either get her transferred to homicide to some low-ranking garda who would take her statement while silently cursing her for interrupting his break then leave the report on someone else's desk where it might be found in a day or two, or it would send some other low-ranking garda to fetch her down to the station where she'd spend a long night answering questions. If her luck held, she'd spend what remained of the night in a cell for wasting police time since she didn't have any hard evidence or witnesses to prove Maire tried to kill her. She'd run the drill with Dunmullach homicide before. O'Reilly would take her seriously, even if he didn't ordinarily deal with crimes of recent vintage.

"I'm hanging up now." The voice on the phone brought her back. "If you call back I'll have you run in—"

"I'm not wasting your time. Tell Inspector O'Reilly it's about his cat."

"His cat."

"Yes, his cat." Using a man's pet to lure him to the phone was low, but she was desperate. Jackson had his smartphone out, about to call 999. If emergency services showed up at the door she'd lose all control of the situation. "Please just tell the inspector Gethsemane Brown is calling about his cat."

A few clicks on the other end of the line and O'Reilly's anxious baritone replaced the angry voice. "What's wrong with Nero?"

She'd forgotten he'd named his cat after the fictional detective. He'd adopted him after he solved his former owner's murder. She hated herself a little bit. "Nothing's wrong."

"The desk sergeant said—"

"Nero's fine. I guess. I haven't seen your cat."

The inspector hurled a string of expletives in plain English. "Gethsemane Brown, if you—"

"Olivia's maid tried to kill me."

Silence. "If this is some sort of joke..."

"No joke. Olivia's maid tried to kill me tonight."

"Which maid? She had several."

"Maire something. I don't know her last name. She tricked me into coming out to the Dunmullach distillery."

"What the bloody hell is it with you and abandoned buildings?"

Gethsemane ignored the question. "She rigged the catwalk and took out the bolts that screwed it to the wall. It fell and I fell. Luckily, I landed in one of the mash tuns. I almost drowned." She said a silent thank you to Captain Lochlan. "But if I'd hit the ground I wouldn't have stood a chance."

More silence.

"You believe me, don't you?"

"If it was anyone but you I'd say you were coddin' and I'd arrest you for it. But I have no trouble believing someone tried to kill you."

She deserved that. Hearing it pissed her off, but she deserved it.

"Where are you now?" O'Reilly asked. "Are you someplace safe?"

"I'm home at the cottage. Jackson's here with me."

"Did you see Maire?"

"No, she called me. I, admittedly unwisely, went out to the distillery on my own." One of these days she'd heed Tchaikovsky's warning. She told the inspector about the will Maire claimed to have. "I figured she'd sell it to the other bidder if I didn't act fast. I assume she meant Curtis Boyle. He certainly doesn't want Olivia's will found. He'll inherit the wind and nothing else if it is."

"Did you see anyone else at the distillery?"

"Just Hank Wayne and Ray Delaney. Hank's thinking of buying it. Ray was showing him around. They helped me out of the tun. Well, Ray did."

"Maire's probably in Ballytuam. A bit out of my jurisdiction, but since the actual crime happened here I think I can convince the fellas over there to let me take the lead. Unless you want me to turn this over to the homicide unit."

"If I'd wanted to be ridiculed, belittled, and humiliated I would have called them directly."

"All right, let me make a couple of calls and I'll head over there. I'll start at Essex House. As long as she phoned you in secret, no one can connect her to the distillery. She'll have no reason to run."

"I'm going with you."

"No, you're not."

"No, you're not," Jackson said behind her.

"You stay out of this."

"You pulled me into this," O'Reilly said.

"Not you. I was talking to Jackson. And I am going with you. Imagine Maire's reaction when you confront her and I walk into the room not dead."

"The woman tried to murder you."

"Long distance. She's not going to do anything with a guard or three standing there." O'Reilly's heavy sigh drifted across the line. She imagined him, eyes closed, fingers massaging a temple. "You admit I have a point?" she asked.

"No, I'm reminding myself that if I don't take you with me, you'll find a way to go yourself and it'll probably be a way that will lead to more trouble. Put your brother-in-law on the phone. Maybe I can talk sense to him."

"I will not put Jackson on the phone." Jackson tried to grab the receiver. She ducked out of his reach. "I am not some helpless delicate flower who's going to wilt if you look at her cross-eyed. I'm not going to sit here and wring my hands while two big strong men decide how best to protect me from fire-breathing dragons."

"Oh, for feck's—" A faint thud followed the expletive. What had he thrown? "How did my investigating your attempted assassination—which is not my department, may I remind you—turn into some sort of feminist manifesto?"

"I'm sorry, Niall. You're right. You're the police and I should leave this to you—Jackson's nodding his head—but you've known me long enough to know I'm not good at sitting back and letting others do the heavy lifting. It's not in my nature."

"I remember."

"I'm not suggesting I go off like a lone wolf and confront

Maire." Although if she ever did get her alone, what she'd like to do to the frizzy-haired cow would have homicide on her case. "But with other people present, gardaí present, what harm could come? In fact, me being with you, where you can keep an eye on me, is a lot safer than me being way out here at the cottage all by myself with Maire unaccounted for."

"You're not by yourself," Jackson said. "I'm here."

Gethsemane shushed him. "What if she's not at Essex House? What if she went to the distillery and found out I'm not dead? What if she's lying in wait on the cliffs or up at the lighthouse biding her time until another opportunity—"

"Don't oversell it," O'Reilly said. "Fine, you can come with me. Bring Jackson, too, just in case your nonsense about Maire lying in wait isn't nonsense. But understand, you do as I tell you. If I sense the situation is even remotely getting out of hand, if there's even the hint of danger—"

"I'll wait in the car like a good girl. I promise."

O'Reilly snorted. "You know lying to the police is a serious offense. I'll be there in fifteen minutes. Be ready."

She hung up to find Jackson frowning down at her, arms crossed. "Don't start. It's not as if we're going after Ma Barker."

"I feel sorry for any fire-breathing dragons we encounter. You'll skin them and turn them into a purse and matching shoes inside of ten minutes."

"Tell me again what happened." O'Reilly kept his eyes on the road as he sped toward Essex House.

Gethsemane repeated her story of the phone call, the envelope, the catwalk's collapse, the foul liquid in the mash tun. Once again, she omitted the captain's rescue. She also didn't tell him about the welts on her palms from gripping the railing or the bruises she'd noticed when she showered or how the sludge she'd washed away clogged the shower drain.

Jackson, in the backseat, hid his face in his hands. "Lord,

Sissy, what's with this place? Your attempted murder, Andrew Perryman's murder, Olivia's unexplained death all in the same week. Southeast D.C. is safer."

"The medical examiner ruled Olivia's death a homicide," O'Reilly said. "She had bruises on her upper back and shoulders. The bruises corresponded to hands." He nodded at Gethsemane. "Hands belonging to someone much taller than you. You couldn't have reached high enough to push her with enough force to send her over the balcony railing. Which is why the guards never arrested you." He smiled a dimpled grin. "Sissy."

Gethsemane mouthed the words, "Don't. Even." Aloud she said, "Someone could have told me."

"The Ballytuam gardaí kept a lot of information from the public. They didn't want to jeopardize ongoing investigations."

"Investigations, plural?"

"Olivia's murder and the art fraud scheme. They knew fake pieces were being sold through local auction houses, pieces from famous collections. They didn't know whether the collectors were in on the scam or if someone else with access to the artworks was substituting fakes without the collectors' knowledge. They also didn't know if or how Olivia's death was connected."

"The Creech miniature could have been swapped for a fake at the auction house," Jackson said. "Any number of people could have accessed it if Ms. Ryan and her house were involved in the scheme. Things get trickier if the auction house wasn't knowingly involved, but the switch is still doable. The Freeman sampler's a different story. It was never out of Essex House and never on public display. A limited number of people knew Olivia owned it. The forger would have to know the sampler existed, know where in the house it was located, obtain detailed descriptions of it, sneak into Olivia's office without her knowing, and make the switch. Couldn't be done without Olivia's involvement."

"But if Olivia was involved, she'd never have willed the Freeman sampler to your museum," Gethsemane said. "She was not a stupid woman. But someone else who lived in the house, someone with unlimited access to Olivia's office, could have made the switch. Someone whose presence would not only *not* raise eyebrows but would be expected."

"Who?" Jackson asked.

"A maid. Maire lives in Essex House. She has unlimited, untimed access to everything. And she probably gets a good look at the artwork when she dusts the frames."

"If she was involved, she must have had help," Jackson said. "I admit I didn't know her, but the few times I saw her she didn't strike me as a skilled forger, and I don't think she's often invited to attend auctions."

"Ryan's involvement in the scam is unequivocal. We haven't pinpointed exactly who at the house is mixed up in this, yet, but we have a short list of suspects."

"I bet that assistant is on the list," Gethsemane interjected. "Something about him rubs me wrong."

"Maybe three or four other auction houses and galleries in Ballytuam are in on it, too," O'Reilly said.

"Including Andrew Perryman's gallery?"

O'Reilly nodded. "The Economic Crime Bureau ran an undercover investigation out of Ballytuam. Besides the regular guards, the Bureau borrowed operatives from other agencies, sent them to auctions and gallery openings and galas and whatnot to try to suss out leads. But the art world is tighter than a nun's—tough to break into." O'Reilly met Jackson's eyes in the rearview mirror. "They appreciated your help, Dr. Applethwaite, even though you gave it under duress. The contacts you provided will be key in setting up dealers trying to unload fakes."

O'Reilly turned onto the road that passed by the Ballytuam train station. "It's not too late. I can drop you both at the station and you can catch the train back to Dunmullach."

"And I can buy us both plane tickets home," Jackson said. "You need to come away to a safer place, Sissy, someplace with a lower body count. D.C., east L.A., New York."

"Jackson Applethwaite, did my parents raise any quitters?"

"No."

"Has my mother ever quit anything once she's started on it? Did my father, when he was alive?"

"No."

"In all the tales you've heard about my long line of ancestors, did you ever hear anything that gave you the indication that any of them ever quit fighting no matter how heinous the crap thrown in their faces?"

"No."

"If you want to leave, Niall can drop you at the station. I'm staying."

"Dr. Applethwaite." O'Reilly grinned in the rearview mirror. "In all the years you've known Sissy, have you ever won an argument with her?"

"No."

"There they are."

O'Reilly pointed to the Ballytuam police car waiting in front of Essex House. Its occupants got out as O'Reilly's car pulled into the drive. Gethsemane recognized two of the four. Yseult Grennan standing near the house's entrance didn't surprise Gethsemane. The man standing next to her did. Kenneth O'Connor, the buyer's agent. How'd he fit into this? Was he part of the undercover investigation? One of the undercover agents? Maybe her Secret Squirrel joke hadn't been such a joke after all.

The third person wore a police uniform. He held O'Reilly's door for him as he introduced the fourth, a thin man in a boring gray suit, as Inspector Mulroney of the garda's Bureau of Economic Crime. O'Reilly introduced Jackson and Gethsemane.

Yseult shook O'Reilly's hand.

"Niall, always a pleasure. You remember Special Agent O'Connor."

The two men greeted each other. Yseult and Kenneth acknowledged Gethsemane and Jackson while the uniformed garda rang the bell. A butler answered and the group followed him inside.

Gethsemane whispered to Kenneth, "Tell me again what kind of agent you are."

"Did I say 'buyer's'? I meant FBI."

"Her, too?" Gethsemane nodded at Yseult.

"Her, too. Our art crimes unit loaned Yseult and me to the Ballytuam gardaí, us being from the ould sod originally."

Did Frankie know his ex-wife worked for the American feds? Would she dare ask him?

Inspector Mulroney spoke to the butler. "We need to speak to Maire Fitzgerald."

"Maire's not here, sir. No one's seen her since yesterday. We've been looking for her. She didn't say anything about going away."

Another maid, a brunette who looked just out of high school, poked her head around the corner. "She's cleared out her things." She blushed when everyone turned toward her. "Begging your pardon for interrupting. I share a room with Maire, least I did. Lots of her clothes and all her jewelry is gone and so's a case. I don't think she's coming back."

"Jewelry?" Yseult asked. "What jewelry did she have?"

"She had lots of nice bits and bobs. Earrings, a bracelet, a couple of necklaces. She claimed they were real, but I didn't believe her. How could they be? I know how much she makes. You'd be lucky to buy a toy from a kiddie shop on our salary. I bet they were cubic zirconia. She said she inherited them, but I didn't believe that either. Who'd she have to inherit from? She came from a long line of nobodies who didn't have a piss pot to leave to anyone. I figured she bought 'em herself with money she got from some fella who was getting a leg over, or she nicked 'em from somewhere. Lady Muck got notions. Shite flies high when it's hit with a stick." She blushed. "'Scuse my language."

"Will you take us to your room?" Yseult asked.

"Sure, it's this way."

The group followed the young woman. "Where's Mr. Delaney?" Gethsemane asked her as she led them through several hallways, past the kitchen, and down a flight of back stairs. "He managed the staff; he's sure to know next of kin, previous employers. Maybe he can tell us where Maire might have gone."

"Sorry, miss, haven't seen him since this morning." She stopped in front of a small brown door about a third of the way along a hall lined with identical doors. "Here we are." She opened the door to a small Spartan double-bedded room. Twin dressers, end tables, and a wardrobe comprised the only other furniture. Disarrayed sheets covered one of the beds. The other hadn't been slept in. Partially open drawers in the dresser next to it revealed absent contents. The dresser top lay empty.

"She stole my case." The young maid pointed to the top of the wardrobe at a worn purple hard-sided suitcase. "I had a matching set, present from me uncle."

"She's cleared out," the uniformed garda announced.

"We see that," Inspector Mulroney said. "Question is, where's she got to?"

"And who helped her?" O'Reilly asked. "I just don't see her pulling off art fraud and attempted murder by herself."

"I don't see her pulling off art fraud at all," Kenneth said.

"What do you mean?"

"Yseult and I have been trying to break this ring for a year and a half now. We've investigated everyone even tangentially connected: Mrs. McCarthy-Boyle, Ms. Ryan and her employees at the auction house, Andrew Perryman, Ronan Leary. Maire never came up in connection with anything. Never saw her at an auction, never saw her name on a gallery's client list, never saw her name on any known art criminals' holiday card lists. Never even bought a ticket to the local art museum. As far as we can tell, she has nothing to do with the art world."

"But there's an insider, you said so yourself, someone with access to the works, someone who knows where they are and how to move them."

"Yes, there is an insider. It's just not Maire."

"The missing will's another story," Yseult said. "We can't tie it to our case. Maire may well have stolen it herself or may be working with whoever did."

"My money's on Curtis Boyle for that one," O'Reilly said. "He's the only one with any reason to get rid of it. Everyone else benefitted from the will's existence."

"Shall I call the station to have them send someone 'round to see Curtis Boyle, sir?" the uniform asked his superior. He received an affirmative and left the room.

"Mind if we look 'round, luv?" Kenneth asked the maid. She reddened and consented to the search.

"Not much to see." Inspector Mulroney pawed through the wardrobe. "Some clothes, few pair of shoes."

"Those are mine, sir." The maid snatched a skimpy red-sequined dress from the policeman. "Mostly. Maire used the other half of the wardrobe."

"Nothing there but a moth-eaten skirt."

"Nothing in the drawers either." O'Reilly pushed against one, but it wouldn't shut. He pushed harder and slammed his leg against it. It remained open a few inches despite his efforts.

"Something must be stuck," Yseult said.

O'Reilly removed the drawer and reached into the space. He pulled out a crumpled magazine.

Gethsemane recognized it. "It's the Christeby's magazine. The issue featuring the ContempoPop auction. I keep seeing it."

"Where did you see it?" Yseult asked.

"At the Perryman Gallery and in Olivia's office. I also heard Hank Wayne talking about the auction. He met Andrew there, I think, or at least worked with him. And he thought he recognized Ray, but Ray denied ever being in New York."

"What's the magazine doing stuffed behind a drawer in the maid's room?" O'Reilly held it out for the young maid to see. "Do you recognize this?"

"No, sir. I've never seen it before. If it's one of Mrs. McCarthy-Boyle's art magazines, I never had nothing to do with those. Maire took care of the missus's office."

Inspector Mulroney addressed Yseult and Kenneth, "You're positive Maire's not involved in art fraud?" They assured him they were. "Who has access to this room besides you and your roommate?" he asked the maid.

"We don't keep it locked. I guess anyone could come in. But no one does except me and Maire."

Jackson reached for the magazine. "May I?" He examined its edges the way he'd examined the edge of the grimoire. "Pages are missing. See here?" He showed the group where several pages had been torn from the volume.

O'Reilly took the magazine back. "Let's assume Maire tore out the pages and hid the magazine behind her drawer. Why? Did she want to keep people from seeing what was on the pages? Did she want to show the pages to someone else?"

"I don't know why Maire cared what was on those pages," Gethsemane said, "but I know how to find out what was on them. Let's go to Andrew's gallery and find his copy of the magazine."

The group of seven—Gethsemane, Jackson, Inspectors O'Reilly and Mulroney, Special Agents Grennan and O'Connor, and the uniformed garda—descended on the Perryman Gallery. A locked door forced them to wait for the building's landlord to arrive with a key.

Gethsemane questioned Kenneth while they waited. "So you made up that story about being a buyer's agent?"

"It was my cover, yes."

"And Yseult's story about being a forensic art and documents examiner?"

"True. The agency recruited her for those particular skills. But she's a field agent, not a lab dweller."

"Where does Ronan Leary belong in this? Is he part of your cover?"

"Ronan Leary belongs in prison."

"Prison?"

"How much do you know about Andrew Perryman?"

"I know he used to deal paintings in New York with his partner, Ronan Leary. I heard he left New York to come back to Ballytuam because—his story—he faced too much competition in an oversaturated market, or—gossip story—he fled a scandal over his relationship with a client's husband. I suspect he and his partner forged paintings in New York, fled when the law started closing in on them, set up shop again in Ballytuam, but this time they forge antique textiles instead of paintings. Am I right?"

Kenneth gaped. "I'm impressed. You're right. Gossip was wrong. Andrew left New York because of a scandal, but it had nothing to do with his love life. We knew Andrew and Ronan were selling both forged and stolen paintings. Andrew handled the forging, Ronan handled the stealing. Andrew would also create counterfeit provenance—bogus bills of sale, exhibit catalogs, magazine reviews, what have you. We could never find enough evidence to prove anything. Word of our investigation got out and hurt their business. Destroyed it. Who'd want to buy anything from dealers suspected of forgery and theft? So Andrew sold his gallery, gave Ronan the shaft in the process, pulled up stakes, hightailed it back to Irish soil, and changed his medium from paintings to textiles."

"Back to Ballytuam with a prolonged layover in Dublin?"

"Right again. You're good at this."

"You thought—knew—Andrew was back in the forgery business. Do you think he's the one who sold Olivia the Freeman sampler? Is that why Yseult had me looking for the bill of sale? To compare it to other examples of Andrew's work?"

"Criminal habits die hard. It's much easier to move a faked or stolen piece if you have papers saying the piece isn't faked or stolen. Riches await a talented forger. When we learned Ronan Leary was in town, we were certain we were onto something."

"He creeps me out. He keeps popping up without warning. And he accused me of theft and murder. Didn't exactly endear himself. How's he fit into this?"

"Ronan Leary hasn't endeared himself to anyone, including his own ma. She reported him after a heist from a gallery in Kilkenny. He slipped through investigators' hands on that one. He was a minor at the time and no one could make the charges stick. He vanished and reappeared years later as Andrew's partner in the New York gallery and his partner in crime. Andrew pissed Leary off when he sold out and fixed things so he kept most of the profit and Leary kept most of the liability. Surprised us when he and Andrew seemed to have patched up their differences and gone back into business together."

"You think Leary killed Andrew? Out of revenge for the double-cross?"

"He's our number one suspect, but he has an alibi for the time of the murder. We haven't been able to break it. Yet. We think a deal went sour and Andrew tried to short-change him again. Leary decided not to be left holding the bag this time."

"Could he have planted the miniature sampler in Jackson's pocket?"

"Yeah. We're almost sure that was him. He'd have stolen the miniature with no trouble—'tis what he's good at—but realized he had no chance to get out of the building with it. We'd have searched him first, second, and third. He must've figured no one would ever suspect Dr. Applethwaite of theft so no one would search him. Your brother-in-law would've walked out of the auction house with the miniature in his pocket, none the wiser. Leary would've stolen it from him later."

Gethsemane shuddered at the thought of Jackson being mugged. Or worse. "One thing I don't understand. Why steal the miniature in the first place? Why go to the trouble of slipping a fake into an auction only to have to steal it back right before it's sold? Insurance fraud?"

Kenneth nodded at Jackson. "For the same reason you wouldn't will a fake sampler to a museum. A crime-fighting museum curator. Leary and Perryman and the rest of the gang figured the fake miniature would wind up with some private collector too arrogant or lazy to have it properly authenticated. Or perhaps too embarrassed to make a fuss when they discovered they'd been duped. When they learned Jackson planned to bid, well, a museum is a different story."

"Because of course Jackson would have the piece independently authenticated, and of course he'd call the authorities once he discovered the fraud."

"Better to steal it themselves before that happened."

"Then destroy the fake, just like with the Freeman sampler, and no one's the wiser. The case gets written off as another unsolved art theft."

"You really are pretty good at this secret agent stuff. I might have to offer you a job."

"Got one, thanks." Something nagged Gethsemane. "Since you attended Olivia's fundraiser, why did Yseult send *me* to find the sampler's bill of sale? I understand why she wanted it, but why send me, the civilian, for it instead of you, the trained agent?"

"I'd tried to get into Olivia's office but couldn't. Could never come up with a valid reason to be in that part of the house. Olivia watched the goings and comings at Essex House like a hawk. She was hardly some sweet little old lady in her dotage. But with your cover as a musician performing at the party, you had plenty of reason to be in the part of the house where the office is located. I also had some, uh, other issues to attend to."

"You were surprised to see me."

"Part of my cover. How would I have explained knowing you'd be there?" The landlord arrived and let everyone into the gallery, ending Gethsemane's questions.

"Do you remember where you saw the magazine, Dr. Brown?"

"Right here on this end table." She rummaged through the stack she'd looked at earlier with Frankie until she found it. "Christeby's magazine, ContempoPop edition." She flipped to the pages missing from the copy Maire had hidden at Essex House. "Oh. My. But he said—" She handed the magazine to Yseult. "It's Ray Delaney."

A four-page photo spread featured snapshots of the auction and the pre-auction preview. Pictures, both candid and posed, highlighted the rich and the beautiful and the notable people who attended the events. Hank Wayne appeared in half a dozen. Two photos immortalized Ray Delaney. In one, he stood next to a man the caption identified as the auctioneer. The other showed him with an elderly woman who favored Olivia.

"Ken, take a look." Yseult pointed at the woman. "Isn't she the woman who died in that awful car accident? You remember."

"Yeah, she collected street art and outsider art, mostly. She owned several pieces by Basquiat and one or two Harings. Car ended up in the Hudson with her in it. Wasn't there something funny about her will? Long-lost relations crawling out of the fog or something."

"No, not mysterious relatives. Her will went missing. Then her assistant found a copy stashed in a closet or cabinet or under a mattress or someplace. Seems he did okay for himself. She left him a pot of money."

Gethsemane laid a finger on the caption. "Says Ray Delaney is her assistant."

"Two old ladies dying from unnatural causes, two missing wills, and Delaney worked for both," O'Reilly said. "I gave up coincidence for Lent. There has to be a connection."

"Hank thought he recognized Ray from the auction. Ray lied. He swore he'd never even been to New York," Gethsemane said.

"If Ray expected to profit from that woman's will," Jackson said, "he'd make sure someone found a copy."

Inspector Mulroney sent the uniformed garda to make some phone calls.

"I want Delaney found. Answers to some questions are in order."

"If Ray attended this auction he probably met Andrew," Gethsemane said. "I know he met Hank, Hank remembered him, and Andrew was acquiring art for Hank. But Andrew denied ever going to Essex House."

"Denied it to you?" Inspector Mulroney raised an eyebrow. "How'd the subject come up?"

Gethsemane blushed. "I, er, may have found something at Essex House that belonged to him."

"You mean you tampered with evidence from a murder scene?" Mulroney asked.

"I wouldn't put it that strongly."

"Just tell us what you found." O'Reilly's eyes took on the storm grey hue that signaled controlled fury. "*Sissy*."

"A custom-made sterling silver button. I came across some documents at the tailor's—"

O'Reilly interrupted. "Came across?"

"Came across." Gethsemane continued. "They proved Andrew owned the button. But if he'd never been to Essex House, how'd he lose a button there?"

"Why not just admit he'd been up there?" Mulroney asked. "Admit he'd been to see Delaney, an old acquaintance. There's nothing odd about visiting a friend who moves to a house within walking distance of your gallery. It would be stranger not to see him."

"Either Andrew or Ray," Gethsemane said, "wanted to keep their past friendship secret."

"Let's have another look around," Yseult said. "We tried to find something to connect Andrew to Leary. We didn't search for anything connecting him to Delaney."

"Or to Maire," Gethsemane added. "She knew more about Andrew's gallery than the average maid."

The group searched the gallery as the sun rose. They went through Andrew's office and his inventory but found nothing aside from the Christeby's magazine that connected him to Ray and nothing at all that connected him to Maire.

Inspector Mulroney suggested they quit. "The homicide unit's already been over this."

Yseult ran her hand under a stack of linens folded on a shelf. She pulled it out and held up a small pink paper. She unfolded it.

"Well, well. We did miss something the first time through. A receipt for a Koors teddy bear painting."

"That god-awful thing at Essex House?"

"Hard to tell without the painting in front of me," Yseult said. "But I can say with certainty it's not a receipt for any canvas sold legitimately through this gallery. I'll analyze it when I get back to the station, but instinct says it's forged."

Gethsemane knocked over a book, an exhibition catalog from the Ibiza Museum of Contemporary Art. "Damn." She bent to pick it up and spied a torn piece of paper in a corner under a desk. She retrieved it. A few words marched across the scrap in Andrew's neat handwriting. "Hey, I think I found something." She read aloud. "'Last will and'...Andrew wrote a will. Or started one." She handed the paper to Yseult.

"Who'd he write it for? Himself or someone else?" Yseult asked.

"It's in his handwriting," Gethsemane said. "I recognize it."

"Could be a draft copy, a working document to make sure he got the details right. That would explain why it was torn up here. He probably dropped this little piece on his way to the incinerator or dumpster."

"So you *do* think he forged a will for someone?" O'Reilly asked Yseult.

She held the paper up to the light. "Not for someone, Niall. For Ray Delaney. It makes sense. A repeat of Delaney's scam in New York. Hire a forger to rewrite your elderly employer's will, naming you as the prime beneficiary, switch the copy for the real will, murder your employer, and live off the inheritance. Money runs out, do it again."

"How do you find a forger you trust enough?" Jackson asked. "What's to stop them from turning you in to the authorities?"

"These people are professionals, Dr. Applethwaite," Yseult explained. "They want money, not trouble. If you pay them enough—"

Gethsemane cut in. "Or sleep with them. Look what I found

tucked inside the book." She held up one half of a torn photo. A shirtless Andrew sat on the edge of a lounge chair beside a pool. A man's arm was draped around him. The hand lay on Andrew's chest in a manner that suggested Andrew and the arm's owner were anything but platonic friends. The rest of the man's image had been ripped away.

"Can't tell who the other fella is," O'Reilly said.

"I can." Gethsemane pointed at items on the half table still visible in the photo. An umbrella-laden drink stood near Andrew. Next to it—a gold-plated cigar lighter. "That's Ray's." She turned the photo over. A partial inscription read:

To my youn—

Thanks for the bes—

Ibiza

"That's Ray's, too. The handwriting, I mean. I recognize it from the playlist he gave me when he hired me for the party." She recalled what the cellist told her at lunch. "Andrew always had a thing for older men."

The uniform burst into the gallery, out of breath, and ran up to Inspector Mulroney. "Sir." He panted. "Sir, we spotted Maire Fitzgerald boarding a train. It departs in seven minutes."

Fifteen

"We can be at the station in less than two." Inspector Mulroney motioned to Yseult and Kenneth. "C'mon." They rushed out behind the uniform.

"You two stay—" O'Reilly began.

"You're not leaving us here," Gethsemane interrupted.

"Yes, I am."

"With Ray on the loose? No one's seen him since Maire disappeared. She didn't run because she tried to kill me, she ran from Ray. She must've blackmailed him. 'Give me money and I won't tell anyone your lover helped you forge a will leaving you your employer's fortune. Your employer whom you pushed over a balcony.' Except Ray decides killing Maire is cheaper than paying her. She figures out he plans to murder her, so she takes off before he gets the chance."

"He killed Andrew, didn't he?" Jackson asked. "Ray had to be the inside man switching fake textiles for the real ones. If Andrew knew the authorities were on to him, he might have offered them Ray to save himself."

"I bet Ray engineered my catwalk misadventure as well. I doubt Maire would've concocted such a plan all on her own, and I don't see her climbing on a catwalk removing screws. He and Maire set me up. She never intended to blackmail me. She and Ray wanted me dead. His showing up at the distillery with Hank at that time in the evening was no coincidence. He wanted to find my body in front of a witness to give himself an alibi." She tapped her watch. "Train's leaving, Inspector."

"Damn it, Gethsemane Brown—All right, c'mon. But you do as I tell you."

A voice cackled over the loudspeaker. "This train departs in three minutes. Three minutes. All ticket holders please board. Mind the gap. Three minutes until departure."

O'Reilly showed his identification to the conductor and boarded the train.

"We're with him," Gethsemane said as she and Jackson hurried after him.

Yseult met them. "Maire bought an unreserved ticket. Second class is that way."

"She could be hiding anywhere," O'Reilly said. "We'd best split up."

"Ken's up front with Mulroney and the uniform. Why don't we start at the back?"

O'Reilly pointed at empty seats, then pointed at Gethsemane and Jackson. "You two stay here." They sat. O'Reilly leaned down with his face an inch from Gethsemane's. "Don't you move. I mean it. So help me, I'll arrest you for interfering with a police investigation if you so much as stand to stretch your legs."

"Niall." Yseult motioned for him to hurry.

Gethsemane waited until they exited the car, then stood. Then sat down again. With Mulroney, Kenneth, and the uniform at one end of the train and O'Reilly and Yseult at the other, Maire had nowhere to go. Neither did she.

Jackson frowned.

"Inspector O'Reilly said not to move."

"I heard him."

Jackson stood. "Switch seats with me."

"Why?"

"So you'll be by the window where you can't get out without crawling over me."

She grumbled as she changed places with her brother-in-law. She leaned her head against the window and closed her eyes. Nothing to do but wait, a task not in her skillset. A wave of fatigue swept over her. She'd been awake since who remembered when, she'd survived an attempted drowning, her bruises ached, her head hurt, "Pathétique" played—

She opened her eyes. Why did Tchaikovsky play? She searched out the window. Maybe Maire was giving them the slip, jumping off the train. No one on the platform except—there! She saw him hop on just as the train began its slow pull out of the station. A dark-haired man with a graying beard and eyes as blue as the Mediterranean. She poked Jackson. "Ray Delaney's on the train."

"What? Where?"

"Ray's on the train. I just saw him get on." She held her breath as she stared at the door at the car's entrance. It remained shut. "He must've gone the other way. We've got to warn the others."

"Inspector O'Reilly said—"

"Jackson! That was before a murderer hopped the train. You go after Niall and Yseult. I'll go forward after Kenneth and Inspector Mulroney."

"Sissy—"

"We're on a moving train full of people. What can he do? But it won't be long before we get to the next stop. So move. We don't want him to get off. We'll lose him. Hurry."

She pushed past Jackson and headed toward the front of the car without waiting to see if he went the other way. A few of the other passengers glanced at her as she rushed past. Most remained absorbed in their smartphones, tablets, books, and newspapers. The train lurched as she stepped onto the platform connecting her car to the one in front of it. She grabbed at a railing to steady herself. How far had Ray gone? Had he reached Kenneth and Inspector Mulroney yet?

She saw the frizzy blonde hair as soon as she stepped into the next car. Maire. No police, no Ray. Where was everyone? Maire pressed the button to open the door at the opposite end. She disappeared onto the platform before Gethsemane could reach her.

Gethsemane followed through to the next car. No Maire. Not possible. The maid couldn't move that fast. Could she? Gethsemane surveyed the sea of headphones and earbuds that filled the car's seats. You could drive an armored vehicle through and no one would notice, let alone a blonde rushing down the aisle. Unless...Gethsemane looked to her right and her left. Toilets. Maire could have ducked into a toilet. She knocked.

"Hold yer horses," a man bellowed. "Someone's in here, ain't they?"

She tried the opposite stall. Empty. She kept going. Maire had to be in front of her. Ray, too. Maybe they planned to meet on the train, Maire being smart enough not to fall for the ruse of an isolated exchange spot that had nearly cost Gethsemane her life. If she had the original will or the forgery and the magazine pages with her she could hand them to Ray, he could hand her the money, and she could get off the train at the next stop and vanish to start a new life. She must have noticed Ray's gold lighter, his expensive clothes—so much nicer than her discount-store fast fashion—his thirty-euro haircuts. She would have held him up for a lot more than five hundred euro.

Gethsemane braced herself against another lurch, then moved on. Plenty of other toilets to hide in.

Gethsemane reached the last carriage before the dining car. Fewer people occupied this one. Some napped, some read, only one wore headphones. She hurried past to the toilets at the far end of the car. The stall to her right was empty. She tried the door to her left. It wouldn't open. She knocked. Silence. She knocked again, louder. No impatient answer telling her to go away or wait her turn. She turned the door handle again and pushed the door harder. It moved a few inches, then stopped, jammed. More pushing gained another couple of inches, far enough to see what blocked the door—Maire, legs splayed, mouth open, eyes bulged, obviously beyond help. A blue-patterned silk necktie knotted around her neck dug into her flesh. Gethsemane stumbled back and leaned against a window as she fought off waves of nausea. She jumped at a noise at the same moment the train lurched and pitched forward toward the toilet. Desperate not to fall on Maire, she spun and flailed as she grabbed for something, anything, to steady herself. Her hands grasped rough fabric and she found herself holding onto the tweed lapels of a chubby man with rosy cheeks and a scowl. His voice had been what startled her.

"I asked if you were going to use that." He nodded toward the toilet as he pried her grip loose.

She shook her head. "Call a porter or the conductor, tell them to stop the train. There are police—gardaí—onboard, get them here."

He looked past Gethsemane into the toilet. He looked as queasy as she felt. "Jaysus, Mary, and Joseph." He crossed himself, stumbled back, and hit the train wall with a thud.

Other people in the car noted the outburst. Soon a group clustered around the grisly find. The volume rose as the air filled with expressions of shock and dismay and calls for someone who "knew what to do."

Gethsemane backed away from the commotion, heart racing, breath caught in her throat. She pressed her hands against her temples and recited Negro League stats. She shook her head to clear the image of Maire's blue distorted face. This was no time to lose it. Only Ray had reason to kill Maire, and Ray still lurked somewhere on the train. A few more batting averages and her heart slowed. The crowd gathered around the toilet blocked the hallway. Gethsemane peered into the deserted dining car for another exit and saw the door at the far end open. The door to the car beyond stood open as well. The baggage car. Of course. Where better for Maire to hide the wills and magazine pages than in her checked luggage, disguised by hundreds of similar bags, in a car only staff visited? Ray must have had the same thought. Or maybe Maire told him before he—Gethsemane shook her head again. A vision of his ever-present gold cigar lighter flashed in her mind. She needed to find that suitcase before he did.

"Excuse me," she said in case anyone stopped staring at Maire long enough to wonder where she'd gone. "I think I'm going to be sick." She ran through the dining car. No one followed. She stepped onto the small platform between the dining and baggage cars and paused, listening. The *clackata-clackata-clackata* of the train filled the air. Light shone from somewhere deep inside the baggage car. Another door must have been open, an easy way for Ray to get off the train without being seen. The light illuminated the car enough for her to see luggage stacked as high as the ceiling along the carriage's walls, held in place by webbing, and in shorter columns on racks throughout the car. Plenty of corners hidden in shadow provided places for Ray to hide. Gethsemane let her eyes adjust to the dim interior and scanned in vain for something to use as a weapon.

"Be the big dog," she whispered to herself. She needed him to say something, make a noise, so she could locate him. She called out. "Give it up, Ray. We found Maire. The gardaí will swarm as soon as we reach the next station. You'll never make it off the train." She didn't tell him about the law-enforcement officers already on the train. No point in showing all her cards.

Ray's voice sounded from the gloom. "I don't have to make it off, do I? I'll just slip into a seat and be ordinary Joe as shocked as everyone when I hear about the terrible tragedies that befell the poor maid and the American woman. It's getting so no place is safe these days."

Ray'd thought this out. Her heart pounded. More stats. Hilton Smith, four thirty-five, Willard Brown, three forty-six, Harry Else, three ten. Of course, Ray didn't know about Jackson. Her brother-in-law must have found O'Reilly and Yseult by this time. He'd have told them about Ray and they'd be on their way. Right? "No place will be safe for you. You shouldn't have strangled Maire with your tie. It's custom-made, isn't it? Tailors keep records. Or had you planned on murdering the tailor and burning down the shop? You've already committed murder and fraud. Why not add arson and make it a trifecta?"

Ray swore. Gethsemane thought she heard movement, then the baggage car fell silent again. She glanced toward the dining car. The connecting doors had closed, but the crowd—which now included several people in rail company uniforms, but none of the gardaí nor either of the FBI agents—clustered around the toilet, and Maire's body in the car on the other side remained visible through the windows. If she made a run for it, she could reach them before Ray reached her, but—she turned to the baggage car as a shaft of light fell on the wall of suitcases. Ray only had to toss Maire's suitcase off the train and with it the proof of his fraud and murders. He could backtrack later, retrieve the case, and destroy the wills and magazine pages and anything else Maire might have against him at his leisure.

"How much was Maire into you for?" Gethsemane asked. Anything to keep him talking. If she could keep track of him, she could keep from ending up like Maire. And Andrew. And Olivia. And the New York widow. She hoped.

"Seventy-five thousand. Can you believe that? The greedy little bitch."

"A regular Lady Muck. What'd she have on you? Did you put her up to luring me out to the distillery?"

"Of course. Do you think she came up with that plan on her own? Can you see her crawling around on a catwalk loosening bolts? She'd have killed herself. Maire and I were partners. She knew everything about the wills. She stole the original for me. Had to seduce that gobshite solicitor's clerk to get it. I owed her for that. She was supposed to discover the forged copy hidden in Olivia's office."

He'd confirmed her suspicion about Maire only being the decoy Ray had used to lure her out to the distillery. "The copy of the will that left everything to you."

"Not everything. Mustn't be too obvious. Others still got their cuts. Your brother-in-law still got his embroideries."

"After you switched the genuine textiles for fakes, no doubt."

"I figured discovery of large-scale art fraud would distract attention from my little inheritance scheme. And it would have worked if Maire'd done as she was told. But instead of giving me my version of the will, she kept both."

"And told you to pay up or she'd go to the gardaí," Gethsemane said. "Did Andrew forge the will for you?"

"Sweet, sentimental Perry. Delighted to help me out for old time's sake. I invited him to lunch at Essex House not long after he arrived in town. A chance for us to renew our acquaintance. We eventually got around to discussing securing my inheritance. All the delicious textiles on display inspired him. He devised a way for me to pay him back for the will." Ray laughed. "An additional way to pay him back."

"You help him steal Olivia's textiles, he helps you steal Olivia's estate. *Quid pro quo*. Why'd you stab him? Found out he was seeing another man?"

"Unlike Perry, I leave sentiment to the rom coms. He told me you'd traced a button back to him. It came from a jacket I'd given him as a present when we moved to New York. He must have lost it during one of his visits to Essex House."

Ray sounded close. She peered into the shadows. She still couldn't see him. Keep him talking long enough to figure out where he hid.

"An expensive gift. You two must have loved each other at some point. I found Andrew's photograph of the two of you. Half of it, anyway. He seemed happy."

"In addition to being sentimental, Perry had a flare for the dramatic gesture. I went to see him at his gallery. You and that button and your talk about the Koors painting made him nervous. He thought you knew more than you did."

"He thought I knew the Koors was one of his fakes," she said.

"Yes. He got quite hysterical. We had a falling out. Perry

wanted to run again. I didn't. He ripped the snap and threw my half in my face."

"Which you destroyed. Before or after you killed him to keep him from skipping out?"

"After. Unfortunately, Maire found my complete copy of the photo hidden among my things. I should never have saved it. Maybe I'm sentimental after all."

"Something for a forensic documents examiner to work with if they ever examined the signatures on the wills."

"Maire wasn't as dumb as I mistook her for. She recognized the added value of the photo and the pages from that damned magazine."

Other copies of the Christeby's magazine existed, but, by itself, the magazine didn't prove anything. Lying to a hotel magnate about not being at an art auction was no crime. The photo provided a direct link between Ray and Andrew, but dating a man who later turned up murdered wasn't a crime either. The wills were key. If Ray burned the original and felt bold enough, he could still substitute the forgery and try to claim the inheritance. Or he could just cut his losses, destroy both copies, let Olivia's estate stay tied up in probate forever, and find a new widow to prey on. She needed to find that suitcase.

Gethsemane pressed her back against the wall. Luggage handles and straps poked her as she inched farther inside the baggage car. She peered ahead as far as she could. No sign of Ray. Nothing but suitcases, rows and rows of suitcases. How would she find a single battered purple case among all of those?

Ray's voice boomed in the small space. "Not polite to keep me waiting, Dr. Brown." Gethsemane froze. "Let's get this over with. I have things to do."

"Like find another widow to sucker. And murder. You were behind that mysterious car accident in New York, weren't you? The car in the Hudson? So nice of your employer to leave you all that lovely money."

"Malicious gossip. You shouldn't believe everything you hear."

"The authorities believe it enough to go back and take a closer look at her will."

"By the time they sort anything out, I shall be residing in a country with no extradition treaty. You can find rich widows everywhere if you look for them. They're always so grateful to have some kind person manage all the tedious details of living so they can concentrate on important things, like hosting parties and lording it over the peons."

"That's why you killed two women and stole their fortunes? To strike a blow for the proletariat? How very populist of you."

"The woman in New York never earned an honest dollar in her life. She lived on trust funds handed down from robber barons. And I only took from Olivia what was mine by rights. The Boyles stole my family's lands and sentenced us to abject poverty. It's taken centuries for us to claw ourselves out of the gutter they left us in. Now I've settled the score. Bloody English."

"Olivia was a McCarthy. She was Irish."

"She married English for money, even worse. Nothing but a glorified whore."

"Why couldn't you wait until she died of natural causes? You probably would have gotten away with the swindle if you had."

"Couldn't wait. There'd have been nothing left. The feckin' wagon was selling off to move to Florida. Florida. Feckin' Disney. All the properties were going. The distilleries, Essex House. Most of the art, too, what she didn't plan to leave to your brother-in-law's museum."

"The brochures I found in Olivia's office. Real estate in Florida. She wasn't involved in art fraud, was she?"

"That prig? Far too self-righteous to be involved in anything so sordid."

"She didn't know the Koors was a fake, and she didn't know you'd switched the Creech miniature for a fake right before the auction."

Gethsemane halted at the edge of the beam of light and looked back toward the dining car. Where was the cavalry? She looked the other way. Where was Ray? She called his name. Only the train's *clackata-clackata* answered her.

The light shone through an open door in the side of the baggage car. The landscape whizzed by at a dizzying speed. Too fast for Ray to jump, but perfect for tossing out a suitcase. The train lurched again and Gethsemane stumbled and pitched toward the open door. She hooked an arm through nearby webbing in time to stop her fall. She pulled herself upright—

A vice clamped around her neck. No, fingers. Ray's fingers, both hands squeezing her throat, cutting off her air. Ray's eyes narrowed, filled with hate and rage, as he tightened his grip. She kicked him, but he didn't let go. He shoved her hard against the luggage and used the leverage to squeeze even tighter. She clawed at his hands, but her nails bounced off his flesh as harmlessly as feathers off steel. The shaft of light dimmed. Her head swam and her arms and legs grew heavy. No ghost was going to rescue her from the depths this time. No one else was going to show up either. If law enforcement was on the way, they wouldn't get here in time. The best she could hope for was them finding Ray standing over her dead body. She'd come back and haunt the bastard. Or she could—she reached up and behind her.

The train lurched once more, harder than the last time. Ray loosened his grip a fraction as he steadied himself. Gethsemane used the reprieve to latch onto the first thing her hand landed on. A handle. She pulled down and forward. Another jolt of the train gave her some forward momentum and she brought a hard-sided wheeled case down on Ray's head. It caught him in the side of his face and knocked him backward. Gethsemane swung the suitcase again and let it fly into Ray's chest. He fell and lay stunned in the baggage car's doorway.

She didn't wait to see if he got up. She ran toward the dining car. She saw Jackson, O'Reilly, and Yseult through the windows, running toward her. Yseult held her phone near her mouth like a walkie-talkie. She tried to cry out, but only hoarse, raspy noises came through her sore throat.

The light in the car dimmed. She looked over her shoulder, expecting to see Ray gaining on her. She froze.

Rock walls, their tops too high to see from within the train, blotted the sun. The train barreled down an ever-darkening chute. A tunnel. She saw Ray stagger to his feet and grab the edge of the open door for support. The tunnel walls narrowed around the speeding train. Ray stumbled as the train lurched. He pitched forward, almost falling out of the baggage car. He grasped the door frame and tried to right himself. His head bobbed out the door, inches away from the tunnel's wall.

"Look out!" Gethsemane shouted.

A second later, a claustrophobic air surrounded her as rock closed overhead and extinguished the light. The car plunged into darkness. In another second, she heard a sickening noise, a noise she'd heard once before, recently, when a man's skull smashed against something harder than bone.

Voices called as the train burst into the sunlight on the opposite side of the tunnel. "Sissy! Gethsemane! Dr. Brown! Are you all right?"

She stared at the gore sprayed across luggage racks. Ray's lower two-thirds lay motionless on the floor. The tunnel wall had annihilated the upper third. This time, "I'm going to be sick" wasn't an excuse.

"How are you?" O'Reilly handed Gethsemane a cup of coffee.

She shifted in the hard plastic chair in the hallway of the Ballytuam garda station. She and Jackson had given their statements and were waiting for someone to drive them back to Dunmullach. "Better, thanks." She sipped coffee. "I only see Ray if I close my eyes. If I can find a way to stay awake forever, I'll be fine." She drained the cup.

Jackson put his arm around her. "Come back to Virginia. Start over, forget all this."

"I've already started over. In Dunmullach. I'm no quitter.

Besides, I have too much to do to go to Virginia. School starts soon. I've got lesson plans to write, I've got to do the music program for Our Lady of Perpetual Sorrows' anniversary concert." Her throat tightened. "I have to find a new place to live."

"Sorry about the cottage," O'Reilly said. "Too bad we couldn't connect Hank Wayne to Andrew and Ronan's scheme. Fraud charges would have distracted him from his real estate ventures."

Gethsemane formed a reply but saw someone at the far end of the hall who distracted her.

"Frankie? What are you doing here?"

The math teacher ambled over, hands shoved in pockets, tweed jacket seemingly more oversized than usual. He looked almost as miserable as he'd looked the day he announced Yseult's engagement. "Hail, hail, the gang's all here."

"You look worse than I do," Gethsemane said, "and I just saw a man get decapitated. What's going on?"

"You tell 'em, Niall. I still can't bring myself to say her name."

"Inspector Mulroney needed to ask Frankie some questions about Yseult's history. Seems she's disappeared."

"Disappeared?" Gethsemane and Jackson asked.

"She and O'Connor went rogue. They worked to bust this crime ring for years with no results, got tired of the crooks slipping through their fingers. Decided the collectors were nothing more than a lot of wealthy gobshites who exacerbated the problem by buying from shady dealers and refusing to cooperate with authorities. They began an affair a few years ago and decided to run away together instead of running after bad guys."

Frankie interrupted, "Run away together? Are you telling me O'Connor is her mystery fiancé?"

O'Reilly nodded. "They kept their relationship secret, of course. They'd have been reassigned different partners if their romance were known. They kept their mouths shut and their hands to themselves when out in public and focused on the Patience Freeman sampler, their ticket to the life they thought they deserved."

"I don't understand," Gethsemane said. "That sampler's a fake. It's not worth anything."

"The sampler you saw hanging in Olivia's office was genuine," O'Reilly said.

"Yseult showed me the fake, in the courtyard when we found Olivia's body. She showed me how the colors had faded the same on the front and back."

"One of your officers let me examine the sampler in the evidence room," Jackson said. "It is a forgery. A good forgery, but still a forgery."

"You're both correct. The sampler in the evidence room, the one Yseult displayed at the scene of Olivia's murder and claimed she'd found hidden in a bush, is a fake. However, the sampler from Olivia's office, the one Kenneth stole and left in the bush for their accomplice to retrieve, was genuine."

"Accomplice?"

"Ronan Leary."

"Let me get this straight," Gethsemane said. "Kenneth stole the genuine sampler and hid it in a bush. Ronan swapped it for the bogus sampler and—"

"Handed the genuine piece over to Yseult."

"Kenneth was supposed to take the fake from the bush, place it in the frame, and hang it back on the Olivia's office wall?"

"Correct. Of course, neither of them planned on Olivia being murdered. Her death threw a curve into their scheme. Especially after you," O'Reilly pointed at her, "noticed the fake sampler in its hiding place. Kenneth hadn't had time to retrieve it. Yseult recognized it right away and had to improvise."

"So all that business about the thief murdering Olivia because she interrupted him mid-heist was nonsense? Stuff Yseult made up to throw everyone off the trail of her own crime?"

Frankie scuffed his shoe against the floor.

"My ex mastered the arts of improvisation and misdirection when she still wore pigtails. She'd have enjoyed showing off and sending this lot," he jerked his head in the direction of the registration desk, "down the garden path. She hates the gardaí."

"She sent me after that bill of sale because she knew Kenneth wouldn't have time to search for it *and* steal the sampler," Gethsemane said. "And I made a perfect scapegoat if I got caught. She swore me to secrecy. It would have been her word against mine. And we all know how that would have turned out." She turned to O'Reilly. "When do the gardaí ever believe me?"

O'Reilly held up his hands.

"You had a better excuse for being in Olivia's office if you'd been caught than Kenneth," Jackson said. "As a party guest, Kenneth had no reason to be in a private area. As an entertainer, you had access to areas off-limits to the public. You could create a plausible reason for being in her office."

Which she'd done. Olivia had still been suspicious. How would she have reacted to finding Kenneth in her office? How far would Kenneth have gone to pull off his theft? "Kenneth didn't expect me at the party. At least he said he didn't. Part of his act? Yseult was the only one who knew why I was there. If Kenneth hadn't acted surprised I'd know he talked to Yseult."

"His surprise was genuine. Yseult hadn't clued him in on that part of the plan."

"The last-minute opening for a pianist?"

"Yseult again. She sent the original pianist a gift basket with his favorite sardines. Unfortunately, the tin was a bit—off."

"What would have happened if I'd discovered the bill of sale for the sampler and photographed it for Yseult?"

"One of two things," O'Reilly said. "Either Kenneth would have slipped into Olivia's office later and stolen it. He'd have known exactly where to find it, so retrieving it would've been a quick in-and-out job. Or Yseult would have used the photographs to phony up a receipt."

"Yseult will have a hard time selling the sampler without paperwork, real or forged," Jackson said. "Even a dealer as unscrupulous as Ronan Leary won't touch it without paperwork."

"Would she have gone to Andrew? If Ray hadn't stabbed him, I mean. Granted him immunity in exchange for forged documents?"

"No need for her to outsource." Frankie slumped into a chair. "She learned how to fake papers long before she heard the term 'forensic documents examiner.' She hails from a long line of counterfeiters. Her da's doing ten years in Limerick Prison for selling the Church phony letters he claimed were written by Pope Pius the Eleventh."

"Honestly, Frankie," Gethsemane nudged him. "Your taste in women."

"Keep it up, Sissy, see where it gets ya."

Jackson smacked his forehead. "Those curators and dealers Yseult had me contact. She didn't want to set up the thief or put an alert out on the sampler. She wanted to know who she might sell it to. And I just handed her their names. Was happy to do it."

"Don't worry, Dr. Applethwaite. We've been in touch with them. They all agreed to notify us the minute Yseult contacts them."

"You thought you were keeping us both out of jail, Jackson."

"About that." O'Reilly wouldn't look her in the eye. "Neither you nor your brother-in-law were ever under arrest."

Gethsemane worked her jaw. "Is it still a crime to punch a cop?"

"Yes." O'Reilly moved out of arm's reach.

"What do you mean we were never under arrest? I remember Sergeant Heaney saying, 'You're under arrest' and reading me my rights. In painful detail, I remember one of the most frightening, humiliating moments of my life."

O'Reilly explained, "All an act for Yseult's benefit. Sorry you had to go through that. Sergeant Heaney's not as incompetent and hostile as she appeared. She's actually a very sweet woman. Bakes brownies for her whole squad on a regular basis. We suspected Yseult of being up to no good for a while now. We tried to give her enough rope to hang herself."

"Looks like she slipped the noose," Frankie said.

"How'd you get involved in the investigation, anyway, Niall?" Gethsemane asked. "You work in Dunmullach, not Ballytuam."

"On loan. I knew Yseult, worked with her back in the day. She trusted me and thought me none too bright. The cold cases weren't going anywhere, so I volunteered to help with a hot one."

Gethsemane leaned her head against the wall and closed her eyes. "So four people are dead because of an inheritance and a five-hundred-year-old grudge, a local art crime ring is busted up, and Kenneth and Yseult and Ronan slither off into the sunset with an antique textile worth the gross national product of a first-world nation. Which they might or might not be able to sell. Did I miss anything?"

"Just a couple of details," O'Reilly said. "Ronan Leary's the one who ripped off the art supply store in Dunmullach. He figured it was far enough away from Ballytuam no one would connect the theft to the forgery."

"Except Jackson." Gethsemane jerked her thumb at her brother-in-law. "Basic forger's tool kit. Is the shopkeeper pressing charges?"

O'Reilly laughed. "After making me put up with her for an hour while she went through every scrap of inventory left in the store, she better. Although, petty theft is the least of Leary's worries right now. Interpol picked him up at Charles de Gaulle airport thirty minutes ago. Seems someone slipped a GPS device and a few hundred euros' worth of counterfeit bills in his bag."

"My ex is almost as good at math as I am," Frankie said. "A fortune beyond your wildest dreams divided by two is larger than a fortune beyond your wildest dreams divided by three."

"But smaller than the same fortune divided by one. The other detail? Only Yseult's disappeared. Kenneth is sitting upstairs spilling his guts. Yseult also neglected to clue him in on the part of the plan where she double-crossed him. He's all piss and vinegar and wants her found as badly as we do."

"Look at the bright side, Frankie." Gethsemane nudged him again.

"What bright side?" He raised an eyebrow.

"Her wedding's off."

Sixteen

Gethsemane drew a demoralized "X" through January fifth on her calendar. One day until Epiphany. Twelfth Night. The night Billy turned Carraigfaire Cottage over to Hank Wayne and Eamon and Orla's home ceased to exist. She'd survived two murder attempts, helped bring down an art forgery and fraud ring and an inheritance swindler, exposed a blackmailer and a multiple murderer, and recovered a will which left her brother-in-law's museum a fortune in antique textiles. She helped a ghost make peace with his past and cleared both herself and her brother-in-law of suspicion of murder and theft. But she failed to do the one thing she'd set out to do: save Carraigfaire. Tears never helped, but right now they sure felt good.

"I can't leave you alone for a moment, can I?"

No mistaking that voice. Or the smell of leather and soap. "Irish!" She ran with open arms to where Eamon leaned against the kitchen table. His six-foot-three frame, dark tousled mop, and green eyes appeared as solid as her own hand. She threw her arms around him and kept going through him to land with a *whump* on the table top. Every inch of skin sizzled and buzzed.

"Careful," he said.

"Eamon Padraig McCarthy, I wish you had a body so I could kiss you. Oh, hell, I'll kiss you anyway." She placed her hands where the sides of his face would be and planted a kiss into his cheek. Her face tingled.

"What's gotten into you, darlin'?" His aura glowed an amused and happy green-red. "I haven't been gone that long."

"You've been gone *too* long. You've no idea how much I've missed you. You've no idea what's happened." It hit her how much she missed having her friend around. She didn't care about the calendar, the cottage, Hank, or Billy. She had Eamon back and nothing else mattered. She tried to hug him again.

"Will ya stop?" His aura turned pink with embarrassment. "That tickles."

"Where the hell have you been? Oh, wait, you weren't, were you? In Hell?"

"No. Thank you very much for your high opinion of my character. I wasn't in Hell. I was someplace much worse. Chaos or limbo, I'm not sure what to call it. Nothing but gray fog and silence, and the occasional aroma of fish and chips. No sense of time, no sense of place. Torture."

"I am sorry." She reached for him, but he dematerialized before she could touch him.

He rematerialized on the other side of the room in front of the kitchen counter. She read the labels on the canisters through his chest: flour, sugar, rice. "I'll keep my distance until you're over the shock of seeing my handsome face again."

"Aren't you glad to see me?"

"Of course I'm glad to see you, darlin'. Beyond glad, over the moon. And not just because I was losing my mind in the middle of all that nothingness. You're the first friend I've had in a quarter century. I hated to give you up so soon after finding you."

"Thanks. That's about the nicest thing anyone's said to me in the past week and a half." She didn't add that almost everyone she met in that time was trying to kill her or charge her with a crime.

She didn't have to. "I know what went on," Eamon said. "Part of it, anyway. I ran into Captain Lochlan on my way back. He filled me in. Did you learn nothing from last time?"

"The gardaí suspected my brother-in-law of felony theft and art fraud. They suspected me of murder. Art was being forged and stolen, inheritances were being swindled, people were being stabbed and strangled. I had to do something."

"I suppose you wouldn't be the Gethsemane Brown I know and love if you hadn't." Eamon blushed and his aura's pink deepened. "Not love, love. You know what I mean."

She winked.

"By the way, Sissy's a ridiculous nickname."

"We agree on that."

"You need a nickname worthy of an Amazon, a superhero, a war correspondent. How about Fearless?"

"Fearless Brown. Has a certain ring to it."

They sat for a while in the comfortable silence that exists between close friends. Then Gethsemane asked, "Why'd you go away?"

"Had no choice in the matter."

"I'm not accusing, I'm asking. I came home one day and you were gone. Guess I didn't really expect a goodbye note, but, I don't know, things felt wrong."

"I certainly wasn't resting in peace. I think I was sent away. Banished. I can't remember the details. I meant it about losing my mind. The longer I stayed in the gray, the fuzzier my memory became. Much longer and I might not have remembered my name, much less my life. Or my life-after-death."

"So how'd you get home? I tried to bring you. I found a summoning incantation in one of Father Tim's books. I recited it, but nothing happened. Well, not nothing. Captain Lochlan happened. Apparently, some music I played created a sympathetic vibration that allowed him to come back to this side of the veil."

"'This side of the veil.' Listen to you. You sound a proper paranormal investigator."

"Nothing wrong with using the correct terminology. Anyway, the captain explained the spell only worked if you played the right music. Or, at least, made the right noise. And the ghost you got was the ghost who resonated to the specific sound you made. I had no idea what to play to call you. I tried your compositions, your favorite composers, your least favorite composers, pub songs, children's songs. Everything. Nothing worked. So how did you get back?"

He didn't answer. He looked as embarrassed as his pink aura.

"Eamon?"

"You played the right tones."

"When?"

"At the distillery. The caterwauling the catwalk made when it spun 'round like a dervish."

"Seriously, Irish? You sympathetically vibrate to creaking metal?"

"We don't get to choose. And the tones had a certain musical quality." Her funeral dirge, she'd called it. "Your tears helped, too."

Her turn to blush. "I'm sorry you had to come back to such grim news."

"Finding you still among the living is not grim."

"But your home being sold to a developer is. By this time tomorrow, Carraigfaire Cottage will no longer be owned by a McCarthy. It will become the latest acquisition of Wayne Resorts, International."

"Epiphany, eh? Billy intends to hand my house over to some gombeen like the magi handing gifts to the Christ child. Well, baby Jaysus got three presents, why should Hank Wayne have to settle for one?"

"Really? You mean it?"

"'Course I mean it." His blue aura backed up his statement.

"This is going to take a full-blown, no-holds-barred, all stops out, party tricks included, full-bodied manifestation. Are you up to it?"

Eamon hurled a blue orb against a chair. The chair exploded backward. Gethsemane yelped and jumped away from the heat. "I'm up to it," he said.

"In that case, let's take the party to Hank. He's in town. Billy, too. They're both staying at Sweeney's Inn."

"I visited Sweeney's many times while I lived." Gethsemane

raised an eyebrow. "The restaurant on the ground floor. The chef did a brilliant shepherd's pie. And shame on ya for what you're thinking. Anyway, it's about time I paid Sweeney's a return visit."

Gethsemane pressed her ear against the door to room twelve. "I don't hear anything."

"Try knocking," Eamon said.

They'd come straight from the cottage to Sweeney's Inn, Dunmullach's only lodging except for two rooms above the Mad Rabbit the barman sometimes rented out. The two-hundred-fifty-year-old hotel had hosted its share of famous and infamous guests over the centuries—statesmen and highway men, runaway lovers and incognito celebrities. On their way in, Gethsemane and Eamon passed a small crowd in the lobby gathered around someone Gethsemane assumed was moderately famous. She ignored them. Hank Wayne and Billy McCarthy were the only guests who interested her at the moment. Green, purple, and gold Epiphany decorations festooned the lobby and reminded her of how little time remained to save the cottage she now considered her home. A star struck desk clerk left the registration desk unguarded. Gethsemane peeked at the registration book and found Hank's room. They'd gone up unannounced.

Gethsemane knocked.

"Who is it?" Billy McCarthy called through the door.

"Oh, good, they're together," she said to Eamon. She answered Billy, "Gethsemane Brown. Something's happened at the cottage. I need to talk to you about it."

Billy opened the door a crack. "This isn't the best time. Actually, this isn't even my room. I'm in fourteen. Perhaps you could come see me later."

She peered around him. "Is that Mr. Wayne? Hi, Hank. Hey, thanks for outing Ray Delaney about being in New York. You helped tie him to the murders. Not that he lived to face charges." She hoped she sounded flip enough to hide her true reaction to the memory of seeing Ray's destroyed corpse lying on the floor of the baggage car. "But you did help."

Her elbow tingled at Eamon's touch. "Steady, darlin'."

She turned her attention back to Billy. "May we come in?"

"We?" Billy, one of the majority of people who couldn't see Eamon, stuck his head into the hall and looked both ways. "You're alone."

"Not quite."

Eamon pointed at the door and it flung inward, knocking Billy to the floor. Hank's eyes widened. His mouth opened into a silent "oh." He jumped from his chair, sending stacks of paper floating to the floor, and jumped onto the bed, where he flattened himself against the headboard.

"I take it you see me, Mr. Wayne," Eamon said.

Hank quivered. Unlike Eamon's nephew, he had the gift of being able to see ghosts. Or the curse.

Billy stared back and forth between Gethsemane and the developer.

She explained, "Your uncle's here and he's pissed about you selling out to Hank. He feels betrayed by his closest living relative and heir."

"This is business." Billy's eyes watered as he fought to keep the tears from his voice. "And I'll remind you that it's none of yours."

A blue orb appeared in the middle of the room and whizzed toward Billy. "Shite!" He dove and curled into a ball. The orb missed him by a few inches and fizzled out in a corner. It singed the carpet. "What the feck was that?"

"Uncle Eamon's calling card. You'll probably have to pay damages for that," Gethsemane said.

"You don't understand." Billy's sobs broke free.

"I understand, Billy, I do. Hank offered you more money than you ever dreamed of having. He offered you so much money that if he'd offered it to the devil, the devil would have sold his soul to Hank. But this is family. And family is more important than money."

"He's not your family."

"But he is my friend. And friends are more important than money, too."

Hank had dropped to his knees on the bed and recited a prayer over and over.

"Hank," Eamon said.

The hotel man prayed louder.

"Hank." Eamon levitated the bed and let it drop, jostling Hank to the floor.

Hank blubbered. "Please don't hurt me, please don't hurt me," he said between sobs.

"I don't want to hurt you. I want you to go away. Forget about buying my home, leave this village, and leave Ireland. And don't come back. If I find you within ten kilometers of Dunmullach limits, I'll haunt you. The party tricks are for Billy's sake. I won't need those with you. I'll just be wherever you are. I won't give you a moment's peace. Do you understand me, Hank?"

Hank nodded at Eamon. He pulled himself up with the bedclothes and stumbled to the table. He picked up the scattered papers and tore them into pieces. He stumbled to the door and collided with a bellhop.

"'Scuse me, sir," the young man said. "We had a report of crying and some thuds. Is everything all right?" He looked at Billy on the floor and both men's tear-stained faces. "Did you fall? Does anyone need a doctor?"

Hank squeezed past the bellhop, careful to keep space between himself and Eamon.

"I'm checking out. Now. I'll send for my things later." He ran for the stairs.

Billy pushed himself to his feet. "No need for a doctor. Business deal went sour, that's all." He stepped into the hall. "I'm going back to my own room. Maybe you can see to Mr. Wayne's things." He handed the bellhop a folded bill.

Gethsemane called after him, "Billy, wait."

"Wait for what? For you to bring the roof crashing in on my

head? Haven't you done enough? By the way, I want you out of Carraigfaire. Tonight."

He slammed his door.

"That didn't go exactly as planned."

Eamon glowed a happy green. "You saved the cottage, got rid of Hank Wayne."

"Yeah, but—"

"That eviction nonsense?" Eamon waved a hand. "Don't worry about it. It's my house, and I say you can stay. Besides, Billy'll come 'round once he stops being mad."

"If he stops being mad. We did just cost him a fortune."

"Like you said, family and friends are worth more than any fortune."

"We three kings of Orient are, bearing gifts we traverse afar, field and fountain, moor and mountain, following yonder star," Gethsemane sang as she chalked the year and "C + M + B" over the cottage's doorway.

"What're you doing?" Eamon materialized beside her.

"You are such a heathen. This is the traditional Epiphany house blessing. C, M, and B are the magi's initials. They also stand for *Christus Mansionem Benedicat.* I figure we can use all the blessings we can get."

"Will you stop worrying about Billy? I told you he was talking mad. He hasn't sent the gardaí 'round to put your things on the drive."

"Yet."

"Did you see him at church tonight?"

"Yes," she said.

"Was he civil?"

She conceded he had been.

"He didn't mention you leaving and he minded his manners. He's over his tantrum."

"His good behavior didn't reassure me. It's hard to evict

someone when the parish priest is preaching about charity and giving and half the village is in the pews watching you."

"Worrywart." Eamon dematerialized.

She found him in the kitchen, oven door open.

"Since when do you cook?" he asked. "I wasn't gone that long, was I?"

"I can cook. One or two things. King Cake being one of the two." She slammed the oven door. "Don't open that. It's not done yet."

"Explain king cakes to me. Why would anyone want to cook a plastic baby in a cake?"

"It's an Epiphany tradition. You serve the cake at your Twelfth Night party and whoever gets the slice with the baby has to buy next year's cake. It's also a choking hazard, so these days the cake's usually served with the baby on the side. It's also more fun when more than one person eats the cake. It being just me kind of kills the suspense of who gets the baby."

"So am I invisible all of a sudden?" Eamon solidified until he appeared as dense as Gethsemane.

"You have to have, you know, teeth and a mouth and internal organs to eat cake."

"I have a nose." He sniffed. "Are you sure it's not done?"

She grabbed a potholder and pulled the purple, green, and gold ring from the oven. She waved away smoke. The cake had a fourth color on the bottom—dark, dark charcoal brown. "Oh, well. I'm not in a party mood anyway." She let the cake slide into the trash, plastic baby and all.

"Is throwing the baby out with the king cake anything like throwing the baby out with the bath water?" Eamon laughed his full throaty laugh. A green aura surrounded him.

"It's not funny."

Someone pounded on the door. They both fell silent. The pounding repeated.

"What if it's Billy?" Gethsemane whispered.

"One way to find out." Eamon dematerialized.

She rushed to the front door and inserted herself between him and it. "Let me. Maybe it's just magi bringing me gifts. But in case it's not..." She grabbed her shillelagh and turned the lock.

The woman on the porch handed Gethsemane a business card and pushed her way into the entrance hall. "I'm Venus James, true crime author." She spoke with an American accent. "I'd like to talk to you about the Eamon McCarthy case."

"Oh, God, it's you." Gethsemane crumpled the card. "You wrote that book."

Before the woman could respond, three men came into view behind her on the porch. Gethsemane stared at the one in the lead. Mid-thirty-ish, slim, hipster glasses, dressed in black. She'd seen him somewhere. The crowd at Sweeney's Inn. He'd been in the middle of it. No, wait. She knew him from someplace else.

"You're—"

He finished her sentence, "Kent Danger." He introduced his companions. "We're the *Ghost Hunting Adventures* boys."

"Paranormal investigators," Eamon said over her shoulder. "Bloody hell."

Photo by Peter Larsen

ALEXIA GORDON

A writer since childhood, Alexia Gordon won her first writing prize in the 6th grade. She continued writing through college but put literary endeavors on hold to finish medical school and Family Medicine residency training. She established her medical career then returned to writing fiction.

Raised in the southeast, schooled in the northeast, she relocated to the west whcre she completed Southern Methodist University's Writer's Path program. She admits Texas brisket is as good as Carolina pulled pork. She practices medicine in North Chicago, IL. She enjoys the symphony, art collecting, embroidery, and ghost stories.

The Gethsemane Brown Mystery Series
by Alexia Gordon

MURDER IN G MAJOR (#1)
DEATH IN D MINOR (#2)

Henery Press Mystery Books

And finally, before you go...
Here are a few other mysteries
you might enjoy:

A MUDDIED MURDER

Wendy Tyson

A Greenhouse Mystery (#1)

When Megan Sawyer gives up her big-city law career to care for her grandmother and run the family's organic farm and café, she expects to find peace and tranquility in her scenic hometown of Winsome, Pennsylvania. Instead, her goat goes missing, rain muddies her fields, the town denies her business permits, and her family's Colonial-era farm sucks up the remains of her savings.

Just when she thinks she's reached the bottom of the rain barrel, Megan and the town's hunky veterinarian discover the local zoning commissioner's battered body in her barn. Now Megan is thrust into the middle of a murder investigation—and she's the chief suspect. Can Megan dig through small-town secrets, local politics, and old grievances in time to find a killer before that killer strikes again?

THE DEEP END

Julie Mulhern

The Country Club Murders (#1)

Swimming into the lifeless body of her husband's mistress tends to ruin a woman's day, but becoming a murder suspect can ruin her whole life.

It's 1974 and Ellison Russell's life revolves around her daughter and her art. She's long since stopped caring about her cheating husband, Henry, and the women with whom he entertains himself. That is, until she becomes a suspect in Madeline Harper's death. The murder forces Ellison to confront her husband's proclivities and his crimes—kinky sex, petty cruelties and blackmail.

As the body count approaches par on the seventh hole, Ellison knows she has to catch a killer. But with an interfering mother, an adoring father, a teenage daughter, and a cadre of well-meaning friends demanding her attention, can Ellison find the killer before he finds her?

FIXIN' TO DIE

Tonya Kappes

A Kenni Lowry Mystery (#1)

Kenni Lowry likes to think the zero crime rate in Cottonwood, Kentucky is due to her being sheriff, but she quickly discovers the ghost of her grandfather, the town's previous sheriff, has been scaring off any would-be criminals since she was elected. When the town's most beloved doctor is found murdered on the very same day as a jewelry store robbery, and a mysterious symbol ties the crime scenes together, Kenni must satisfy her hankerin' for justice by nabbing the culprits.

With the help of her Poppa, a lone deputy, and an annoyingly cute, too-big-for-his-britches State Reserve officer, Kenni must solve both cases and prove to the whole town, and herself, that she's worth her salt before time runs out.

CPSIA information can be obtained
at www.ICGtesting.com
Printed in the USA
LVOW13*0535120218
566112LV00010BA/92/P